D1608072

Also by Joe Moore

Believe Again,
The North Pole Chronicles

1st in The Santa Claus Trilogy

Glaciers Melt & Mountains Smoke

3rd in The Santa Claus Trilogy

Return of the Birds

Santa's Elf Series

Santa's World,
Introducing Santa's Elf Series

Jamie Hardrock, Chief Mining Elf

Shelley Wrapitup, Master Design Elf

To Ann

Faith, Hope & Reindeer

Have faith!

Joe Moore

By Joe Moore

Published by The North Pole Press

Published by The North Pole Press

Smoky Mountains, Tennessee
ISBN13:978-09787129-2-1

Cover design by Mary Moore
Artwork by Brenda Harris Tustian @ 2011 Faith, Hope & Reindeer
Copyright © 2011 by Joe Moore

Library of Congress Catalog #2011910278

Information about and for this book may be obtained through
contacting North Pole Press at: Info@thenorthpolepress.com.
Printed in the United States of America

Dedication:

To my loving and beautiful Mrs. Claus, my Mary, who has kept me focused and gotten us both through all our adversities. She has been the only lighthouse I have needed to bring me back home through all the storms we have encountered. She has always been the twinkle in this Santa's eye. Thank you, my love, for all you do for me.

Acknowledgements:

I need to say a special thank you to my many dear friends that have always believed in this project and have contributed pearls through the various readings. To all of you I give thanks. My dear friend and fellow Santa, Fred Selinsky, for his unwavering support of this book. My friends from California who appear as characters in this book including Bill, Julie, Marshall, Jonathan, Graham and Regina, along with several others. And to my dearest friend who has made me look so good to so many, the lovely and gentle Brenda Harris Tustian who painted the cover. She has painted me so many times with her lovely watercolors. She always brings out the best in Santa time and again.

Scan code
and get your
FREE Color Digital Copy

of

Faith, Hope & Reindeer

Table of Contents

Preface

When they read the will they hadn't heard of this company before. He may have mentioned it to them while he was alive, though they couldn't remember it. But for such a large sum of money to be given they would have thought they'd have greater knowledge of the firm.

When they contacted the company, it sent a very short but pleasant man who said he was in charge of endowments to the firm. They pressed him for information, strictly out of curiosity, and the smallish man in his forties said that their firm had contributed significantly to Ruth and Elliott Handler's efforts a long time ago. "Many of their innovations were accomplished through our assistance," the man stated.

Fearing an upcoming copyright fight for some of Mattel's products they started to protest his statement. The man held up his hand and said, "We consider the matter long past closed, and payment for our part was made in full many years ago. This is why we consider this check as purely a donation from two very special philanthropic individuals." He placed the check in his coat pocket, thanked them and left.

Thursday December 15th

"Doubt is a pain too lonely

to know that faith is his twin brother."

Khalil Gribran, Author and Lebanese Poet

Chapter One

"This is so useless!" Jared Grady moaned. He stood up to his full 6'1" frame and rubbed his sandy brown hair with both hands. While he was only 42, he felt he had aged a good ten years this past year. He had rugged features, but he had began to look more weathered in recent months.

Julie gave her husband of twenty years a sympathetic look, knowing his frustration all too well. "Something is out there for you," she said. "It's only a matter of time. Right now I need to get the kids."

Julie jumped into her SUV and backed out of the driveway of their modest, but pretty, Cape Cod home. She pulled up in front of the high school a few minutes later.

Her daughter, Susan, stood out front with some friends. Julie again admired her striking daughter. She was proud of how much Susan looked like she did at seventeen. Same shoulder-length auburn hair, same high cheekbones and the beautiful figure Julie had at her age. Julie had kept that good shape all her life and thought Susan would, too. Susan spied her mother's car and said a hasty goodbye to her friends. She hopped into the front seat. "Hi Mom."

"Where's Marshall?" asked Julie.

"He forgot his Chemistry book and since he has a test Friday, he thought it might be a good idea to bring his book home to study."

As soon as she had said this, Marshall came jogging around from the far building. "Sorry." he said scrambling into the back seat. "Hey Mom, did you remember to sign that release for the band concert on Saturday?"

Julie said, "The paper is on the counter, now don't forget tomorrow, or they may not let you go."

Marshall smiled broadly. "Naw, they'd never think of leaving their best tenor sax behind!"

"You'd be surprised at the things they'd do in the name of school policy." Julie was proud of both her children and was pleased that Marshall's looks emulated her husbands, except like Susan, he had her soft green eyes and long fingers.

Both of the Grady kids were in great moods. This was that special time of year. They only had a few more days, then no school for two whole weeks while everyone celebrated the holidays. Even final exams would be held later than usual and wouldn't begin until the latter half of January.

Marshall was more animated and he seemed to sense something particularly special about this upcoming break. Had you asked him, he couldn't say what – only a feeling deep down. Susan always loved the Christmas holiday, and thought it was her special time of year.

Neither of them could possibly guess what was about to take place as they were getting into the car.

Chapter Two

Jared thought to himself, *This is going to be a very different Christmas indeed, but for an entirely different reason.*

As he moved away from the computer again considering their plight the doorbell rang. He opened the door to a FedEx envelope addressed to "The Gradys." Jared supposed it might be an early Christmas present, but couldn't imagine from whom.

He retrieved the package and opened it. He scanned its contents and read and reread the cover letter. The return address simply stated "Alaska Authentication Department."

Julie and the kids returned to see Jared standing in the entryway reading and scratching his head.

Marshall eyed the FedEx envelope and asked "For me?"

His dad looked past Marshall at Julie and said, "Can I talk to you for a moment?" Julie feared bad news. They walked into the office and Jared closed the door.

"What's up?" asked Julie looking worried.

"Did you enter any contests or fill out any forms for prizes?"

Julie shook her head. "No, you know I don't believe in those, they exist to get people on their mailing lists and other marketing ploys."

Jared thought for a second. "What about the kids?"

"I suppose it's possible. but I've told them the same thing and I discourage them from doing anything of the sort. Jared, what is this about?"

He handed her the contents of the FedEx envelope.

Julie read it and said. "This can't be right. Obviously this is in error or belongs to another Grady."

"Look at the cover letter and who it's addressed to."

Julie perused the cover letter. Dear Jared, Julie, Susan & Marshall: She was puzzled, "Well it still must be wrong. But let's ask the kids just in case?"

They left the office and called Susan and Marshall down from their rooms. Both said they heeded their mother's advice and didn't enter anything.

Then Marshall groaned and said, "Oh wait. I did sign up to win an iPad one time on the computer." He seemed hopeful, "Why, did I get one?" His parents looked again at the mysterious contents.

Susan asked, "What's this all about? Why the questions?"

This time Jared spoke up. "It seems we've won a trip to Alaska. A one week. all-expense paid trip including airline and train tickets and we leave next week when your vacation starts and we'll be gone over Christmas."

"COOL!" "GREAT!" Both kids cried out.

"Now wait a minute." said Julie, "We don't know if this is legitimate or how we got this. It may be a scam or something."

Marshall took the letter from his father's hand and read it.

Dear Jared, Julie, Susan & Marshall:

Congratulations! You are invited on a special trip for the four of you to Alaska. Your tickets are enclosed. You will be traveling by Alaska Airlines to Fairbanks on December 19th then will board an exclusive train following the directions below. This train will take you through some of the most rugged and spectacular terrain with the widest abundance of Alaska's wildlife you are ever likely to see.

You will stay at a magnificent five-star resort for six days and nights, where your every wish will be attended to and return December 26th via the route you came. All meals, lodging, tips and transportation are included. The only thing you'll need to bring is plenty of warm clothing.

Please make certain you allow extra time to make your flight from Orange County's John Wayne Airport, as changing flight times or days cannot be allowed because it will affect the train schedule as well.

We know you will enjoy this trip of a lifetime and we wish you all a very Merry Christmas.

Sincerely,

Alaska Authentication Department

"It must be for us," Marshall said excitedly, "It has all our names on it. Cool. Are those the tickets?"

Julie stopped him in his tracks. "Now wait a minute

young man. We can't go off to Alaska in the middle of
winter on a whim, especially at Christmas."

Susan was now reading the letter and said, "Wait a
second, it IS over the Christmas break, and it says
everything's included." She looked at her father, "Dad,
you did promise we would take a trip to Alaska before
things went crazy with your job."

"Yeah but sweetheart, I was talking about a cruise or
a summer trip to Denali, and not as Mom said 'in the
middle of winter'!" He looked at the ticket information
for the airline and train again. It certainly seemed
authentic, then he said more to himself, "We aren't even
sure this is real."

The next half hour consisted of a family debate.
Susan reminded them (several times) how she would be
going off to college next summer and how this might be
the last 'family' vacation that they could all take
together. Marshall's argument was centered on a more
simple 'nothing ventured, nothing gained' attitude.

The final decision for that day was that Jared and
Susan would look into this more carefully and at least
verify the legitimacy of the "trip", and what strings
might be attached. Then they would discuss this further
when all the details were available.

To this Marshall said, "Wow! I'm going to go see what
kind of warm clothes I've got," and took off for his
room.

Chapter Three

"I'm sorry sir, I cannot give that information over the phone," said the immovable Alaska Airlines representative.

"Look, I'm trying to verify whether you have tickets in our name or not."

"I can verify that the flight number, day, time and destination are all accurate, but I cannot give you passenger details. If you wish, you may come to the Alaska counter with picture ID and we can verify any other information."

Getting the information about the train was even more nebulous. The only thing he could find out was that, yes, there is a Northern Express train, and yes, it left from somewhere in Fairbanks. But its route, destination and schedule were some strange secret, or at least not known by any normal line of inquiry.

Julie tried calling the Alaska Department of Tourism, but got no further than Jared. No they were not giving away trips, and yes, it was possible someone else was. No they did not have an "Authentication Department". Yes the cruise ships and trains generally stopped by September. But there could be a few special promotions and companies that did events over the holidays to get through the long quiet months of winter. It was suggested she search the Internet for more information on those.

Most of the next morning they tried to secure whatever information they could about the package contents. The "resort" itself wasn't listed by name or address in the letter. Also, with no actual destination of the train, there was little to go on.

Susan and Marshall had left in high spirits that morning and Jared and Julie were not pleased with the aspect of dashing their hopes when they came home. But it seemed like everything led to a dead end. They weren't very comfortable heading off to places unknown and unverified. Around 11:30 that morning the doorbell rang again.

Julie opened the door to a large box dropped off by UPS this time. When the Gradys opened the box they found four beautiful ski suits with matching gloves, each a different color and size. They were labeled for each of them. Jared's was a rich dark blue with light blue piping, Julie's white with red trim, Marshall's a dark forest green, and Susan's white and sported an eggplant trim. The enclosed card contained a hand written note, which said:

Hope this helps for the trip. We look forward to seeing you here.

The labels on the jackets read "The Warmth of Faith Company" of Alaska. Jared tried on the jacket over the sweatshirt he was wearing and it fit beautifully. He knew by looking at the ski pants and gloves that they would fit equally as well.

Julie looked at him and shrugged. This was getting a little eerie. If someone was out to get them, they were going through a lot of expense and trouble to do so. The

Warmth of Faith. Well they certainly would have warmth now, so she thought maybe they could supply the faith.

When the kids came home Jared and Susan filled them in on the whole story about trying to research the tickets and destinations and expressed their concerns. Then they finally showed them the suits and gloves. Susan agreed with her mother that this was one of those times when they had to put faith before cynicism. She reminded her Dad that often he reiterated what the Pastor at church said about how a little faith would go a long way.

Meanwhile, Marshall was already in his ski pants and putting on the jacket. In his mind, he was already halfway to the airport. Jared finally said that if the tickets on Alaska Airlines were good, they were going. If not, it would be the shortest vacation on record. All the same he might try going to the airport to at least get a secure answer for that part of the trip.

The kids weren't sorry about leaving over Christmas, and they would be home for the second half of vacation anyway. Everyone was suddenly in vacation mode, and for the first time in a long time, Jared wasn't transfixed on being unemployed.

Chapter Four

The next several days were spent tying up loose ends,
going to Marshall's holiday concert, taking tests at
school, securing vacation time at Julie's job, and getting
together with friends to exchange what gifts they could
before leaving Monday.

There was no time to shop for clothes and only time
to restock essentials from the health and beauty
departments. The Gradys were thankful for the new ski
suits, and wondered how cold it might get. Jared looked
on the Internet for weather and temperatures, but
without an exact location, it was impossible to gauge.
The weather varied widely throughout the state, from
−35° F with blizzard conditions to 42° F and sunny, with
everything in between going on in that massive
wilderness. The nearest he could guess was their arrival
in Fairbanks where it was a brisk −10° F with snow on
and off. What he did know was that they needed to
pack anything they owned that was warm.

From quick trips on the Internet, Jared learned that
Fairbanks was one of the best spots on earth to see the
Northern Lights, and he hoped that the kids would get
to see this most awesome display of nature. He was
frustrated at not being able to plan properly for the trip
and felt that he didn't have much control, which of
course was correct.

But then again, it was rather exhilarating to not have

to worry about the details and to go "sight unseen" into this vacation. He did try to locate rail lines and such around Fairbanks, to no avail. He hit a whiteout trying to gain any new information. He also never got to the airport, and figured if everyone else could muster up some trust, he would too. Besides, the worst that could happen was that the tickets weren't real, but for some reason he didn't believe it.

Faith is a marvelous thing.

Monday
December 19th

*"I can't think of anything
that excites a greater sense of childlike wonder
than to be in a country
where you are ignorant of almost everything."*

Bill Bryson, Author of *A Walk In the Woods*

Chapter One

Monday came quickly and without much time to even think about it. The Gradys were off at 5:00 for their 7 am flight to Fairbanks. According to the flight information they did have, they had to change planes in Seattle.

The airport was already crowded, even at this early hour, from passengers trying to get away on their vacations. Many people made their plans for the week after school let out, and it seemed that most of them were in attendance.

The Gradys were relieved they had allowed more time than they needed, as the long lines ate up the clock in big gulps.

It turned out by the time they checked luggage and verified their tickets, it was already 6:15. Getting through security took another thirty minutes and by the time they got to the gate they were already in the process of boarding. They got aboard and settled in for the roughly three-hour flight to Seattle. The plane pushed back from the gate at 7:03 and Jared and Julie were surprised that they actually found themselves heading out on vacation. It was very different from what they had expected this December.

The flight to Seattle was without incident and they landed within five minutes of their scheduled arrival. As it so often does, it was raining in Seattle, but that didn't

dampen any of the Gradys' spirits. The first leg of a
long trip was over. Now it was time to change planes and
head for Fairbanks. They had approximately two hours
before their next flight lifted off. They grabbed a
breakfast wrap in the terminal and strolled to their next
gate. More than at Orange County, people were bustling
all through the airport trying to get to their
connections. It was later in the day and more people
were heading through the airport at a breakneck pace.

The plane they got on was a small, close-quartered
737 with three across seating on each side. Despite the
busy airport, their flight wasn't very full and they were
able to spread out and have open seats beside them. In
fact there were only about fifty to sixty people. Jared
and Julie secretly wondered if any of these people
received a similar cryptic invitation and tickets like they
had received. It was mostly all families and a few older
couples on the flight heading north. A couple of the
families had young children around four to eight. Jared
wondered if it was wise to bring such small children to
such an inhospitable climate. But he realized that people
live there all year round and surely there must be
children that live in the town.

After takeoff they were informed that this flight
would last about two hours and forty minutes, and
would arrive in Fairbanks on time a little after 3:00 pm.
Once again Julie ran through the questions in her head
about when they arrived in Fairbanks. They hadn't even
tried to book a hotel as a backup, in case there wasn't a
train, or if that's where their trip suddenly ended. She
wasn't even sure about how they were supposed to

connect with their train.

   Jared had said he assumed they would have information at the Fairbanks terminal since the letter hadn't really addressed that part of the 'tour'. She hated that word 'assume' and always thought of what people broke it out to mean. Nonetheless, she cleared her mind as the plane rose through the clouds and reminded herself how good it was not to see Jared all tied up in knots over his job prospects. He still showed his worry lines, but at least for now it was over something else entirely. Even if they went no further than Fairbanks, this had to be better than staying at home and beating the computer in frustration. Especially, since few companies would be interviewing over the holidays anyway. She murmured a little prayer of thanks for taking them away from their situation, even if temporarily.

   A common, yet unspoken thought went through much of the airplane. *Exactly where are we going, and what are we supposed to see when we get there? It was on the minds of many of the passengers.*

Chapter Two

The arrival into Fairbanks Airport made the Gradys feel that they were literally off the edge of the map. It was already dark. There was only one other commercial airliner and a few private planes that were heavily tethered to the tarmac. The terminal itself was the smallest any of the Gradys had ever seen. The fact that there was snow everywhere making it difficult to see anything past the immediate runway gave them a serious pause in their jubilation at being on vacation.

For the first time Marshall thought maybe this wasn't such a hot idea. *'Hot', oh brother, that was a word that probably wasn't used much up here,* he thought to himself.

As the plane taxied up to the terminal they saw the ground crew pushing the rolling stairs to the plane.

"Well I guess it's time to road test these ski jackets," Susan said flatly.

"How do you think the resort will cater to our every whim?" Julie whispered to Jared.

"We better keep our 'whims' to the small and basic," he whispered back.

The look of concern was on more than the Gradys faces. A quick look around would have told them who else was visiting Fairbanks for the very first time.

When the door of the plane was opened, a blast of cold air whipped through the entire plane. The temperature was an extremely frigid -12° F, and it caught everyone's breath. Even the people who looked like they may have come from colder climes than Southern California looked stunned.

As they descended the icy stairs, nobody dawdled getting into the structure. The Fairbanks terminal was kind enough to hit its visitors with a blast of hot air as they came in. It was like some kind of perverse Swedish spa.

As they gathered around the sole turnstile to await their luggage a small army of impeccably dressed skycaps suddenly converged on the crowd. Each was holding a sign with a different name professionally printed in big bold letters.

The Gradys found a short but strong looking young man with soft features and a broad smile approach them holding their name.

"We're the Gradys," Jared said.

"Ah yes, Mr. Grady, my name is Conrad. I was told to look for an attractive couple and their two teens. Hello Susan, Marshall. Now if you will stand in back of me and point out your luggage, I will handle the rest."

He produced a cart out of thin air and carefully stacked the luggage onto it. Along with Conrad, it seemed that almost every family had a skycap at their disposal. The Gradys wondered if he was with the resort, and Marshall asked him.

"I will be your personal valet during your trip to and from the Inn. I will also be your waiter aboard the train."

Waiter! That meant food! Whatever they served it couldn't be any worse than what they had coming up

here in the plane and terminals. The long ago breakfast
wraps were little more than a memory by now.

Conrad retrieved the last bag for the Gradys and filed
in line with a procession of other 'personal valets'
leading out of the terminal.

"Bundle up now," he advised. "It's a short walk but a
chilly one."

Susan thought, *Chilly? Chilly? What the heck did this
man consider cold?*

As they were met with another Arctic blast they
raced off to one of two waiting luxury buses. Conrad
urged his passengers to get on and get warm as he placed
the luggage aboard the lower part of the bus. A few
minutes later he reappeared and said that the train
station wasn't far, but they certainly wouldn't want to
walk there. Even on a nicer day than this one.

About ten minutes later the buses lurched and moved
away from the terminal. The buses were warm and
comfortable. Each passenger had their own TV screen
and there looked to be a bathroom and type of bar in
the rear. It seemed a shame that the trip only took
about ten minutes. The bus went through the downtown
area and down a road into another structure. It
resembled a large barn more than a train station, and at
first some of the passengers thought the driver took a
wrong turn. As the first bus approached the building a
large barn door opened going up into the structure and
the bus drove in followed by the second bus. It was
deceptively large on the inside and seemed to almost
grow double in size to one's perception.

At the far end of the building stood an old time

passenger train complete with a large steam locomotive, three coach style cars and a caboose. It reminded Jared of the old Lionel set he and his Dad had set up when he was a young boy. The cars were dark green with bright red trim throughout. The windows looked large and spotless. The writing on the side stated simply: THE NORTHERN EXPRESS.

Jared thought it was one of the most beautiful things he'd ever seen.

Chapter Three

As the passengers disembarked the bus they found
the building was neither cold nor draughty as it looked.
In fact. they couldn't feel a breeze stirring inside and it
was cold but comfortable temperature wise. As the
valets again loaded the luggage onto the carts. the pace
seemed efficient but leisurely as if the whole world had
begun to slow down.

Conrad beckoned them to follow him to the second
car. He said. "Hop on in there and after I stow your
luggage I will come find you to take your order for
dinner." The Gradys did as they were instructed and
embarked onto the old train.

The car was immaculately appointed inside. Tables
with white linen tablecloths and stuffed comfortable red
tufted benches on either side awaited the passengers.
The windows were adorned with curtains that rolled
down. Jared guessed it could get pretty bright out there
on a sunny day with all that snow.

Like the bus. there looked to be a type of bar and a
bathroom in the rear of the car. There was a small but
warm potbellied stove in the center of the car and it
seemed to radiate heat throughout the interior. The
Gradys settled on a table about two-thirds toward the
back of the car.

Other people were boarding and Julie wondered if
their own faces and looks were like the people coming on

board. Each person was filled with surprise and wonder
at the beauty of their transportation.

One young man about five or six years of age, got on
the train and shouted excitedly, "See Mommy, it's like
my dream! I told you it would be like this!" The mother
looked dumbstruck around the inside of the car as if her
little boy had described it blindly and in exact detail. A
slightly older boy and his father followed the mother
and little boy. They also carried a rather stupefied look
on their faces. That family sat across and up two tables
from the Grady family.

The next family to get on their car looked nothing
alike. The first girl had almost whitish blond hair,
piercing blue eyes and very fair skin. Her sister had
brown hair and hazel eyes with a much darker
complexion. A third girl, younger than the first two,
followed and had Hispanic features with very large dark
brown eyes and raven black hair. They looked to be
about seven or eight, five and three, respectively. Their
parents followed and both looked Irish in origin.

Dad had reddish hair, green eyes and a ruddy skin
tone, while Mom was also red haired, brown eyes and a
little on the heavy side. Both looked extremely pleasant
and carried half smiles and excited gazes while looking
around at the car.

Jared thought they looked as if they had won the
Irish sweepstakes and this was the ceremony before the
award. They plopped the girls down at the head of the
car and took the table directly across the aisle from their
girls.

The last family to join them in this car was a young

man, his wife and their toddler, who was dressed in a
pale blue ski suit and looked to be about two years old.
This family looked as if they had come from an area
more rural in nature, and the young man looked very fit
and muscular. His angular face spoke of hard chiseled
lines, but his eyes were soft.

His wife was beautiful with high round cheekbones
and stunning gray eyes with a hint of blue in them. Her
shoulder length hair was more of a strawberry blond
color and contrasted her eyes beautifully. They sat at the
next table up from the Gradys.

Everyone gave each other a polite nod and a half
smile as they got themselves situated. Not one person
had the look as if they had been through this experience
a time or two before. There were certainly no 'ho-hum'
looks as they stepped onto the train. It seemed like each
person had the same question on his or her minds.

Where are we going and how did we get here? That is all
but the one little boy, who seemed to have all the
answers, if only the adults would *listen!*

A few moments after everyone had found their place
and settled in, Conrad and other valets appeared with
hot cocoa, tea and coffee. They offered these and said
other beverages were available should their guests prefer
it.

Susan and Marshall opted for the cocoa; Julie a
strong cup of tea and Jared had the coffee. It was his
personal favorite, Kona coffee from Hawaii. Conrad
explained that as soon as the train got going they would
be able to order dinner.

Jared finally found enough of his wits to ask Conrad

how long of a train ride this would be. Conrad replied long enough to have dinner, relax for a few moments afterward, meet some of the other guests, get to know them better and then they'd pull in to the station.

Jared asked if he could put that into minutes and Conrad responded. "Time takes on a slightly different perspective up here. Minutes and hours don't quite measure the same.

"For instance we don't see the sun set for months on end, same is true in reverse, and we don't see it all for months either, like now. Think about what you'd like for dinner and I'll be back to take your order."

Julie said, "I'm sorry Conrad, but we don't have menus, yet."

"You don't need them, just think what you would enjoy most and ask for it." They all looked at him as if he had grown two heads. From another table they heard one of the girls say "ANYTHING?" And their valet/waiter said, "Yep, give me your favorite food, and we'll serve it up."

Conrad smiled again and said, "Start thinking," and was off.

The Gradys looked at each other and started to laugh and snicker. 'Anything we want.' Boy, could they get this poor lost Northern soul scratching his head. Suddenly, they felt the train begin to move forward ever so gently. It was as if the engineer thought everyone was asleep and didn't want to wake them. The train pulled out of its comfy cabin and lurched into the bitter cold outside.

The Gradys felt like they were on a game show trying to come up with the wackiest meal imaginable and see if the staff could throw it together. They were having a good deal of fun coming up with unreal combinations and crazy concoctions, and they weren't alone in the fun. All over the car they could hear the adults and kids throwing ideas all over the place. Some of the ideas were crazy, some plain absurd (like theirs) and some on the edge of culinary genius (like roast Duck with an Asian ginger sauce over a chestnut and date stuffing).

Marshall said, "Yeah, but whatever we order it will all taste like chicken!" This made not only Jared and Julie, but the other adults howl with laughter.

A few minutes later the personal captains returned, and Conrad said, "Good, you are all having some fun. That's as it should be, now what may I get you for dinner?"

Julie said what was on all their minds, "Conrad, really, could you give us a hint what you have?"

Conrad beamed. "Oh, if I did that I might influence your decision. Please order whatever you are in the mood for, or something you really love but don't get very often."

Marshall tried first. "Okay, I'd like a rack of baby back pork ribs with barbequed beans and a chocolate shake."

Conrad said, "Very well, do you like the BBQ sauce spicy or smoky?"

"Uhhh, smoky."

Conrad nodded as he wrote. "And you Susan?"

Susan scrunched up her face as she seriously considered all the possibilities. "How about golden fried shrimp, with coleslaw and a piece of chocolate cream pie?" she asked.

"Anything to drink?"

Susan thought again, "Just more of this hot cocoa, its wonderful!"

Again a quick nod and a smile.

Julie was ready and waiting for her turn. Jared saw her get that look, as if she had the most delicious idea and couldn't wait to launch it on the world. Conrad looked at her, and she shot forth, "I would like a spring rack of lamb with rosemary seasoning and a little dab of mint jelly. Could you also bring a spinach salad with hot bacon dressing, some spiced apples – cored of course, and (she paused) a hot fudge sundae, no nuts but a cherry on top."

"I'll make sure there's two! And for you Mr. Grady?"

Jared never had the culinary excitement Julie had, so he ordered his most pleasing staple, "I'll have a prime rib medium rare with horseradish sauce on the side, a twice baked potato and salad with honey mustard dressing. And Conrad if you are going to be with us through so much of the trip, please call us Jared and Julie."

The obedient servant smiled broadly. "They told me you were extremely nice. Thank you Jared. May I bring you anything else to drink or for dessert?"

He thought a moment. "Why yes, I'd like a dry martini with a double olive."

Conrad's smile evaporated. "I'm sorry Jared. We don't serve alcohol or allow tobacco products on the train."

Jared gave a casual wave of his hand and said with a

little too much enthusiasm. "No problem, bring me
some more of this wonderful coffee!"

Conrad's smile returned. "Right away, sir!" Then he
spun on his heels and was off.

The Gradys looked at each other as if they had pulled
the best practical joke on poor Conrad, and snickered
and giggled about the outrageous requests. Jared said to
Julie, "Spiced apples? Cored — of course?" He could
only shake his head and have another guffaw over the
idea.

Susan said, "I at least hope they have cream pie, even
if it's not chocolate." A few seconds later their happy
waiter returned with Marshall's milkshake, more cocoa,
coffee and tea. The Gradys kept a straight face to the
best of their skill though Susan started sniggering as he
was leaving. At the other table the little boy said,
"You'll see, they'll bring it!"

After a while something happened that they could
never explain as long as they lived. From both sides of
the car the waiters burst in with two assistants each
carrying a cacophony of dishes that defied explanation.

Conrad bustled up to the table and laid before the
Grady family everything they ordered and precisely the
way they ordered it, right down to Jared's horseradish
sauce, Julie's spiced apples and Susan's chocolate cream
pie.

The little boy cried out with delight, "SEEEE, I told
you he'd bring me dinosaur besghetti with meatballs!"
But that wasn't the craziest. There was the Asian Duck
as it had been described, and over there were lobster
tails, and the young girls had cheeseburgers, French fries

and pizza (some things never change). There was pheasant under glass and Baked Alaska for desert, and filet mignon and deep-dish pecan pie.

It seemed the joke had been on them. It was so unbelievable that everyone sat stunned for a moment before the loud clanging of forks, knives and spoons rang like silver bells through the car.

Chapter Four

"It's about the best I've ever had," said Marshall. The rest of his family couldn't agree more.

And it was the consensus across the train. Everyone raved about their individual choices, and the tastes they stole off each other's plates. After the airport industries best, this was definitely Five-Star quality. Everyone had cleaned their plates down to the last bite of dessert, and they settled back to watch the little bit of scenery they could see, which wasn't much.

As Conrad said there are six months where the sun is not seen at all in these parts. And they were right in the middle of those six. That was another thought that had escaped them while hastily packing for their trip. The only wildlife they'd get to see would have to come up and tap on the window.

Julie walked over to the family with the little boy. "And who's this handsome young man?" she said with a smile.

"My name's Patrick."

Julie returned, "Well Patrick, my name is Julie, and it's very nice to meet you."

Patrick said, "Did you get a 'vitation from Santa Claus, too?"

"Excuse me?" Julie asked. "What invitation would that be?"

Heather Conner came up to Julie and introduced

herself as Patrick's Mom and said that Patrick was convinced that this trip was not only a gift from Santa Claus, but that Santa's Workshop was their final destination.

"He keeps telling his father and me about his dreams, and how Santa personally told him about the trip," said Heather. Julie watched the little boy grinning and playing with a car he'd brought with him for the trip up.

Heather whispered to Julie, "So far he has described everything very accurately right down to the different types of food."

Julie looked surprised and then regained herself. "I must admit that the variety of cuisine was pretty unusual even for a luxury train, but I'm not quite ready to submit to the Santa theory no matter how far north we are."

Heather asked the magic question. "How did you get here by the way?"

Julie fidgeted but thought it safe to tell Heather.

After she recounted the story, Heather nodded. "Exactly the same with us, I thought your ski jackets looked similar."

Heather was sporting a soft green jacket with darker green trim and her husband had a black jacket with silver piping. "These are our favorite colors, too."

Julie hadn't thought about that before, but realized that her entire family liked the colors of the outfits they'd received, which was nothing short of miraculous in Susan's case. Jared almost always wore blue if he had a clean blue shirt in his closet. And Julie really liked the red/white combination and thought it was stunning.

They were joined by the Irish mother of the three daughters, who each sported different combinations of pink and cream on their jackets.

"Hi, I'm Maureen O'Reilly. We were wondering if you might happen to know exactly where we are going? Our package didn't explain it clearly, or my husband, Jim, and I missed it if it did."

Jared had walked up during this exchange. "Oh, you didn't miss it, at least not if it was the same package as ours. It was distinctively absent of information."

Jim O'Reilly came up behind Maureen and introduced himself and his three girls. Being a large man he filled up the space behibnd Maureen. He was tall as well as big, and resembled a moving mountain with the sun setting on his peak of red hair. After everyone else introduced themselves and hands were shaken all around, Jim said, "We weren't going to 'fall for it', until the ski outfits and note showed up. In fact, I had to retrieve the package out of the trash. Truth is, we can't afford vacations, as we are trying to raise our three foster daughters."

Julie immediately gave a knowing nod and thought to herself. *No wonder they don't look very much alike.*

"Three girls, yeah, I'll bet the clothing costs kill you alone!" said Heather's husband as he wandered over to the group. "Hi, my name's Brian Conner. I was thankful from that end, that Heather and I had boys."

Jared laughed. "You may not be so happy when they are a little older and become eating machines."

Brian scoffed. "Yeah, well I still think food is easier to replace than all the clothes girls go through, so I'll take my chances with John and Patrick."

Maureen rebutted. "Well nowadays boys or girls don't seem to matter. Everything is designer-labels with designer price tags. The old days of buying jeans and a decent shirt doesn't cut it anymore."

To this all the adults nodded, knowing how true it was.

"Can't even pay a decent price for shoes, as everything has to be the hottest brand of the month," argued Jim.

"Or week," replied Julie. They all chuckled at their own experiences.

About that time one of the other valets, the one for Maureen and Jim, stepped through the door and Maureen called to him. "Fred, we were all discussing our final destination, would you care to enlighten us?"

Fred was tall and thin, but held the same demeanor and pleasant smile that Conrad sported. Fred smoothed his moustache. "Well it is a very exclusive resort town. In fact, it is one of the most exclusive in the world. No more than a couple hundred people a year are ever invited, and only once."

So, Jared thought, *It was one of those types of promotions! They got you up there and soaked you for every pampering service they could think of. And why not? What else will you be doing in the ever dark of a town out literally in the middle of nowhere and with no escape until the train comes to take you back?*

It was almost as if he said these thoughts out loud. "Now don't worry Mr. Grady. The invitation said there would be no expense and believe me, there will be no

expense. If you didn't need your ID for the airlines, you
could have left your wallet at home." Jared looked a tad
sheepish as if he had been caught telling a lie.

Then Patrick jumped up and again put forth his
argument. "We're goin' to see Santa Claus!"

Fred smiled at the little boy. "Well you never know
who you might meet in the village, Patrick." He turned
as if he had urgent business and was gone before anyone
could think of another question.

Another young man, one of the assistants Jared saw
earlier, came in the coach car and asked if anyone would
like any beverages or dessert, to which they all replied in
the negative. They were still trying to move their
sumptuous feasts around in their body.

He said they would be arriving soon and left.
Everyone spoke to each other as if they were old friends.
Susan and Marshall were talking and playing with the
three O'Reilly girls who were Ellen (8), Renee (6) and
Annie (4½ - with emphasis on the ½!). Maureen and
Jim had adopted them when tragedies struck each of
their biological families. As they were filling in the
blanks of their lives and backgrounds, Jared noticed the
train had begun to slow.

Chapter Five

The adults and children alike moved over to the windows as they all noticed the train decelerating. The view outside surprised them. They were going through a heavily wooded area that was thick with trees, and not only pines and evergreens, but maples, ash, oak and more.

Brian Conner said, "This doesn't make sense. I thought all there was this far north was tundra and snow."

Heather said, "That's what the Internet site I saw said, too."

Indeed it was hard to fathom such a rich forest in the middle of the Arctic. When they saw the soft lights of dwellings their curiosity bordered on disbelief. Who could live in such a place? Then through the darkness they saw a small boy (or maybe a girl) leading what looked to be an elk through the forest. In the dim light none could make out any distinct details. Off in the distance there was a glow from what looked to be a large campfire, and more children moving very rapidly as if gliding across the snow in circles.

"Boy they must be of hardy stock to be outside around here," said Jim O'Reilly.

"I can't see any adults. Where are their parents?" questioned Brian.

"Maybe it's a birthday party or something," Susan added.

"Outside?" asked Marshall.

Suddenly a wall of white covered the windows. As the outside scene disappeared, the valet/waiter/porters appeared again and said they would be arriving at the station in about five or six minutes and everyone should start gathering their things.

They had gone into the tunnel that would take them to the village on the other side. Everyone asked about the woods and the dwellings and the children. The valets simply said all their questions would be answered at the orientation once they disembarked and were made comfortable at the lodge.

Surprisingly even after the very long day of travel, none of the Gradys felt exhausted. In fact, they each felt pretty good and didn't complain at the thought of an orientation meeting to learn about this strange excursion. Jared, for one, thought that perhaps he would finally get some answers to his myriad of questions.

So he and his family went over to their table and started gathering jackets and belongings. Jared felt sorry to be leaving this magnificent train so soon, and would have enjoyed a much longer trip, though it was obviously not designed for sleeping. But then again, after the meals they prepared on board he thought maybe he hadn't seen the length and breadth of this train's secrets.

"Oh my God!" It was Heather Conner who exclaimed.

As the train came out of the tunnel it was as if the white curtain was being drawn on a surreal Christmas scene. Heather was the only one to exclaim, as the rest seemed devoid of speech. A couple low whistles were the most that were heard, and Julie couldn't be sure if those hadn't come from the train.

Everyone's eyes seemed bigger than the sockets meant to hold them. They all tried to take in the full measure of what they were seeing. The scene even seemed to have gone over and above the dreams of little Patrick, as he stood on his bench in rapt fascination like the others.

It was finally Maureen O'Reilly who made the next comment, "Have you ever…?" was the most she could muster.

Marshall and Susan rejoined their parents and were peering through the window with the same awe that was on the faces of the other passengers.

For Julie and Jared, it was as if they'd returned to their wildest dreams as children. Even then it was hard to imagine the variety of buildings and architectural styles that stood before them. And the colors!

Every color and roofline you could dream up was here. But the most amazing thing right off was all the children…except wait…they weren't children. They were dwarves… no that's not right either; they were…

"ELVES?" Susan asked out loud the question they were all thinking.

Chapter Six

"Welcome everyone, welcome to the North Pole!" said Conrad, Fred and the other valets.

"The North Pole?" asked Jared, Jim and Katy.

"Yup," answered Fred, "you are officially at the top of the world and in Santa's Village. Mr. and Mrs. Claus and all the people of the Pole welcome you. Now if you'll follow us over to the Reindeer Inn, we'll get you settled."

Everyone seemed to be in overload between the scene outside the window and the formal announcement of their location. Of course the children were as excited as kids can get and little Patrick Conner was jumping up and down saying 'I told ya, I told ya!' over and over.

As they got off the train they were met with smiles along with "Welcome" and "Merry Christmas" from all the passing elves on their way to other places. The air was crisp, but certainly not the -12° they met in Fairbanks. This felt like it was at or around the freezing mark, and there was no wind or even a breeze to contend with.

It was cold but pleasantly so.

Jared looked up at the sky and said, "Will you look at that?" Covering the entire area as far as one could see was a dome like substance, and yet there were some billowy clouds inside at the top. A little ways off you could even see snow falling from one of the clouds.

Maureen asked, "Do you think they can make their own weather in here?"

"Since this place doesn't exist in the first place, I would guess anything is possible," Julie laughed.

There were high hills around the Village and houses and shops were on two different levels. Beyond these hills and shops were mountains that seemed to reach up and connect to the domed roof. Looking around there were shops and stores everywhere. Jared thought it looked like an old time Solvang, which is a little Danish town with multiple quaint shops and retail stores that he and Julie used to love to visit and stroll around.

Every store here was different. From the rooflines and trim down to the colors, shape and style of each structure. Some looked Russian or Cyrillic in nature, and he could swear that one was German, and the bakery he couldn't figure out. The roof and the towers looked like a big but gentle roller coaster from the front. Some buildings looked more like candy shacks or old hot dog stands taken to a much grander scale.

They followed one of the valets from the train car that was in front of them. The valets walked carefully keeping their eye on the guests with children to make sure they didn't travel too quickly.

They approached a large edifice that had so many gables and towers that its true size couldn't really be determined from any one direction. There were little reindeer statues mounted on the top of each tower. The building was a caramel color with smooth walls and windows everywhere. The roof was scalloped with dark red tiles that ended in soft curves. A very inviting structure, as were the rest, each seeming to say "come on in and take a look around at your leisure".

The valets grabbed the two large arched oak doors and opened the structure for their anxious guests. As they all filed into the expansive lobby they saw a fireplace large enough for a man to lie down inside with room to spare. However, on this particular day it had a large roaring fire going in it. The wood smelled of a hint of eucalyptus and it gave off enough heat to warm the whole lobby to a pleasant temperature. The room had seating all around and could comfortably sit twenty-five or more without leaving any one standing.

A sprite small lady came out of the back with a huge smile on her face.

"Welcome honored guests to the Reindeer Inn. My name is Christel Bunkinstyle and I am the Chief Resort Manager," the elf said. She stood approximately four feet tall, and had a long face with soft dark blue-gray eyes. Her nose was slightly longish and ended in a cue stick point. Her ears were long as well, but not pointed, as one would expect an elf's to be.

She said, "We will be having an orientation in the lobby in forty-five minutes, but you may all go up to your rooms to check your accommodations and register any questions or concerns about them. Your luggage will be placed in your rooms while you are at the orientation. Now all the room names are marked clearly on the walls and doors and you should have no trouble finding them on your own. However, we shall take you to them personally this first time."

She produced a two-inch gold sleigh bell from her

pocket and rang it. Several elves filed in from three
different ground floor locations into the lobby.

Christel called out the name of each family and
announced their room. "Billings – Donder, O'Reillys –
Chestnut," with that Maureen, Jim and their three girls
went trotting off with their 'bell-elf' leading the way.
"Fredricks – Prancer," and a family of four walked
toward the staircase. "Wus – Vixen," a younger Asian
couple headed off with their elf. Christel then called out,
"Peters – Cupid," and two young adults with a toddler
walked toward the stairs.

The young lady with toddler in hand turned to
Christel and asked, "Excuse me, does she have our key?"
indicating to the young elf heading off in front of them.

Christel said, "We don't have keys here. Terrible
waste of time and energy."

Katy replied, "Well, how do you lock your doors?"

Christel looked at the young woman and smiled.
"Dear, you are in the North Pole. You do not need to
lock your doors or bolt your windows. We are all on the
'honor system' up here. And you may rest assured that
no one will disturb your room, or steal from you. They
wouldn't be here if they had even the smallest inkling of
that in their heart. Enjoy the Cupid Room."

As they turned to go Christel returned to looking at
the group and continued calling out names and rooms.
"Gradys – Rudolph, Thomas – Alandale."

Jared, Julie and the kids marched behind an elf
toward the stairs. "I'm William," the four and a half
foot dwarf said, "You should really enjoy Rudolph."

Julie said, "I don't wish to seem ungrateful, but all

four of us in one room? Is there any chance we could get a second room so the girls and guys can share a room together?"

William said, "Oh I wouldn't worry there, it's plenty big enough for all of you. You'll see."

The Gradys walked up onto the third flight of steps and there were two rooms on this floor, Rudolph and Pocatello.

"Pocatello?" Marshall asked.

William said matter of factly, "Why yes, that's Rudolph's Father. Here you go," as he pointed to the room adorning Rudolph's name and opened the door.

Chapter Seven

"It's a suite, and a really big one at that," said William. They stared in stunned silence. The main living area was large and filled with beautiful antique furniture from the French Renaissance period.

The sofa was modern, the kind that is overstuffed so that you sank into like a giant pillow. A small but beautifully adorned dining table with four chairs stood at the opposite end of the room. It had a flowered centerpiece of fresh red roses and evergreens wrapped up in the most stunning ribbons and bows the Gradys had ever seen. A smaller seating area made up of two matching Queen Anne winged chairs and a small 17th century lamp table sat off the other side under large windows overlooking the village. There were three doors and a smaller opening that looked to contain a kitchen off both sides of the dining room.

William said, "Mr. And Mrs. Grady, your room is off to the right, next to the kitchen. Marshall, yours would be the far left, and Susan, the nearer left. Enjoy your stay with us."

Marshall didn't need to hear anymore, he immediately walked to the room at the rear and opened the door. "Oh, this is too cool." He walked into a room with wallpaper festooned with all types of musical instruments and even a gold tenor saxophone in the corner gleaming in its stand. Marshall loved playing in the marching, concert and jazz bands at school and hoped that maybe he'd be good enough someday to make it a career. He caught sight of a new mouthpiece lying on the dresser with a note that said, *"We love Christmas music, and you'll find some sheet music in the drawer."* Marshall didn't even know what to think. He looked at the four-poster overstuffed bed, and already wondered if there was a way they could extend their stay.

Susan opened the door to a smartly decorated room filled with different college pennants from around the world. Everything from Oxford and Harvard to William & Mary were hanging from the walls. Below the pennants were quotes from many of the world's scholars touting the virtues and abilities of humanity to succeed and accomplish great things. On one wall was a bookshelf with writings of some of the greatest politicians and thinkers in history. She pulled a book from the shelf that looked particularly aged and saw it was *Poor Richard's Almanack* written by Benjamin Franklin, and dated 1755. It looked to be an original copy.

She hopped onto her white four-poster bed and carefully looked through the pages. She read some of the proverbs and quotes that she and so many others had heard growing up in their lifetime.

Julie and Jared opened the door to a rustic but very comfortable colonial style room. It was simply furnished and was decorated in soft pastel hues. The most interesting thing in the room was the high ceiling. It contained soft clouds of white throughout and they

looked very real as they floated around the top of the
room. The bathroom (there was one in each bedroom)
contained an oversized claw tub and two pedestal sinks.
The bathroom and bedroom were spacious enough for
two, but not wasteful in area.

The whole feeling of the room was serene, but
practical. There was a large set of windows that
wrapped around three sides and they realized they were
in a turret shaped room that looked out over a good
portion of the village. There were a couple smaller
seating areas and each looked out on a different view.
Their room had a carved four-poster Williamsburg
styled queen size feather bed directly in the center. The
bed did not have a canopy. Instead you viewed the
clouds that were rolling slowly across the ceiling.

Julie placed a few things from the overnight bag she
had carried in the large armoire located next to the
bathroom. She felt happier than she had in years and
said to herself; *If this is a dream, please don't let anyone
or anything wake me for another day.*

Jared was staring out the window. He was afraid to
say anything. His practical nature was making it very
hard for him to accept all this. Julie and the kids seemed
to be going along with this as if it had been known and
planned all along. He wished he could be getting as
much enjoyment as the rest of his family. But he still
knew that whatever this place really was, he would have
to return to reality next week. It wasn't a pleasant
prospect, thus not all of the clouds in the room were of
the North Pole's making.

A knock on the door and Marshall strode in, "You

really should see my room!" he said grinning. "You'll
never guess the theme – MUSIC! Is that amazing or
what?"

Julie smiled back and said, "Well I'll bet they bring a
lot of budding 'Carnegie Hall' musicians here. Have you
seen your sister?"

Marshall threw his right thumb backward and said
"Yeah, she's in her room reading some dusty old book.
Hers looks like a college dorm room or something. I got
the best room," he said looking around. "But you have
more windows and chairs."

Julie pointed up at the ceiling and said, "Did you see
this?"

Marshall looked up, laughed and said, "Wow, I hope
it doesn't snow at night!" and went off to explore the
rest of the accommodations.

He made a right into the kitchen and flipped on the
light. It was an efficiency kitchen. Not really the kind
in which you would make a large dinner for friends and
family. But it had many of the usual small appliances:
toaster, coffeemaker, blender, microwave and the like.

The refrigerator was adequate for a short stay, but
didn't look like it held much. He opened the door and
inside were sodas, juices, milk, cream, water and coffee
drinks. When he opened one of the cabinets and found
a variety of coffee mugs and glasses. The next contained
almost every kind of hot cocoa mix imaginable: double
Dutch chocolate, vanilla cream chocolate, caramel
crème chocolate, mint, raspberry, milk, dark, and even
white chocolate were there. The upper shelf contained
ciders, including apple, cranberry, and more.

The next cabinet had all types of snacks and nuts, and...chocolate candies! There were several boxes each marked with its contents, "crèmes and chews", "nuts and fudge", "truffles" and more. He thought, *"Boy, wait 'til Mom and Susan see this!"*

In other cabinets he found boxes of cereals (including his Dad's favorite Granola style), soups marked with the North Pole label, different flavors of coffees (even egg nog flavored), a large number and types of tea, spices, baking goods, etc.

Jared walked in and Marshall gave him the tour, showing him first all the goodies, then the more practical items.

Jared chuckled and said, "Why do I feel like I'm going to be paying for this at the gym until next summer?"

Susan walked in and said, "Did I hear something about chocolate?"

Marshall laughed and opened the cabinets and said, "Welcome to heaven!"

Susan gasped in wonder and joy. A few minutes later Julie walked in and announced that it was time to go to the orientation and that any further exploring would have to wait until later.

Chapter Eight

"Where do you think they found those porcelain houses?" asked the lady of Asian descent to her husband. "I have never seen so many perfect recreations."

Everyone was filing back down the steps and was being joined by other families, all discussing their incredible rooms.

"How could they know my hobby was aircraft?" asked one.

"Did you believe all the books on New England crafts? I thought I had every one in print!" said another.

The children were even more animated than the parents. On the way down, Jim and Maureen's youngest daughter Annie was pleading, "Why can't I ride the rocking horse some more, Mommy?"

Maureen assured her daughter she would be able to ride it a great deal more later on, but they needed to meet the nice lady again.

Their other two girls were busy comparing notes about all the dolls and accessories that were in their bedroom. Renee said she swore she saw one of the Barbies on eBay as an original worth a ton of money.

They all filed into the massive seating area by the fireplace and took seats in the large sofas and chairs. Cookies and fruit of several varieties were laid on a tray at the table in the center of the area. Some of the elves

brought tea, coffee and hot cocoa from the back and
offered it to the guests.

As they were getting their refreshments, Christel
bounded out of the back and said, "Thank you all for
your promptness. I'm sure you have many questions and
I shall address each one in turn, but first let me address
all the obvious ones that you share. After you settle in I
will tell you what you want to know."

With that announcement the adults were unusually
swift to get their beverages and drinks and be seated.
Their need for information even outweighed the desire
for sweets.

The children also became quiet as Christel stepped
into the center of the group. They were all waiting to
hear what they would be able to do if they ever decided
they'd want to leave their rooms. With an almost
storyteller quality she began her tale.

**"It began a little over a century ago. The
North Pole had been in operation much longer,
but we noticed that people had begun losing
faith in the magic and wonder of Christmas.**

**We were finding that not as many people
believed in Santa Claus, and worse, had lost
faith in the real reason behind Christmas – the
birth of the Savior, Jesus Christ. It was decided
after so many centuries of secrecy that we
would allow certain people to visit the North
Pole, to see its reality and spread the truth
about Christmas to others. Of course we had
strict guidelines to adhere to, and they are still**

in force today.

The first and most important is that anyone invited must have shown that they already know how to keep Christmas alive. Not only in November or December but throughout the year, every day.

Secondly, they must be people who may be trusted with secrets. They must understand that while they know the truth about certain things, they cannot disclose it to win an argument or gain an upper hand on someone else.

Third their children (if they have any) must demonstrate the same qualities and values, as they possess themselves.

Fourth they must not hold any malice intent in their hearts toward others.

And lastly, they must give of themselves to others as unselfishly as we try to do here in the North Pole.

It is because of these outstanding qualities that each of you is here. It is very difficult some years to find many people with all these virtues. Many people we watch lose their faith. Some are driven toward material things, get everything they want and become selfish or stop sharing their gifts. Well, that's the sad side."

Many people raised their hands as if in a classroom, but Christel raised her own and said,

"Please hold your questions for now. There is more to say and I need to address some other things before we get too far afield.

Now the wonderful news! You are all here to enjoy yourselves. You have the opportunity to learn all the things that you and everyone else have ever wanted to know about Santa Claus. You'll learn his history and heritage, along with truths and non-truths and the myth and legend behind the greatest gift givers in history.

Someone couldn't wait on that one and asked, "Did you say 'givers'?" Christel continued firmly,

"Yes, the Santa Claus that you will meet this next week will be Nicholas the Eleventh. His father, Father Christmas, also still lives up here but retired over 100 years ago. The first Santa Claus, St. Nicholas, was a very wealthy Bishop in the country now called Turkey around 300 A.D. He lived a virtuous and wonderful life and instituted the legend of Santa Claus. When he died, his son felt it necessary to carry on the traditions and continued giving from his father's inheritance.

Soon, people contributed to Nicholas II in return. This allowed him to give and do more for others than even his father had done. The legend spread as did the family. Nicholas II also had a son who carried on the tradition. Then he had a son, and that son went to Germany. There, Nicholas the third began several

traditions among the people in Europe, including the Christmas tree, its decorations and adornments like holly inside the home.

A couple generations later, Nicholas the Fifth traveled into France and Italy, and so on and so forth. The population of the world spread into North and South America and it grew exponentially. It was in the latter 1700's that we found Nicholas the Tenth in the Netherlands and invited him to the North Pole. When we explained what we could do for him he agreed to move here. Here we are able to produce more gifts and create more magic, plus because of the environs we have the ability to maintain a much longer life.

Here the average person lives about 400 years, give or take. We are not immortal, but we have seen a lot more by the time we become adults than most people of the world see during their entire lifetime. Having lived so long we are actually way ahead of you in technology and production, but we produce items to match the speed of your individual cultures. We are happy, and concerned, to see it's finally beginning to make some leaps to get a little closer to ours.

Now, anyone is allowed to roam at their leisure day or night through the North Pole Village. Most shops and the few factories in the village are open the usual hours of 9 until 9. You need not worry about your children becoming lost. They are free to meander wherever their feet take them. The elves will keep watch over them, feed them if they become hungry and return them when they are tired. Our staff here will also help watch your children. So if you wish to go somewhere without them it is not only permissible, but encouraged. Of course anyone of George and Marshall's age and above will not be monitored, as they are old enough to go unescorted through the village.

Next, food is available to you anytime you are hungry. We do not have set times or menus. Like on the train, you tell us what you would like, when you would like it and we will have it made available to you. I will caution you about overeating, as you could still get a stomachache. You are free to use your own judgment.

Now the best part, because of the special air and magic that is here, you may eat anything you'd like and it will not add weight, and if you are allergic to some foods, they will not harm you here. Even if you would have a deadly reaction to nuts or are lactose intolerant, it holds no sway here. So anyone having special dietary desires is free to indulge. You have our promise no ill effects will occur.

I will tell you 'photo buffs' in the crowd that because of the magnetic effects of the

North Pole your photographic equipment will
be all but useless. So while we won't prevent
you from taking photographs and videos, we
will tell you that they will not reproduce well.
We sometimes even have trouble with battery-
operated items up here. You will find that nearly
every item is hooked to an AC adapter, because
batteries only last nanoseconds in the strong
magnetic pull of the Pole. Similarly, your cell
phones will not function, as there are no cell
towers. Even satellite phones do not receive a
signal up here so no calls will be able to be
made while you are here. That goes for any
computers as well, sorry, no Internet.

Each of you is able to acquire a gift of
your choosing for each member of your family
at no cost. You may choose any gift from
anywhere around the village, but I advise you
to choose wisely. These gifts are to be given on
Christmas Day and not before. Other gifts may
be 'purchased' but you will find the price tags a
bit unusual. You will see what I mean when you
leave the inn and begin shopping.

And now for the "rules".

Rule number one. No one is allowed to
venture past the Nutcracker Guards into the
Manufacturing or Woodland areas. This is off
limits to visitors for safety and technology
reasons. Some secrets must remain when you
leave here, mostly because your culture is not
yet ready to receive some of the breakthroughs

and gadgets that we have developed. We estimate as much as another 50 to 75 years will pass until you are ready for some of them. Much of that time will depend on how your countries and its leaders begin to keep peace with other nations.

Rule number two; any secrets about production and distribution must remain secret. We cannot take the chance that someone may use that information to sabotage Santa and his deliveries to the Christian people of the world. You will be given a "debriefing" during and at the end of your stay as to what is safe to discuss and what is not. To tell you now wouldn't make sense, and you would not understand some of the things until you learn more."

"You mean we can't talk about the reindeer?" asked Renee.

"Yes you may, but there are other parts of the distribution secret beyond our reindeer. We would want you to share about our wonderful reindeer. This brings up the last rule, as there are only three.

You MUST try to pass on many of the things you learn here, as enthusiasm and knowledge are the best ways to grow Christmas spirit. Like any living thing, it needs to be nurtured and given plenty of light, water

and room for growth.

If Christmas is allowed to take root in other places and survive the harsh years, it will develop and grow, wherever it is spread, into a beautiful world of love and understanding. Now I will take your questions."

The room exploded with hands and voices. "Please, please one at a time," said Christel laughingly. "Yes Mr. O'Reilly."

Jim stood and said almost sheepishly. "Ah, well, I don't wish to sound like I'm making a confession, but Mo and I aren't very religious and we can't understand why you chose us, unless it was for our girls." He sat down and stared at the floor.

"Mr. O'Reilly, Jim if I may, you and Maureen took three children that had suffered tragic losses. You gave them a home and love, taught them not to be angry with God for their loss, but to respect all life as precious because it can be precarious. Every day you give them love, shelter, and hopes. You teach them that adversity doesn't prevent dreams; it just changes the architecture of them. How much more of the spirit of Christmas can you be expected to give? Each of you has lived and continues to live a very unselfish life."

She looked over at the Gradys and continued.

"You do things for others when there is no financial or personal gain, and you face problems without losing your faith or asking 'Why me?'"

She looked over to the the young couple with the toddler named Peters. "You fight to protect others

rights and you help other families in need without
asking anything, not even a favor, in return. This is
giving and keeping Christmas all year long. Please take
my word that you all belong here, and you all deserve
this. We want you to be able to spread the good news of
this trip. Next question."

It was Fred Wu, half of the younger Asian couple the
Grady's saw that asked, "I thought that Santa and the
North Pole were all about wooden toys and stuffed dolls
and the like, how do you mean that you are more
advanced than we are?"

"Mr. Wu, we were about carved toys and stuffed dolls,
when your country was carrying muskets and hitching
horses. Yes, we still do some of those, but if we brought
you a powdered wig today, you would say it is of no use
— and you'd be right. Similarly, if we suddenly stuck a
computer under the tree that could fly to a particular
address on the moon by itself, carrying a grocery list of
items you need, it would be equally absurd. There is a
time for all things, past and future, and to do either in
the present wouldn't make sense to you. For a time we
were banned in Boston, because of religious heretics and
concerns of witchcraft. Imagine if we showed up in a
GMC pickup loaded with toys at the time to help *them*
out!"

Questions followed about everything from some of
the legends to where they could get diapers if they
needed them. Christel Bunkinstyle handled all questions
tirelessly. She responded to most, but put off questions
on operations and legends, saying there would be a
better time to ask those. After a period she said that it

was about time that they all got some rest and that they
would be much fresher to learn things tomorrow.
Everyone seemed disappointed, but admitted the steam
had gone out of their engines. They finished their drinks
and snacks and moved their now-tired bodies toward
their rooms. Tomorrow would bring exciting discoveries
and even more questions. Some would have trouble
sleeping, or so they thought.

According to Jared's watch it was about 11:30, but he
thought it felt more like 8:30 or 9:00. Though he felt
tired enough for it to be that late. As he got ready for
bed he felt it strange to seem late and yet so much
earlier. It was as if he was waging an argument with
himself.

Julie had unpacked everything for their trip, in short
order, as if everything had a special place to go, just as
in their own home.

Soon he and Julie climbed into the big featherbed,
and before he could ask Julie about her opinion of the
days events, they were both sound asleep.

"Ask and believe and wondrous things can happen.

You just need to become a child once more,

and have a child's faith."

Noel Hottentot, Balloonist

Chapter One

He woke to what seemed like a bright sunny day. When Jared realized where he was, he told himself that would be impossible. "The days are without sun this time of year," he thought out loud. Jared looked at the clouds floating in his room above him and shrugged. Julie had said earlier, 'if they can control their own weather under the canopy, probably they could control the lighting as well.'

Julie had come out of the bathroom looking refreshed and happy. "Hey, sleepyhead are you gonna loaf around all day?" she teased. Then she jumped on the bed and tousled his hair. "Come on, the coffee's already made and waiting."

When he got out of bed the room was cool but comfortable. He found the slippers and robe that Julie packed and while tying his belt swaggered into the kitchen.

Julie poured him a cup of coffee and said, "Guess what, they have Kona coffee here, too. Boy, are you getting spoiled." Her mood was playful and contagious. Soon they were discussing the amazing events of yesterday. Julie said, "I feel like I fell into a storybook, and I'm in no hurry to get to the end of it."

Even Jared had to admit he felt the best he had in a long time. "Kids still asleep?"

"Oh good heavens, no," she responded. "They were

both dressed and out as if they had to catch the bus for school."

Jared asked, "Did they know where they were going, or what the plan was?"

Julie laughed. "Plan? What plan? They were all ready to go exploring and couldn't wait to get out. I asked if they wanted something to eat first, and they said 'We'll get something in the village.' And off they went." She sipped her coffee. "Personally I think it's a great idea, except I seem to have some dead weight."

He smiled back at her and said in a mock-resigned voice. "Okay, okay, I got the message. I'll go shower quickly and we can be off, too." He picked up his coffee and shuffled off to the bathroom.

Julie watched him head off. Then she noticed a phone on the wall she hadn't seen before next to the doorway. She wondered if they let you make phone calls from here. She picked up the phone expecting a dial tone and before she could breathe, a voice came from the other side saying, "Good morning Mrs. Grady. What can we do for you today? May we bring some breakfast to you and your husband?"

She was so shocked she didn't immediately respond. Remembering what was said last night and the dinner on the train, she said that Jared would probably enjoy steak medium rare and eggs over easy, and she would like some French toast and a baked apple.

The voice on the other side said, "That will be up there in short order, will you be ready in ten minutes?"

She thought of how slowly Jared was moving. "Better make that twenty."

"Very good, Mrs. Grady," said the voice and she thanked them and hung up the phone.

Jared had just finished pulling on his shirt when there was a knock at the door. Julie opened it and a cute elf with bright red hair and freckles walked in carrying a tray that looked larger than her.

She laid the tray on the dining table and said, "We also added some potatoes to Mr. Gradys order. I think you call them 'home fries' and fresh strawberries for you, Mrs. Grady."

Julie looked surprised and said, "Where did you find fresh strawberries in December?"

The elf said cheerily, "Oh, we grow them year round here in the horticulture center."

Jared took a deep whiff and said, "Man, everything smells so good!" He pulled up a chair.

The little elf said, "I'll get you some more coffee if you'd like."

Jared gave a nod and murmured a quick thank you as he moved the plates closer.

Julie said she was fine. The elf returned with Jared's coffee and said, "Enjoy your breakfast. Leave the dishes and we'll take care of everything when you're finished." Then she was gone as fast as she had come.

Everything tasted even better than it looked and smelled, and they again enjoyed every morsel.

Jared said, "I really hope Christel wasn't lying about not gaining weight, or you may need to carry me around in a wheelbarrow by the time we leave."

After the sumptuous meal, they felt guilty leaving everything there, even though they were instructed to

do so. Instead they carried the dishes into the kitchen
and placed them into the sink.

Jared who seemed to get renewed energy from the
shower and meal said, "Well, are you ready to explore
our little fantasy land?"

Julie smiled and nodded. She was indeed.

As they reached the lobby another elf was picking up
a couple glasses from the seating area they were at last
night. He introduced himself as Fergie Keepitneet, the
daytime innkeeper. "Is there anything special I can
point you to or any questions you may have?" Fergie
inquired.

First they said 'no' then Jared thought again and
turned to Fergie, "Well before we run off, perhaps you
could tell us where best to go?"

Julie was stunned. Jared had never asked directions
in his life!

Fergie asked what they were in the mood for?

Julie said, "That's kind of tough since we don't know
what is here."

As if on cue, Fergie pulled a small disc out of his
pocket. It looked like an old style compact case, round
with a little gem in the center. He set it on the table and
pushed the jewel.

Instantly a holographic image of the entire village
burst in the middle of the room.

Jared felt as if he stepped aboard the Enterprise in
Star Trek.

Fergie pointed to the Reindeer Inn and said, "Here
we are. Now if you would like to see the village from
above, you can ride the gondolas over here." He moved

his long index finger down. "Or you can see Santa in his Visiting Cottage over here. Most of the shops and workshops are over here in this area."

Jared pointed to a large circular looking structure and asked, "What is this, this looks interesting?"

Fergie said, "That's the best way to see the entire North Pole! That's our hot air balloon ride. You can float over the whole place; even see the manufacturing and woodland areas, which are restricted on foot."

"Why is the area restricted on foot, but not by balloon?" questioned Julie.

Fergie said, "Oh we don't mind you seeing the structures and areas, we just can't allow you seeing some of the technology, plus it is extremely busy and you might get hit by a running sleigh or squibble."

Jared raised an eyebrow. "A squibble?"

Fergie said, "Yes sir, it's a form of transportation that looks kind of like a snow saucer but floats about two feet off the ground. They vary in size, but some of the freight squibbles are quite large and could cause an injury if it bumped into you."

Julie questioned Fergie further. "Aren't there any 'squibbles' in the village, and why do you call them that?"

Fergie shrugged and said, "We don't use them in the village as we don't want accidents with the children."

He reflected for a moment on her second question and asked, "Why do you call your vehicles 'cars'?"

Julie shrugged.

Jared asked how to best get to the balloon rides. Fergie indicated they'd need to take gondolas to the

upper level and then they could take a sleigh to the
Aviation Center at the end of the village.

"A sleigh?" responded Julie excitedly.

"Oh sure," said Fergie. "They're all over the village.
You can take them anytime you'd like. Look around and
you'll see one will be going your direction. It's kind of
our mass transportation system, except we don't have
too much mass." He laughed at his own joke. Fergie
advised them to turn right from the Inn and walk about
two blocks to the gondola.

They thanked him and turned to leave. As they
moved away, Fergie pushed the jewel on the disc and the
village disappeared from view, and he slipped the disc
back into his pocket.

Chapter Two

The Gradys stepped into the brisk air and zipped
their ski jackets a little higher. They turned as
instructed and moved through the village. As Fergie
promised, there were reindeer and horse-drawn sleighs
everywhere. There were also elves scurrying to and from
shops and carrying everything from boxes to stacks of
pies. Julie wondered how they kept from collapsing in on
themselves.

As they moved past a scarf and mitten store, Julie
asked Jared if they could take a peek inside.

"What if we miss our balloon ride?" questioned
Jared.

She said, "I have a feeling they'll be ready to go when
we are."

Jared knew she was right and motioned to the shop.
He opened the door for his wife and they both walked
inside.

There were mittens, scarves, socks, sweaters and the
like. Everything looked handmade. The beautiful
crochet and knitted work was flawless. Some had
multiple colors and patterns and others were solid.
There were both tight and loose knits and weaves. And
the variety of weights covered everything from very
thin and lightweight to bulky, heavy knits that would
protect one from the worst blizzard imaginable.

Julie picked up a nice weight scarf that she thought

would go well with her jacket. She found the price tag and looked. Then she looked again, "What the..." was all she said.

Jared came walking over holding a pair of leggings for a child and said, "Uhh, you need to see this price tag."

Julie looked back and showed him the one on the scarf. She looked at the item he was holding and wasn't surprised. Hers had said 'one meal to a homeless person', and his had said 'two good deeds for someone you don't know'.

They looked at other items and saw there was not a monetary "price" listed on anything. Each tag came with a particular request. They included the small, like for a pair of mittens that asked to 'say a prayer for a friend in need' to a larger 'donate 40 hours to charity' and so on. The more valuable the item the bigger the request on the tag.

The 'biggest' price tag he saw was to establish and chair a large fundraiser for a nonprofit health agency. This was for matching his and hers crocheted jackets. They now knew what Christel meant when she said 'the price tags were a bit unusual'.

They left the store without 'purchasing' anything right now and walked on to the gondolas. They boarded as Heather and Brian came running up.

"Isn't this the most beautiful place you have ever seen?" exclaimed Heather.

Brian said, "If I fell down the rabbit hole, I don't want to find the exit." He was clearly more animated than when the Gradys had met him on the train.

"Where are the boys?" asked Julie.

"Two elves knocked on the door very early this morning," said Heather. "We were up and dressed already. I guess we were excited about getting going, anyway the elves said they were there to help the boys get ready, eat and take them down to Santa later. So they said we were free to leave and go explore on our own."

Brian said, "I was a little hesitant at first, but Heather convinced me. We ran into them a little while ago coming out of one of the shops. They were all excited, especially Patrick, as they were on their way to a personal audience with 'the big guy'."

They all boarded the Gondola and as Julie and Heather compared rooms, Brian and Jared tried to pretend they were still grounded in reality.

"All I know is this is like no other place I've ever seen. And I've been around to a lot of places," said Brian.

Jared asked what Brian did for a living, and Brian said, "I am a sales manager for a sporting apparel company. And believe me working in sales I've heard and said most of it, though I have always tried to be honest in my representations..."

Jared raised his hand to stop him saying, "As the lady said, if you were dishonest you wouldn't be here. Which brings up another nagging question, how do they know...I mean really know, how we've lived our lives? I don't wish to sound paranoid, but talk about big brother! I can't figure out how they seem to know things. Like what kind of coffee I like, what I like to eat, about me losing my job..."

"You lost your job?" asked Brian. "Gee, I'm really sorry to hear that. What do you do?" Jared lowered his head and shuffled his feet. "Well, I was the Controller for my last company. Now it seems I'm not worthy of a clerk's position." He looked back at Brian. "Sorry, I get kinda melodramatic as I've been looking for quite a while now."

Brian looked sadly at him and said, "I know it's tough but you hang in there, especially for your family. Something will turn up, and probably from the least likely place you'd expect."

Jared gave a weak smile. "Yeah, I'm sure your right. It gets so frustrating sometimes. I mean look - fantasy all around me and I still can't get into the spirit."

Then Julie sidled up beside him and squeezed his hand. "Can't you let it go, even for this week?" she pleaded. "I think you could genuinely go back with a new attitude and a stronger resolve if you did."

Jared forced a smile. "When was the last time you ever heard of a Controller giving all their cares away and living in a Fantasyland?"

Brian laughed out loud and said, "Yeah, you're right – that's the job of the sales team!"

They all got a chuckle from his remark and the mood lightened considerably after that.

Chapter Three

As they reached the upper station they came out of the tram laughing and making jokes about the state of bewilderment their friends would be in when they got home and explained where they've been. They joked about how they will probably be locked away after relaying their experiences about the meals by itself, let alone the village and all the elves.

Heather and Brian decided to take the balloon ride together with the Gradys. As promised by Fergie, a reindeer drawn sleigh was waiting as they came off the tram car, and an older elf with warm brown eyes and wearing a mountain hat with a long feather said, "Can I offer you a ride, folks?"

They all hopped into the sleigh and pulled the blankets around them.

Jared called over his shoulder, "To the Aviation Center my good man."

"Right-oh," the elf called back and they were off.

It was a very pleasant ride and neither Heather nor the Gradys had ever been in a sleigh before. All four of them were enjoying the ride so much; they secretly hoped the Aviation Center was a ways away. The driver, who was named Bristol, told Julie that there was a thermos of hot tea and some mugs by her feet if anyone would like some. Julie and Heather enjoyed a mug, and it was the perfect accompaniment to their sleigh ride.

The reindeer jingled on for about fifteen minutes and then slowed.

Bristol called out, "Here we are! The Aviation Center awaits."

They jumped out of the sleigh and everyone thanked Bristol for the enjoyable ride. They turned and went into the building before them.

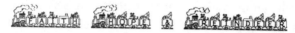

As their parents were pulling up to the Aviation Center, Patrick and John were walking into Santa's Visiting Cottage. There were flagpoles all around the area each representing a different country. John asked one of the elves if every flag in the world was there. The elf said, "Every country that celebrates Christmas, anyway."

The Visiting Cottage itself was rather small in stature, and looked little more than a couple rooms with some chairs. There weren't even any windows to speak of.

Patrick wondered out loud why Santa wouldn't have a bigger place.

The other elf laughed at his comment and said, "Santa only does his appointed visits here. His castle and workshop are at the other side of the Pole in the Woodland area. That's where he spends most of his time. He also has that house there." The elf pointed to a large two-story structure that looked Victorian in style. "He spends a lot of time there. That's his 'Village Home' where he rests and eats."

They walked through the door and Patrick's breath caught in his chest.

There he was, wearing his red pants and green suspenders. His shirt had different Christmas ornaments on it and looked comfortable and soft.

"Well, right on time. I've been looking forward to seeing you for a long time."

Patrick and John hardly knew what to say. In fact, both were silent as tombs.

Santa laughed his patented 'Ho, ho, ho', and motioned for the boys to follow him. He walked into the other room where a large chair was sitting. He sat down and motioned to the boys to join him on his lap.

He then spoke in much quieter tones and told them how proud he was of each of them and why.

Chapter Four

"I see it, but I don't believe it," said Brian as he walked into the building.

"Do you think they really mean it?" asked Julie.

"I doubt they would have a sign for it if it wasn't true," said Heather.

Jared said, "It's probably a mechanical ride, you know like the octopus at carnivals or something."

They gazed at the sign next to the directional sign for the Hot Air Balloon Rides. It simply read *Flying Reindeer Rides* with a large arrow beneath it pointing to their right.

"Which do we want?" asked Jared. Immediately Brian and Julie looked a little unsure about the reindeer side.

"I think we should stay with the original plan, but it wouldn't hurt to go take a look, would it?" pleaded Heather.

"I'm not sure I will believe it, but yeah, I've always wanted to see a flying reindeer since I first knew Santa used them," said Brian.

"Why not?" urged Jared. "Maybe one more incredible fantasy will be proved right at last!"

So they all turned right to get a peek at the impossible.

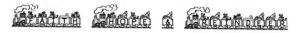

"Do you believe this stuff?" said Marshall to his sister.

"I never had any idea there were so many Teddy Bears in the world, let alone in one store," replied Susan.

They were standing in the middle of the store marked 'Santa's Friend Theodore', a four-story structure that was taller than it was wide. It had every kind, color and texture of Teddy bear stacked from the floor to the third floor.

George Mendez had joined them a couple stores back. George was six months younger than Marshall, though several inches taller, thin and with dark brown hair. He also was a sophomore in high school. George was in the band and played trumpet "fairly well" according to his own assessment. He said he was second chair at school.

Marshall told him of his love for music and the saxophone. He and Marshall hit it off instantly and found a good deal in common, with regard to band, classes and school in general. That would have been enough for George, but he was infatuated with Susan.

She didn't seem to mind a couple 'lower classmen' hanging with her. George thought that she was as pretty, or more so, than any of the girls at his school. Plus she didn't carry an attitude about it. In fact she was quite personable and friendly.

George had come with his mother and nine year old brother, Hunter. They had lost their father in an automobile accident a year and a half ago. They were going through some tough times as their Dad's money was running out. His Mom had gone back to work immediately afterward, but wasn't pulling down the salary his late father had.

When they got the invitation, both boys begged their mother for an opportunity to get away, anywhere for a week. It had been tough going through Christmas last year missing their Dad, none of them wanted to repeat the misery of it.

The three teenagers were looking up at the fourth floor which was devoted to "manufacturing." It was comprised of elves stuffing the bears and sewing them up.

"So much for 'high tech'," said George.

"It's not about technology, here," said one of the elves and all three jumped in surprise. "Oh, sorry about that," he continued, "but really it has a great deal with using a loving touch to put these special bears together and not 'mass produce' them as fast as you can. There is a time for technology and robots and cloning, and there is a time for hand crafted work."

"Cloning? Robots? At the North Pole?" questioned Susan.

The elf gave a knowing smile and said, "You would genuinely be amazed at what we can do and how we could do it. But back to our bears, you see every one of these bears has a special person in mind. Each will be loved and needed by one, and only one, individual. For instance," he pulled down a plush pale yellow Teddy from one of the shelves and showed it to Susan. "What do you think?" he asked her.

Susan felt a little uncomfortable critiquing the bear but said, "Uh, it's nice, but yellow isn't exactly my color."

"Exactly." replied the elf. "This would not be for you at all." He excused himself and said he would return shortly.

The three high school students went back to looking at some of the larger bears. They found one that was about twelve feet tall. "This must be for a store display," said Marshall. He looked at the price tag.

Even though this was the third store they had gone through. Marshall still wasn't used to the unusual price tags they'd seen. This one was marked, "Take several children from a local orphanage to the zoo." He shook his head. He thought he was a pretty good egg, and tried to think of others, but some of these tags made him realize there is so much that can be done for others and he hadn't even scratched the surface.

Suddenly, the elf returned and produced a medium-sized, light brown teddy with deep plush fur.

Susan gasped when she saw it. She almost ripped the Teddy from the elf and exclaimed, "He's so soft! What a beautiful color! Oh, how much is THIS one, I really want this little guy!"

The elf looked at her. "This one hasn't been marked. That means it has already been sold to someone."

Susan looked completely deflated. "Do you have another – exactly like this one?"

The elf said he was sorry but again, each Teddy was unique.

Susan felt like she was the brunt of a cruel joke and said a little impatiently. "Well, thank you, I guess I'll be going now." She left rather upset and dejected.

George followed immediately, hoping for the chance

to cheer her after watching the exchange.

Marshall came up to the elf. "You kinda took a rough road to make your point, didn't you?"

The elf smiled at him. "Yes, but I had to be sure it was the right one. You see I'm selling you this bear to give to your sister. That is of course if you would like to give it to her."

Marshall looked confused. "Really? Is that why it had no tag?"

"Exactly," replied the elf, "We can't have her knowing the value, because it is *in-valuable* to her!"

Marshall suddenly looked concerned. "Well, how much is it exactly?"

The elf said, "This gift will cost you nothing, as long as it is the only one you give her from the North Pole."

Marshall remembered now that Christel told them that they could get a gift for each member of their family. "Great, but uh, won't she notice it when I go carrying it out of here?" he asked.

The elf bubbled. "It shall be waiting in your room upon your return. It will be wrapped and ready to be given. BUT, you must wait until Christmas Day! You may not give it before then and no telling or hinting to her about it."

Marshall thanked the elf and tried to look solemn as he left the store and caught up to Susan and George, but inside his heart was leaping.

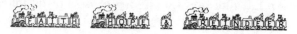

They marched down the corridor without really

saying a word, waiting in almost breathless anticipation and hoping not to be disappointed. They came to a large double door and an elf dressed in a blue flight suit and a cadet style hat.

As the four adults approached the elf said, "I'm sorry, really I am. But the flying reindeer ride is for children and not grown folk. It's because these are smaller reindeer in training. You see this is how we get them to build up stamina."

The adults almost as one breathed a sigh of relief.

Jared said, "Actually I don't think we are as anxious to ride one as to see one, may we?"

It was the elf's turn to show relief. "Why of course you may." Then he pulled open the door.

The two couples walked through the door and Julie felt as if she had walked into a Walt Disney dream at full throttle.

There they were — several small reindeer, about two-thirds the size of their fully-grown relatives. They wore saddles that contained strong belts for holding their passengers securely in place. Three of the reindeer were flying around the outside of the building and one was over the cliff with children yelling and screaming with two parts joy and one part terror.

It was a remarkable sight — reindeer being mounted and then sent on their flights with a cue from one of the other blue clad elves. As one took off, another returned. It was like watching some crazy carnival ride without wires, cables or strings.

Heather thought about little Patrick, and hoped he hadn't heard about this as of yet, for that matter, John either.

One of the elves saw the concern on Heather's face. "There's absolutely nothing to fear. We have never had an accident or even a close call. We train these reindeer for fifteen years before we let them fly with real passengers."

Jared pulled his eyes away for an instant to the elf and asked, "Okay and <u>how</u> exactly do they fly? That's something that has baffled everyone for a century or more."

"Actually," the elf said, "for a little over two centuries now. It really isn't a huge mystery. We grow a special feed of alfalfa that works through their body and makes them almost weightless. This alfalfa can only be grown in one part of the world, which we keep secret. Unlike normal alfalfa, this variety grows very slowly and takes almost ten full months to mature and be harvested. When we bring it here, we cold store it and then put the reindeer on it exclusively for a couple days straight. By the third day we can barely keep them from flying all over the place. In addition to making them fly, it gives them tremendous energy.

"Because we have a limited supply of alfalfa, and of course for safety reasons, we won't allow most of the reindeer to fly. Actually very few of our reindeer at the North Pole ever have had more than two hooves off the ground at the same time. The exceptions are here at the flying reindeer rides, the reindeer flight training school, and of course the big guy's Christmas Eve team.

"We have to rotate the reindeer because we can't keep them on that alfalfa for more than a couple weeks. They miss out on too many nutrients otherwise, so it's back to corn, oats and regular alfalfa and keeping their hooves on the ground for a while."

The adults couldn't take their eyes off the reindeer.

"I still don't believe it," said Brian.

"That's the problem with adults, even when they see something, they still don't want to believe it," sighed the elf shaking his head. "That's what makes kids so special, even without the magic alfalfa, these kids could will the reindeer into the air, by their complete and total belief that they can fly."

The four adults suddenly looked embarrassed by their skepticism and what they saw with their own eyes. They thanked the elf for his help and turned on their heels heading for the balloon rides.

"Magic alfalfa?' said Heather.

Jared chuckled. "Yeah, think what *that* could do for rabbits!"

They all stopped and stared at each other.

Brian said, "Oh you don't think…"

Jared finished his thought saying, "If there are flying reindeer and Santa Claus is real, how much more of a stretch is the Easter Bunny? Maybe he's on that stuff, too."

They all laughed and shook their heads at the idea while heading to the balloons.

On the opposite side, the elves were clad in white jumpsuits with blue striping down one side.

"Welcome to the balloon rides." A smallish girl elf with a big smile said to the aproaching group.. She also wore a cadet style cap in white. "Will there be two or four of you in one balloon?"

Julie said, "Yes please, four if you can fit us."

The elf said, "Well of course we can, your balloon is
waiting right over there." Julie passed a knowing smile
to Jared, who nodded and smiled back. The elf pointed
to a large balloon with red and white candy stripes
swirled around the entire surface of the envelope.
Attached to the envelope was a giant wicker basket large
enough to hold all of them and more.

Jared understood little about lift and physics and
wondered if it would really get off the ground since the
size of the basket and four adults with an elf or two
looked beyond the balloon's capability.

One of the 'ground' elves said, "Welcome aboard. We
are ready and waiting to give you the best tour of the
North Pole we have to offer!"

The four of them climbed in and the elf closed the
gate on the basket and secured it. There were two elves
inside the balloon and one was already dropping ballast
weight, while the other was firing the flame jets into the
balloon. Very shortly the craft eased away from the
station.

Chapter Five

"Oh how great is this?" said George upon seeing the store marked "Electrons For Pro-tons". They could clearly see it was a store that dealt with things more sophisticated than Teddy bears and Dolls.

They walked into the store and filled their senses with the buzzings, beepings and actions of various computer games, handhelds, and other electronic marvels. They went through the store as if conquering a country, grabbing this and that. Trying different games and testing their skills against products they or their friends had at home.

They were heading toward the latest video game cubes when an elf approached and reached out his hand.

"At last!" he exclaimed. "Some others who understand what this store is all about!" Marshall shook his small hand in his and said, "How do you do?"

The elf said, "I do amazingly well, thank you."

He looked a bit nerdy thought George. He was wearing large heavy black-framed glasses that made his head look too big for his body. His hair was a little wild and his clothes a bit disheveled.

"In fact, I am unbeatable. They have all tried, but no one has bested me yet. Ion Crosswire's my name. And most of what you find in here I created or wrote the programs for."

To that Marshall guffawed. "Yeah, right! You made

'Take 'Em Down' and 'Crosshairs'!"

Ion looked at him over his glasses. "Actually I wrote the programs, I didn't 'make' them. And yes, I developed those, as well as 'Meteorite', 'Hellacious Rides' and 'Rollover', too."

Ion waved his hand across the room. "Almost everything in here has had my hand in the creation of it, in one form or another."

Now it was George's turn. "Except the computers and stuff, you mean."

Ion turned to George. "Including the computers and stuff, I mean."

"Wow, this place really covers some area," said Brian.

They could see buildings, hills and even the heavily wooded area they saw coming in on the train.

The elf handling the ballast weights said, "Approximately fifteen square miles."

Jared spun at the statement. "Not all of it is under this dome is it?"

The elf looked up and nodded. After he tied off another sandbag he said. "We'll give you the full tour in a moment. Ramsey Hampton is your pilot there, and I am Noel Hotentot. I'm waitin' for Ramsey to get into position and then we'll begin."

The four guests introduced themselves to the elves using first names only.

Ramsey said, "We're almost to the back end of the dome in the far corner of the village. Pretty much ready when you are, Noel."

Noel moved toward the other end of the balloon. He had a fairly significant swagger, and Jared figured it was the result of many balloon trips. His face barely cleared the top end of the basket and he had large round eyes that matched his round face. He reminded Brian of the illustrated face of Bilbo Baggins in Tolkien's book *The Hobbit*.

Ramsey was taller and leaner than his partner. He had a more stretched appearance and his face was that of an old sailor. He was only missing the pipe in his teeth to complete the look.

"Now starting over there is the Candy Cane & Mint Shoppe," Noel commenced.

As they looked they saw four boys come out of the shop. No wait, not *four* boys, but two boys being flanked by two elves.

"Look honey," Heather said to Brian, "its Patrick and John." They yelled to the boys and they looked up and waved excitedly.

Patrick had a bunch of different colored candy canes, and John had one very large peppermint stick.

They looked very happy and Patrick yelled up, "I saw Santa!"

They gave them a nod and a wave and the boys disappeared behind the balloon.

"Now over here is our administrative center. Visitors are allowed to see some of our operations like the Naughty and Nice Record Hall, the Post Office where you can actually mail a letter to someone and have the cancellation and postmark of North Pole, Alaska on the envelope. Over there is our daily newspaper office *The Polar Times*. You can get copies all around the village and it lets you know of any special events or tours takin' place."

"Of course over there is the first building you saw, bein' the train station. Next to that is the 'Loomin' For A Knit', a shop with woolens, scarves and other outdoor wear. Behind it in that circle there begins with the Sentry Shop & Factory..."

"Excuse me. What's the century shop?" Heather asked.

"No ma'am, not century, *sen*-try. It's a store and factory where they make all the tin, wooden and plastic soldiers."

"Oh, like nutcrackers?" inquired Julie.

"Uh, actually no. The Nutcracker factory outlet is down over there at the other end of the circle."

Brian asked, "Where do they make the trains? That's what I'm looking for. I have a train set from my grandfather that I would like to get a new locomotive for, and I think this might finally be the place to find one."

Ramsey said from behind him, "That's in the manufacturing center. You'll be able to see it from here but not go into it."

Brian asked, "Don't they sell any trains in the village?"

"Oh sure," replied Noel, "Lots of train sets."

Brian was becoming impatient, "I don't want a whole set, I only need the locomotive. The rest of the set is in vintage working order."

Ramsey said, "Why don't you ask Santa, then?"

This caused all four of them to turn around and look at Ramsey.

Brian paused for a moment and said, "Don't you think I am a little old to be asking Santa for toys?"

Ramsey snickered and said "Why, do you think he is getting too old to bring them to you?"

Heather intervened, "I believe what my husband means is we thought Santa only gives to the children. Once you were an adult, you were out of 'radar range' for Santa's gifts."

Noel jumped in, "The reason people think that is because they quit asking. They also quit believing. Oh sure, they play it up for their kids and buy toys and say they're from Santa. But it's only because they lost their faith in him growing up."

Ramsey spoke again, "Santa brings presents to those who believe and those too poor to provide their own. But the truth is, he will do his best to provide anything in his power when he is asked. Sometimes he gets asked the impossible, like bringing back a relative that passed away or reuniting divorced or separated parents.

"He tells the children the truth that he can't bring back someone who has gone to live with God, and it wouldn't be fair or nice to ask them to leave God's side. And if the parents are separated, he tells them to pray to God and ask Him, and if it is right for them to get back together, God – not Santa will grant their prayer."

Noel looked at all four of them and said almost to himself, "Ask and believe and wondrous things can happen. You just need to become a child once more, and have a child's faith."

As they walked over to a table of Macintosh computers, pointing to the Apple logo George asked, "What did you work on for *them*?"

Ion exclaimed, "My cousin and I came up with the Macintosh design. In fact, it's named after him. Macintosh Gelfeeny is the smartest technology elf we have next to me," he said with a grin. "I'm not boasting, it's fact. We worked on it together and then he took it down to Apple and sold it to them for the royalties."

Susan said, "Now wait a minute. You make royalties off of Apple Computers?"

Ion shook his head and said, "Not me personally – we! How do you think the North Pole pays for everything and gets the supplies it needs? Through royalties, licenses and the companies it owns! Since every country still requires some form of currency, we have to barter by creating companies or selling discoveries, otherwise we couldn't last a year with what we produce and give to others."

The three of them stared at Ion as if he had told him he was from Jupiter.

"You mean the North Pole owns Apple?" asked Marshall.

Ion shook his head, "No, we don't own Apple. Look, it's a simple case of economics. We make things or produce technology and we sell that technology for a percent of the profit. We only own a couple companies anymore. We've sold most of them off. We prefer to have licensing agreements, now. With the exception of the one firm our most brilliant Supreme Toy-maker elf helped get off the ground, we don't have much left. After we sold our share of the Hasbro company, and we asked that other company to buy out Bill Hewlett's share..."

"Whoa! Stop! You mean Bill Hewlett of Hewlett-Packard was an elf? That's absurd!" declared Susan.

Ion corrected her, "I didn't say that, exactly..."

But Susan didn't even hear him and went on, "And Hasbro Toys used to be a North Pole company? Next you'll be telling me you own Mattel!"

Ion laughed, "Interesting story that one. After we helped them launch Barbie the company decided to 'go public'. It is Rory Mattle, who is our Supreme Toy-maker, that worked with the Handlers, who owned Mattel at the time. It is even rumored that the name Mattel came from Rory. But Nick told us the name was already there and Rory's was a coincidence. Even Rory can't believe Barbie is still going so strong. Who knew?" Ion mused.

"Nick who?" asked George.

"The current Santa Claus." Ion said.

"So Mattle, I mean Mattel is owned by the North Pole?" asked Marshall.

"Technically it is owned by the shareholders, but yes we still have some control over it," professed Ion.

"If you're so advanced do you have anything new you can show us?" asked George.

Ion Crosswire looked at them with a gleam and

smiled. "I have more 'new' things than you would
believe, or understand." He shrugged and said, "But I
can't show it to you because it's ahead of your culture."

Marshall said, "There must be something you can
show us. Maybe something that's not too far off, you
know, maybe only a little advanced."

Ion looked at the three of them and whispered
conspiratorially, "Okay, but you can't blab about it or
try to patent it yourself, okay?" They all nodded and
stared at the little man. He reached into his pocket and
produced – a pen.

They all looked as if he had pulled off a good joke on
them. He said with a twinkle through his thick glasses,
"It's not what it seems. Yes it writes, but it is also
this…"

He turned the cap slightly and music filled the room.
He lowered the volume by sliding his thumb down the
pen clip. "Think of it as a combination of the world's
smallest iPod and BOSE stereo. It can hold the
maximum gig, and it even has tiny wireless earbuds that
no one can see. You click the top three times for earbuds
or three times to turn them off."

"Oh, man, do I need that. Hey Susan you can get
that for me for a Christmas gift! Remember we can get
each member of our family something from the North
Pole at no cost and…"

"Not this she can't!" Ion chortled loudly, "The
technology for this is estimated at another two years
away! I can't let you go traipsing off to high school with
this in your pocket, and no explanation how it got there!
Sorry, this is for demonstration purposes only!"

Ion stuck the music machine back inside his shirt pocket.

After Marshall recovered from his disappointment, he asked if Ion had anything on the edge of 'his culture's technology'.

Ion thought for a moment and looked around the 'shop'. "Ahhh, I may have something that might interest you." He walked over to a small square box and lifted the lid. It looked like a miniature laptop. He pushed a couple buttons and up popped the movie *Elf* with Will Farrell.

"What is it?" Marshall asked.

Ion puffed up with pride and said, "This is the first personal, portable movie library and player. You can save up to a hundred full movies in it and play the one you want at the touch of a button."

Marshall completely forgot about the pen/music system. "Incredible!" he said and stared at the machine with awe. "This is today's technology?"

Ion said, "Well it's about six months out, but that's pretty close."

Marshall looked at Susan pleadingly.

Susan scoffed, "Not so fast little brother. A moment ago you wanted that music thingy. What happens if you want something even more in the next store? I only get to give you one thing and I want to make sure it's **the right one.**"

Ion looked admiringly at her and said, "She's absolutely correct."

Marshall for the second time in a very few minutes had the wind let out of his sails. "Fine, but tell me, is that the only one you have?" he asked with a worried tone. "Why of course not, we have multiple units in the back. We put only one on the floor to show and tell about the unit."

Susan said they had spent enough time in this store and told Marshall and George it was time to go.

George protested, "I wanted to challenge Marshall and Ion to a game of 'Rogue 2'".

Susan said that was fine with her, but she was moving on. The boys said they would catch up later.

Chapter Six

"Getting back to our tour," said Noel. "Now after we pass the 'Rocking Horse Stable', and 'Santa's Friend Theodore', we come to 'Electrons For Protons' – that's where you will find most of the kids from age nine up. They love to check out the newer computer and video games and toys."

As they came up to the store, Susan came out the front door. They called down to her to get her attention. Susan could hear her name being called, but kept looking around behind her.

They yelled louder as she looked up, she ran full force into another person in front of her and they both went tumbling into the snow. "Ooooh, sorry," Julie called but they were already moving too far out of range to be heard.

"I'm so very sorry," Susan said to the innocent passerby, "Are you hurt?"

The young man got up brushing himself off and said, "Well I never thought I'd be happy to land in a snow bank before, but yes, I mean no, I'm fine. No broken bones."

Susan looked at the tall, handsome young man before her, and decided she better explain quickly, "My parents were calling to me and I couldn't see them because they were above me. When I looked up it I didn't see you, I mean your back, so I couldn't stop."

The young man laughed and said, "Above you? Like what, in a plane?" Susan turned him around and pointed at the candy cane swirled balloon floating away to the south.

"Oh," he said, "I see what you mean. I didn't know they had balloons here."

She replied, "Yeah, neither did I until a minute ago."

The young man turned back to Susan and said, "No harm done. My name is Bill Fredrick, we arrived last night."

Susan held out her hand. "Susan Grady, nice to meet you." Then she said, "We got in last night, too. But I didn't see you at the orientation."

"I decided to skip it and get something to eat in the village." He blushed and continued saying, "I wasn't smart enough to order much on the train. I really thought they were joking about the food. My parents filled me in on what I missed at the meeting when I got up this morning. Speaking of food, I was going to go over to that café over there to get something to drink. Would you like to come along?"

Susan looked at the shop shaped like a giant coffee mug and nodded.

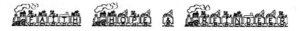

When John and Patrick had seen their parents in the balloon, they had come out of the Candy Cane shop and were following the elves with complete devotion. Elves Sid and Hildegard had given them a wonderful day so far, in fact one of the best they could remember in their lives. John even thought it wasn't too bad hanging around Patrick today.

Something he enjoyed less and less, lately. He really loved Patrick, and sometimes it was fun having a little brother, but at the age of nine, life was becoming more complicated, and it was tough having him tag around with him and his friends. His friends were becoming ever more vocal when Patrick would show up with John. But today was different: he was having a blast, especially when he saw Patrick with Santa.

The two of them looked to be having a very serious and deep conversation that John couldn't really make out. Santa looked up at John at one point and gave a wink and a smile. Patrick was even more animated than normal, but his voice was low and respectful.

When it was John's turn to talk with Santa, he was a little uncomfortable. He knew he was too big to sit on Santa's lap. Santa seemed to sense this and motioned to one of the elves nearby. She brought a nice sized chair and set it right in front of Santa's immense throne.

Santa told John to take a seat and said, "You know Patrick is very proud of you and thinks the world of you."

John blushed, shrugged his shoulders and murmured, "Yeah, I guess."

Santa crowed, "Now no false modesty here, John. Patrick has told me that you even take grief from your friends when he is around you. That's a very noble sacrifice." John looked surprised. He didn't really think that Patrick knew about the ribbing and snide comments that were made about his being about.

He suddenly felt bad about how he wished Patrick would disappear.

Santa spoke, "Now don't be too hard on yourself. Everyone wishes situations were different at times. And we all have occasions when we don't want our siblings hanging around. But to not take it out on them personally, or treat them badly for it, is what is most important." He smiled broadly and said, "The key to living a good life is to hold hands and watch out for each other. Whether brother-to-brother, or sister-to-brother, or friend-to-friend, everyone needs someone to watch out for him or her. You need to be a shining light that draws people to you and makes them feel safe. I know you are only nine, but you have that light in you now, and I believe you will continue to have it. Let it shine so everyone can see it."

They then spoke of lighter things and talked about some of the wonders of the North Pole. Santa had told him how wonderful it was to be here, and how joyful it was to bring so much happiness. He indicated that John would do the same in his life.

John left feeling taller than he would ever reach physically. He decided he would take a different tact with his friends, then and there. If they didn't like Patrick they could go their own way. But he thought the better thing to do was to let them invite their siblings so everyone could play together, and not be selfish.

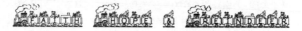

They walked up to the large mug that was dark

brown with a cream colored round roof. It read "Cocoa's Mug O' Nog". Bill and Susan laughed at the double meaning and walked inside. Everything had a rustic charm to it, right down to the potbelly stove in the center of the room. It was a blending of a 1950's malt shop and a western style saloon.

The tables were small and round with iron chairs and round red cushions. But there was also a large bar stretching the length of one wall. A very pleasant looking elf with very long chestnut hair was drying soda glasses and wiping off the counter. "Treasured guests, how may I serve you?"

Bill asked, "What do you have to drink?" Susan knew the answer before the elf behind the bar said it, but kept silent. "Anything you want, within reason," answered the elf. Bill undeterred by her response said, "Perhaps I should ask, what do you recommend?"

That brought a large smile to the barmaid and she said as she extended her small hand, "I'm Cocoa Nicenhot; it's a pleasure to meet you. And if I'm not mistaken, you two would be Bill and Susan, am I right?"

They both stared at her incredulously and asked, "How did you know?"

Cocoa laughed. "There are no secrets in the Pole. Besides you were both described as very attractive young adults."

They both blushed at the compliment, and Bill tried to regain his composure by saying, "So about that recommendation?"

Cocoa laughed again. "Alright let me see." She looked

them up and down as if trying to decide what species they resembled. Then she said, "Okay, have a seat over there and I'll bring your drinks."

They looked at her as she shooed them away. They took one of the tables closer to the stove, as the heat felt welcoming.

They talked and discovered they were both seniors in high school. Bill and his family hailed from Western Michigan, around the Grand Rapids area. He had a younger sister of 11, named Hailey who was off with some of the others. Bill wanted to go to college in the west somewhere, and had applied to USC, UCLA and UNLV.

Susan told him she tried Stanford and got shot down, but she was hopeful about some of the other schools she'd applied to, which also included UCLA and USC, like Bill. She said, "I'm a little concerned though. My dad lost his job almost a year ago, and my mom only works part time. I'm getting the feeling they are running out of money and I don't know how they are going to handle it."

Bill said, "Yeah, I get told the same from my parents. They keep telling me I'm aiming too high on the tuition scale. Have you received any scholarships or help?"

Susan shrugged, "I don't know, I think I might get something. My GPA and SAT's are pretty good, and I've applied for a few scholarships, but I won't hear anything until next year. Right now all my babysitting and part time clerk work is going toward a car."

They we're discussing Susan's choices for a car and how she'd like to get into Political Science. Bill was after an electrical engineering degree.

Without a noise Cocoa suddenly sprang out from behind the bar and said, "I think you'll like these." She placed two mugs on the table. Bill's looked like it contained a greenish liquid. Susan's was more cream colored.

"What's in these?" Susan asked.

"Give 'em a try," said Cocoa, "If you don't like 'em, I'll give you your money back!" She laughed out loud, turned and walked away.

Chapter Seven

"We are now crossing over into the Manufacturing Center. For obvious reasons the busiest place in the whole Pole," said Noel. He was now really into his tour guide mode now and spoke as much by rote as by sight. "We'll begin with the first row of structures, starting with that closest building which is the Light House. It is where we work on and perfect indoor and outdoor lighting. We also string and decorate the Pole from there.

Next to that is the first of three general toy factories. This one is the second in chronological order and has twice the capacity and output of our first one. Next is the gumdrop and taffy shop. Here we used to produce all the gumdrops from past years. It is currently being retrofitted as gumdrops no longer have the appeal they once had."

Jared asked, "What's it being retrofitted for?"

Noel smiled. "Flash-pop candy!"

"What's that?" asked Heather.

This time Ramsey spoke up. "It's the best stuff. A while back people noticed that if you crunched wintergreen mints they would spark in your mouth. We kicked it up a notch or two. Now flashes fly out of the mouth and make popping sounds. Kinda like a mini-thunderstorm in your mouth. Tastes pretty juicy, too."

"Next to that is our Lego plant, and then our Crayola

factory," continued Noel.

"Legos, Crayolas, isn't that trademark infringement?" questioned Brian.

"Not if we have licensing agreements," chuckled Noel. "You see we do a lot of R&D for these companies and in turn we are allowed to assist in the production and distribution of their products. We have developed many new breakthroughs for them and many other firms, besides our own."

Ramsey said, "Rock Candy Mine coming up at eight o'clock."

Noel relayed, "Right. Now coming up is something very interesting. We have a mine that yields vast amounts of compressed and already formed candy."

Heather looked at him for the joke and said, "You're trying to tell us that the mountain there is made of candy instead of rock?"

"Actually it made candy into rocks. Or at least that's what our geologist told us. See above on that hill? They are moving tons of sugar, cream, flavorings and other ingredients back and forth. Apparently we spill quite a bit of stuff on the paths and trails. Because this is all snow and we get more every year, the stuff melts into the path the way salt would melt snow, and over time was kinda mixed and stirred and got compressed into the mountain."

They watched as a freight cart pulled by a horse came out of the mine with two elves on either side carrying picks. In the cart were all different colors of what looked like sugary colored rocks.

Noel asked them a question, "That mine was

originally dug for a different purpose. Any guesses?"

The four balloon occupants looked at each other and guessed, "Gold?" "Diamonds?"

The elves shook their heads.

Ramsey finally said, "When little boys and girls are naughty...."

Brian yelled, "COAL!"

"Right you are," said Noel, "But about thirty years ago it played out and we hit the candy vein instead." Ramsey added, "Just as well, Santa said he was done luggin' bituminous along with the presents. Now if they are that bad, he skips 'em, and flies on."

At the Mug O' Nog, Bill and Susan were having fun guessing the flavors in their drinks.

"It has a minty taste, but with something else I can't place," Bill was trying to explain to Susan. He was looking toward the ceiling trying to place what the flavor was.

Susan had finished telling him hers tasted like vanilla and toasted almond, and said it was one of the creamiest and most flavorful tastes she had ever had. Bill seemed to be enjoying his just as much.

Cocoa strode up and said, "So? What do you think?"

Both patrons started raving together and then both fell silent trying to let the other speak first.

All three burst into laughter at the moment.

Bill gestured to Susan, "Okay," she said. "Vanilla and toasted almond? Is that what this is?"

Cocoa smiled, "Very close, its vanilla and amaretto flavoring – non-alcoholic, of course. And yours, young sir?"

Bill said he was stumped except for the mint. Cocoa grinned. "Yours is Bailey Irish Crème with a dash of wintermint flavoring, also non-alcoholic. You seemed the type that would like mint but needed something creamier." Bill said that her hunch was dead-on.

She smiled at Susan. "You're a sugar and spice girl if I ever met one, and believe me I have, but I thought you also would like nuts."

"Bingo!" Susan exclaimed. "Especially almonds, I'm not wild about peanuts, but I love almonds!"

Bill made a mental note, *almonds - no peanuts*. It was about the fourth or fifth note he stuck in his head about Susan. He really was glad she ran into him - literally.

Chapter Eight

"Look there it is — one of those 'squeegees' are down there!" Julie called out almost making the others jump.

Noel looked at her then followed where she was pointing. He laughed. "SQUIBBLES, not squeegees!"

Ramsey snorted as well.

Noel said, "Yes, that's a squibble, we find them very useful around here. That one's headed for the docking station."

Jared looked puzzled, "What do you mean?"

The elf said, "A docking station or warehouse is where we ship products to a particular staging area in another part of the world and hold them for their respective Christmas deliveries."

"Now wait a minute," both Heather and Julie protested.

Julie asked, "You mean Santa doesn't take the presents in his sleigh and deliver them on Christmas Eve?"

Heather piped in, "There goes all those wonderful fantasies about Santa flying all over the world!"

Noel started waving his hands frantically trying to get the two women to calm down. "I didn't say any of that, you are not understanding me. Please give me a couple minutes to explain."

They both crossed their arms and waited while the elf drew a deep breath. He turned to Ramsey and said,

"You better hold here for a few...this could take a little while."

Ramsey had seen this happen more than a few times before and he pulled up a little stool and got comfortable while he steadied the balloon.

Noel embarked on the subject by saying, "This is complicated and there is a lot to it, so try to follow along and we'll both get through it."

They nodded and watched the elf as he pointed to the 'docking station', and said,

Okay, in much the same way as other freight forwarders like FedEx, DHL, UPS and so on, we have warehouses where we stage Santa's gifts at. When we get a letter, email or fax from a person with a request on it, we make or package that item (if it's already made), wrap it and then put it in the docking warehouse. From there it will go to the staging area for that country or part of the country.

For instance, Ireland has one staging area, France has three and the U.S. has twelve, like you have twelve federal bank branches servicing the nation. Santa leaves here in his sleigh pulled by the reindeer with the first load for that night. When he finishes that area he stops and picks up the next load at the next station, where the elves have already packed it by geographical reference. This goes on four separate days.

"FOUR days. I thought he did this all in one night," questioned Jared. Noel nodded his head and continued,

"He could but that would go against the different cultures and beliefs they have for Santa. For instance, in much of the Scandinavian countries he arrives on his ancestor's holiday. They celebrate the Feast of St. Nicolas on December 6th each year. This is also one of the times he doesn't take his reindeer."

"No reindeer - in Scandinavia? That doesn't make sense." Brian declared.

Noel kept going as if he knew they would catch on sooner or later.
"See in that part of the world St. Nicholas arrives by boat the day before the Feast day or on December 5th, it works kind of like Christmas Eve. It's mostly based on the culture of the country. You would find it a little hard to grasp if Santa showed up on a Harley instead of sleigh, and wouldn't want to accept the concept."
"Yeah, look how you reacted at the thought of the warehouses," snickered Ramsey.
"In South America he is referred to as 'the child'. And comes on the day the three wise men presented their gifts to our Christ child.

That date is twelve days after we celebrate His birth at Christmas. And traditionally they give gifts to mark this event.

Then of course is our traditional Christmas Eve delivery."

"That's only three," said Jared.

Noel said cheerily, "You forgot the international dateline. He can deliver his gifts on the other side of the world on a different day."

"So he really doesn't go all over the world in one night," said Heather thinking for a moment.

"That seems to make more sense to me, now," said Brian.

Noel clarified further, "Especially when you factor in that more than two thirds of the world isn't Christian. Could you imagine what would happen to a large man in a red suit who suddenly appeared without invitation in a Muslim's house in Iran?" They all shuddered at the thought.

"Thanks so very much, Cocoa, we'll be back again later," called Susan. She and Bill headed out of her Mug 'O Nog onto the bright pathway and moved down the street looking at the different shops.

A few minutes later, Marshall and George came running up and asked Susan where she had been. "We've been looking all over for you." Marshall said somewhat exasperated.

"Bill and I stopped for some, uh, refreshments," she said in a rather grandiose way. George looked at Bill and Susan, and was watching the way they were laughing and looking at each other. While he didn't really hold any hope for he and Susan in a romantic setting, he couldn't help but feel a little crushed anyway.

Susan introduced her brother and George to Bill and told him they had been out since early this morning.

Marshall was in a hurry to show Susan some of the shops he had seen in her absence, but Susan said she was tired and wanted to return to the inn and relax for a while. She offered to have Bill go with them, but Bill said he was wearing out also, and offered to walk her back.

Marshall asked if he should head back as well, and Susan told him he was free to do whatever he liked as Christel had said.

"I don't think Mom and Dad will be concerned, either." she said. "You and George go on exploring. I think I'm still a little tired from traveling yesterday." Yesterday. It didn't seem possible they had only left — and arrived, yesterday. She thought it felt like several days ago, but in a very pleasant way.

Chapter Nine

"We are now entering the Woodland area," said Noel. "This is generally most people's favorite part of the tour. Over there, in the largest building behind the creek, is Santa and Mrs. Claus' residence and right next to it is his private workshop. Besides working on concept toys and gadgets, that is where he holds his meetings and discusses many of the cultures, mores, and changes taking place across the globe." It was truly a magnificent edifice and looked like the type of place where Santa and his wife would reside.

"Look there, look at all the reindeer!" said Julie.

Noel said, "Yes, that area contains the reindeer flying school, the reindeer training center and that large structure and pen are the stables."

"So that's where Dasher and Dancer live?" asked Brian.

"Yep," replied Noel. "They're all there, which is why it takes up so much area. At last count we have about three hundred, though for obvious reasons they are never all there at the same time. A good many of them are working in shifts throughout the North Pole."

"How do you feed them all?" asked Jared. He was still trying to take in the logistics of running such a large operation. He desperately wanted to buy into everything, but his analytical mind was working overtime. Especially with all the input he was receiving.

"That train track you came in on carries other things besides people," said Ramsey. "We get at least one freight train per week up here and two to three a week around this time of year. We have a lot of stuff to bring up and ship down."

"How have you kept this all secret for so long?" Jared asked. Again the obvious questions bothered him.

Noel said in an almost sad way, "Not all of Santa's helpers are lucky enough to live up here. We have about 6,000 elves in other parts of the world. Plus there are hundreds of people that know about us, but have sworn vows of secrecy to prevent the goings on from becoming public."

Ramsey added, "You have obviously been told many things about Santa and the operation here, but many of the 'inner workings' and truths are either skewed or some vital facts are missing to prevent most of the world from seeing the whole picture."

Heather said, "Yeah, like warehouses around the world."

"Precisely!" Noel cried out. "Imagine if everyone knew **that** little secret! Besides searching for the North Pole, they'd be trying to find the staging areas as well."

Continuing the tour Noel pointed to what resembled a large college campus with a stately building in the center of some taller apartment style structures. "Now down there is the elf training center and school. This is where most elves learn their craft and where new inventions and ideas are explored. The larger buildings are dormitories so the elves do not have to keep jumping back and forth."

Brian pointed to a large clearing that had several elves skating on the surface. "I think that's what I saw coming in on the train. At first I thought it was a bunch of children moving around."

Ramsey smirked and said, "And that's where I'm heading as soon as we are done today. They have the best hot chocolate in the Pole! They also have sleds, skis and toboggans over there. It's a great way to relax."

The O'Reillys were stepping off the gondola and the three girls ran over to the ice walls at the edge of the overlook. They were able to see all the places they had moments ago walked by and visited. The building with various flags on flagpoles surrounding it they knew was Santa's Visiting Cottage, and the building next to that was his "village residence" where he took rest and got something to eat during his busy day.

There was the store with all the dolls, next to the one with all the Teddy bears. And over there was the "Big Bounce" house which not only had a place for kids to go bouncing in, but also every size shape and style of ball they had ever seen, from soccer and footballs to huge playground balls and even fitness balls.

It was from outside of that shop that Renee saw what brought them up here. She spied the flying reindeer and their passengers. Ellen was also told that the best place for milk and cookies was at the "Cookie Cottage" on the upper level, and that they should definitely give that a try.

Jim had already "bought" a couple items. Not so
much because he 'had to have them', but because he was
so enamored with the price tags, and felt they were
things he could and really wanted to do. He found a
nifty digital camera that he had been wanting for a
while. And while he couldn't afford the six hundred
dollars he'd seen this full kit go for in stores, he thought
he'd be able to organize and run three community clean-
ups over the next year, which was its price tag. What a
wonderful thing that he could buy things up here with
public service offerings instead of worrying what bill
might not be paid if he spent his tight monetary
resources.

The other item was a rocking horse for Annie. She
almost refused to dismount from the one in her room.
Jim and Maureen found the exact same one in the
window of the Saddle Up Rocking Horse Store. While
Maureen took the girls into the doll shop, Jim went into
the store and used one of his 'free family gifts' to secure
it for Annie. Like Marshall he was told it would be
wrapped and waiting in their room and not to give it to
her before Christmas.

He almost bought a new winter outfit at the "Polar
Fleece," but Maureen pleaded with him to wait and see
what else was around before he donated an entire year's
activity on their first outing.

Chapter Ten

"This is the last thing before we return," said Noel. "A quick look at Mount Elfish. Here is another place we unwind and have some fun. Plus the Claus' allow us to safety test and try out some of the toys down the mountain."

They were watching as about a dozen or more elves were sliding, snowboarding, skiing and in general having a wonderful time. Suddenly an elf came shooting by on what looked like a sled with stubby wings.

"Hey Ramsey, Noel!" He shocked Julie almost off her feet.

"What was that!" the startled Julie yelled.

"Oh. sorry," said Ramsey, "That's one of the new sleds we are testing. You shoot down the hill and if you can pick up enough speed you can launch the sled and ride it like a hang glider. You can even glide back to the top of the hill and start all over again."

"Ooooo, I'd like to try that!" said Brian almost with the voice of a young boy. He was following the path of the flying elf with rapt attention.

"Problem is we can't build it big enough for grown folk," said Noel. "In fact, most kids are too big for it except toddlers and young ones. Needless to say, they are not the safest to be taking off from a mountain."

Heather thought it would be better for her and Brian not to mention *this* to John, either.

"Is that a Ski Resort at the top of the mountain?" asked Jared.

Ramsey swelled with pride, "The finest resort we've ever known. That would be Mount Elfish Ski Resort & School. That's where we learn skiing, boarding and sculpture."

Julie looked at Ramsey and asked, "Sculpture?"

"Yes, ma'am, many of us take up ice sculpture. If you look around you will see many of the finished pieces throughout the village, but up there is where we really learn many of the techniques. We must start with hammers and chisels, and work with those for twelve years at least. Then we graduate to power tools and finally lasers." Noel said, "Ramsey there has been at it for thirty-eight years, and he's really doing wonderful things with the lasers."

Ramsey blushed and bowed to his partner. "Yeah, but I still like using the hammer and chisel best of all. The others are faster, but that's the best way to feel one with the ice and do your most personal work."

They began their descent back toward the Aviation Center as they watched another balloon lift off the take-off and landing platform. They set down as softly as they left.

They thanked Noel and Ramsey profusely. Heather even gave the elves a hug and said how much she learned on the trip. They both blushed and grinned, and thanked her and the other passengers for their kind attention.

Bill and Susan finally returned to the Inn by way of a very circuitous route. They had gotten turned around a couple times, whether accidentally or on purpose to extend their time together shouldn't be speculated. Possibly a little of each, as they were in such deep discussion, that they weren't always aware of turns and changes on the pathways.

They discussed graduation, colleges and working over the summer and at college. Like Susan, Bill's parents told him they could probably cover tuition and board for a state school, but he was going to have to pay for some things like books, food, entertainment, gas and car insurance, himself.

They both discussed student loans, but were concerned about being heavily in debt after completing school. Each was enjoying their last year in high school, but they were also in a hurry to get "out from underneath Mom and Dad."

"I like my folks and sister," said Bill, "but I am really ready to strike out on my own."

Susan agreed, though she was always still a little concerned about Marshall. He had Leukemia as a toddler, but had miraculously recovered. She felt as long as she was around, he wouldn't relapse. She knew that was nonsense, but she thought of herself as kind of a safety blanket for him.

They had reached the inn and walked into the warm lobby. The fireplace was going pretty well, and looked inviting, but Susan felt dog-tired. It was only 3:30 in the afternoon, but she desperately needed to lie down for a while. She told Bill she'd meet up with him down here around 7:00, if he'd like.

Bill was awash with disappointment at her leaving and yet, excited at the prospect of seeing her later. He tried to hide both emotions, but was walking around with a silly grin on his face. He went up to his room that had all his sports heroes that he grew up admiring.

FAITH   HOPE   &   REINDEER

George and Marshall were walking around, each holding a snow cone. It was the first one Marshall ever had in his life, and he thought this was the very place to try one out. They had already done the cursory tour of the different shops. They had visited the 'Digital Dreams' store where Jim had bought his camera set. And Marshall saw a few things they both thought his Dad would appreciate.

He made a mental note to drop back there again (along with the 'Electrons for Protons' store). They had wandered past the other stores without much enthusiasm, but both knew they would have to get something for their Moms as well, just not today.

They came up to a large arch that read "North Pole Manufacturing Area, Sorry no guests allowed."

George said, "We won't go in but we should at least take a look," and proceeded to walk under the arch, before Marshall could say anything to deter him. He began to follow George toward the Manufacturing Area when two enormous Nutcracker Soldiers stepped into the archway.

George stopped dead and said, "Whoa!"

The two soldiers looked wooden in appearance and stood twelve feet tall. One was clad in yellow and the other blue. They held rifles in their hands, but Marshall thought they looked more like props than actual weapons. However, the rifles were adorned with bayonets that looked like they could inflict a serious wound. When they stood together, there was no way to get past them and they were as effective as a large gate. They were so tall that they almost bumped the top of the arch.

Marshall said, "I guess they weren't kidding about not leaving the village." On either side of the archway was an ice wall that stood about seven feet tall with no handholds to grab and a curved and slippery looking top.

The guards stood mute and immovable. George tried a few platitudes, but this was ignored by the wooden structures before him. They stood with large grinning teeth that Marshall thought looked more like a grimace than a smile. Their eyes didn't move, either. They looked straight ahead beyond the two boys.

Marshall turned and started back toward the village.

George stood there looking like he was trying to solve a riddle. Marshall called to him and George slowly, but finally, turned and came back with Marshall.

"There must be a way in there," said George.

"Why do you care?" asked Marshall, "It's a bunch of factories. Who knows, if you get in there they may make you stay and work the rest of your life." Marshall brightened and laughed saying, "Yeah, in fact I'll bet all these elves were once kids like us who snuck in and became trapped. They got older but never grew any more. It started with a couple and then every year they trapped a couple more. Remember what they say, 'Be careful what you wish for!'" He was doubled over laughing at the thought.

George looked at him with a sneer on his face and said, "That's so lame. Didn't you hear what the lady at the inn said? 'That we are light years ahead of you in technology.' Wouldn't you like to see what's over there? Wouldn't you like to see what's in our future?"

Marshall was getting over his joke and wiped his eyes. He said "I suppose, but not enough to try and tackle those two telephone poles!"

George said, "Maybe there's another entrance somewhere. Do you think there's a way in up there?" He pointed to the upper level.

Marshall shrugged and said he'd be willing to look, but they should head back for now and get something to eat. Suddenly he was starved and tired.

Chapter Eleven

Everyone finally filtered back to the Reindeer Inn. It seemed that each person had stories they couldn't wait to tell others about this wonderful place. One or two even took on an almost scholarly air, like they could now debunk all the myths and tales and speak with authority about Santa and his magical land.

There were also many comments like 'I found the most perfect gift for you.' and 'I couldn't believe my eyes when I looked at the price tags,' and of course an occasional, 'I saw what I'd like, if you want to get it for me.'

There is going to be a good deal of chatter tonight mused Christel, who was back on duty. At least until about 8:30 tonight and then 'CRASH'. She already saw one give out early. She spotted Susan and Bill when they came in and she saw the look of Susan.

Well no surprise, the most intelligent always gave out first, too much sensory overload. It had nothing to do with believing or not, it had more to do with how active their brain was under normal circumstances. Add this place and – wham – instant exhaustion. She figured Jared Grady wouldn't be far behind his daughter.

Christel watched as they came stumbling in, waiting to provide any assistance they requested. A couple asked for food as soon as they walked in. She sent their orders to the kitchen below, immediately. Several others fell into the sofas and chairs, wanting to tell all, but too tired to start. She glanced up at the giant three-foot Black Forest Cuckoo Clock on the wall. It read 5:15 pm, about right for the first day of a visit.

Julie, Heather, Brian and Jared filed into the lodge and were still talking to each other about all the things they had found out. They were getting on famously. They all felt in the mood for a big mug of hot tea and Heather invited the Gradys to their room. They accepted and went up the stairs after briefly acknowledging some of the other patrons in the great hall.

A few minutes later in came Marshall and George, and Marshall had asked Christel if she had noticed his parents come in. She advised him that they had gone to the Conner's room for tea. She gave him a quizzical look and said, "You look hungry, would you like something to eat?"

His eyes got big and he said, "Boy would I!"

She asked the boys what they would like.

Marshall thought a moment and said, "Maybe I should check with my folks first and make sure they don't have any plans."

Christel smiled. "That's very considerate of you, Marshall. I'll ring the Conner's room and ask them." She picked up the phone on the desk and said, "Dasher."

A moment later she said, "Hello, Mrs. Conner, this is Christel, I have a question for Mrs. Grady regarding a request from her son."

Julie got on the phone and Christel relayed the exchange she had with Marshall. She ended the discussion saying, "Very good, ma'am, I'll let him know." She hung up and said, "You are free and clear to navigate as you'd like, but she'd like you to meet up with them later. It seems she wants to convey some information about their day with you. Now, what'll it be and where would you like it – in your room or in the back dining area over there?"

Marshall could have sworn there wasn't a dining area over there before. But he motioned to it so he and George could eat together.

A few more minutes passed and the O'Reilly gang blew in. Annie and Renee bolted in and fairly screamed to anyone who was in earshot, which was nearly everyone, "WE RODE A REINDEER! IN FACT WE <u>FLEW</u> ON A REINDEER!" Jim and Mo tried to get them to settle down, but soon realized it was not in their power on this day.

Ellen was a little more reserved, but just as happy. She looked on the verge of busting wide open, herself. They saw Marshall sitting down and Renee ran over to him.

While Marshall and George listened to Renee regale her tale of riding a reindeer named Henry, who would finally be old enough next year to try-out for the Christmas Eve team.

"He'll never make it. Everyone knows Santa uses the same reindeer every year," quipped George.

Renee said that wasn't always true that sometimes they put in new ones. George rolled his eyes.

Then Christel came up to them holding their suppers. "It's true, what Renee said."

Renee gave George an 'I told you so' look and nod.

Christel continued. "While many of the years he may use the same team, sometimes he uses a different pair or will even swap out several. It depends on the tryouts."

Renee said, "Yeah, and next year Henry gets to tryout."

Christel smiled at her and said, "And I see he has a cheerleader to spur him on."

George was insistent, "What about the *Night Before Christmas*?"

Christel said, "The year Mr. Moore wrote that poem that was the team Santa used." She explained that every room is named after a reindeer that has pulled the sleigh at least three times on Christmas Eve.

"Including the one next to our room?" asked Marshall.

"Oh, especially Pocatello. He pulled it many times before his famous son was ever born," replied Christel.

"Which famous son?" George asked.

Marshall said, "Rudolph."

"You're kidding," said George, "There really is a red nosed reindeer?"

"Absolutely," smiled Christel, "In fact a few of them. One will be coming by here the day after tomorrow."

Renee almost swooned, "Rudolph! Here?" It was almost more than she could stand and she ran off to tell her family.

Christel moved off, too. She had spied the Peters family coming in with their toddler who was very soundly sleeping in his dad's arms.

She approached them and said, "I'll gladly have some

dinner brought to your room while you get Todd settled in for a long winter's nap."

They thanked her deeply, ordered a light supper for themselves and dragged Todd off to their room.

Almost everyone was accounted for, and she knew that things would begin to calm down in the next hour or so.

Chapter Twelve

Susan got up from her rest about the same time that everyone started filing into the resort. She felt refreshed but hungry. She thought it might be nice to get a bite to eat, but wasn't quite ready to socialize downstairs. She walked into the kitchen and opened the refrigerator. There on the top shelf sat a scrumptious Chicken Caesar salad. It was exactly what she was in the mood for, but she could swear that it wasn't there earlier. She had gotten some juice before she went out and would have noticed. She wondered if her Mom ordered it. Except her Mom didn't like Caesar, she was more the Oriental Chicken type.

Her dad? Definitely not. Certainly no more than Marshall would, and Marshall didn't go for what he called 'rabbit food'. She took the salad and a soda to the table, sat down and ate every bite. She mused about how hungry she always seemed to be here. "Must be the air," she said aloud to herself and chuckled.

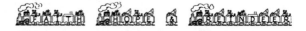

Bill decided to take another shower after reading a book from his room on the greatest baseball legends in the history of the game. He had taken one that morning, but he felt like he wanted to 'freshen up' before meeting Susan again later.

Earlier, he had found the same phone Julie discovered that morning and ordered up a taco dinner to quell his hunger. The tacos were the most authentic he ever tasted, nothing like the Mexican wannabe restaurants in Michigan. He wondered if they had Hispanic elves, and pictured a bunch of elves in sombreros and long moustaches fixing up tacos. He thought this a little too wildly absurd even for here and laughed to himself.

The Gradys and Conners had decided to dine together. Heather and Brian were not too concerned about John and Patrick. They guessed the elves had been taking good care of them, and that either they wouldn't be hungry or they'd have something when they came in.

So they all ordered completely different items. Heather ordered a triple hot fudge sundae with whipped cream, nuts and cherries. She looked at Julie and said, "I have avoided practically every sweet since Patrick was born. I'm going to put the theory of no weight gain to the ultimate test. I figure if they lied, I'll have to go back on the 'after baby' diet again."

Brian ordered a pizza saying the one on the train that the O'Reilly girls ordered looked and smelled so good, that he had been craving one ever since.

Julie requested scallops wrapped in bacon and au gratin potatoes and Jared ordered a Filet mignon and a baked potato with lots of butter, sour cream, bacon and chives.

Jared said he was doing the same thing as Heather except his craving was for red meat and 'taters.

Not long after their meal came, there was another knock on the door and in came John and Patrick with Sid and Hildegard. The two elves introduced themselves to the Gradys and then turned and remarked to the Conners what wonderful boys they had. The boys seemed thoroughly satiated and their parents were told that they'd had their dinner and would probably be fine until morning.

Patrick fired off the days events in rapid succession, and his mother thought he was going to turn blue before he got everything said. Poor John never had a chance but he was so tired it didn't matter to him. He thought he'd wait until morning when he could think clearer.

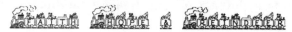

While Marshall and George ate their dinner they listened to some of the stories going around the hall. They all thought they'd made some amazing discoveries, but soon realized they had only scratched the surface.

The comments of what was seen and told made George even more determined to learn all he could of the secrets of the North Pole. Marshall told him he didn't need to know everything, and that it was better for both of them if they didn't. George bought none of that, and thought about how he might yet get around the massive guards.

When they finished their dessert, Marshall said he was going to go up into his room and check out the saxophone there.

He asked George, "Why don't you come up with me and try out the trumpet and maybe we could jam together for a while?"

George said, "Naw, not tonight. We'll have plenty of time later this week. I'd really like to listen to some more of these stories. Maybe we can hatch a plan of attack on where to go tomorrow."

Marshall thought George might have meant that a little too literally.

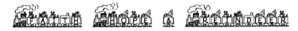

As Marshall left for his room, the Wu family came in almost dragging their bodies from exhaustion. Christel motioned to two young female elves waiting nearby. They dashed over to Fred Wu and his wife Kaileen and suggested that they relax by the fire for a few minutes while they brought them some herbal tea.

They thanked the two elves and Fred smiled weakly at their assistance. Christel came over. "Busy day?" she asked with a smirk. Fred replied, "You have no idea...oh wait, you probably do, don't you?"

Christel chuckled and said, "You folks weren't the first to try to conquer the entire village in one day, and you won't be the last. It's deceptively bigger than it looks.

Kaileen said, "We didn't even cover the whole upper level. In fact, we had barely gotten up there and our feet felt like lead weights."

As Christel turned toward the back of the resort she

said, "That's why he gives you five full days, here." She
then disappeared into the back.

Chapter Thirteen

"Waiting for someone?" Christel asked Bill slyly.

The Cuckoo clock on the wall read 6:40 pm. Bill said slightly flushed, "Uh, yes Ma'am. I'm meeting Susan here around seven."

Christel was glad to see he wasn't going to be coy and pretend nothing special was going on. She asked if she could get him something and he said "No, thanks."

She studied him for a moment and said, "She's very pretty."

Bill agreed silently.

She said, "The North Pole is beautiful at night. Especially if you go to the upper level and look out over the village. In fact, you can even see as far as the Woodland's lights."

"How does that work exactly? I mean the lights. We are in a dome, right? And I heard someone say that the North Pole should be dark during the whole day and night this time of year."

Christel laughed. "Whoa boy, that's a lot of information you asked, and I'm only a simple Innkeeper. You need to see Neutron Kilowatt. He's in charge of our power supply. He can explain and even show you the source of our power up here. He's off now but you could catch him tomorrow. In the meantime why not enjoy the show?"

Bill looked puzzled. "The *show*?"

"Of course," said Christel. "As you may guess we control nearly everything that happens up here, so in a way it's like a giant stage production every day. We bring up the lights and make things happen. Then we lower the lights and set the mood for a quiet evening."

Bill caught on. "Yeah, I see where you're coming from. But....," he hesitated, "It's all real isn't it? I mean this isn't make-believe, is it?"

Christel smiled moving close to whisper. "Kiddo, it's as real as you and Susan." She left him pondering this and walked off.

As the Cuckoo sounded for the seventh time he saw Susan descend from the stairs. He couldn't believe she was right on-time. This was the first girl he'd met who was punctual.

He noticed that she also changed. She was wearing the matching ski pants to her jacket and a pretty lavender sweater that set off the purple contrast of the outfit. She gave a warm smile when she saw him and his heart skipped a beat.

He walked up to her and she said, "So? What did you have in mind?"

"I understand the lights are very nice on the upper level. Interested?"

She nodded and they headed off.

Most of the rest of the crowd downstairs had dispersed and gone to their rooms. Christel did not expect to see most of them again until tomorrow night.

She spied George sitting in a corner listening to another couple talking about their balloon ride over the Pole.

"I still can't believe all the things we saw today," said the woman.

Her husband responded. "All this time I pictured nothing but dolls and wooden soldiers. That is when I would allow myself to picture it at all. Who knew?"

George couldn't stand it anymore. "Excuse me," he said to the couple, "Did you see an entrance into the Manufacturing Center?"

The man looked sternly at George. "There isn't an entrance. They don't allow us in there. I'm sure it's for good reasons."

His wife spoke to George a little more kindly. "If you take the balloon ride, you can get a terrific view and see many fascinating things from the air."

George nodded and murmured a quick 'thanks'. He then headed off to his room.

Christel watched him go and shook her head to herself.

The Gradys bid the Conners good night and headed back to their room.

Julie looked out the bedroom window onto the village. "It's all so beautiful," she said almost in a sigh.

"It's certainly surreal, isn't it?" replied Jared.

She looked at him and furrowed her brow. "Can't you buy into any of it? You really shouldn't be so cynical of the whole thing."

Jared protested. "I'm not being cynical…well okay, maybe I am a little. But you have to admit the whole thing is so far-fetched, who wouldn't be?"

"Me for one. You know they say seeing is believing, but you are seeing this and still not believing. For a man of faith, you're not giving too much benefit of the doubt, are you?"

Jared suddenly felt as if he was raining on his wife's parade. "You're right," he said apologetically. "I'm sorry. I guess I have lost my faith and it's spilling over into everything." He suddenly brightened. "Starting right now, no more Mr. Skeptic. I'm really sorry, honey."

She punched him playfully, "That's better, now I'm wiped. I think I'd like to get ready and hit that wonderful bed again."

They heard the sound of a saxophone in the other room.

FAITH HOPE & REINDEER

Marshall thought this instrument produced the sweetest sound he had ever heard. He played a couple tunes from the recent concert. Then he pulled out the sheet music in the drawer as promised by the note.

He began playing *Silent Night*. Again, the music came out as if a master sax player had previously recorded it. He played quietly, as he did not want to disturb the other people in the inn.

Those who heard it thought it was the loveliest music they'd heard at the Pole.

Chapter Fourteen

Susan and Bill stepped off the gondola and walked over to the ice wall where the O'Reilly girls stood earlier that day. But the view was very different. All the various colored Christmas lights were aglow throughout the whole village with every color of the rainbow glowing from lighted paths. Many of the shops were still open and while there didn't seem to be many shoppers; their lights added another level of softness onto the village paths and surrounding snow.

Bill pointed out what Christel had told him. Off in the distance they could see faint lighting through the trees in the woodlands. They could even make out the elves skating on the pond with a circle of lights outlining its shape.

"I know I'm dreaming, but wouldn't it be wonderful to be part of this all year long?" Susan sighed.

Bill said, "I'm still trying to get over the fact I'm not dreaming now. I mean I gave up believing in Santa Claus and the North Pole quite a while back."

Susan laughed. "Imagine how our parents must feel! When my dad told me 'the truth' about Santa Claus, he was very apologetic that he'd lied to me. Which reminds me, my parents said they had always given all the gifts to me. I wonder why Santa skipped our house all those years? I'll have to ask him that one."

"My parents told me they always bought us the gifts,

but every year they swore that neither one of them had bought one gift or another for us. I think they really believed in Santa before they got here. I think Hailey still did, too. Though I don't believe she would have admitted it out loud. Boy, this will be interesting when we get back to school. Do you think we'll be branded as outcasts or end up in an institution?" He smiled at this last question, but also looked a little concerned.

Susan said, "I wouldn't worry too much. I don't think they will make us carry signs saying that Santa Claus is alive and well and living at the North Pole."

"I'm not so sure," replied Bill, "My parents told me what the Innkeeper said. We have to spread the word.'"

"I think she meant spread the word about Christmas, and try to teach others to keep it all year long."

"I certainly hope that's the case. By the way, how do you keep it?" Bill asked.

She told him about helping out at the Senior Center and tutoring kids at school, but she couldn't think of anything else she did. She asked him the same question.

"I don't do that much, either. I have an uncle that works for Goodwill and I help him out occasionally, especially summers. I also help with Sunday school at our Lutheran church, and my family helps feed the homeless at Thanksgiving."

"That sounds like a lot to me. Especially considering how many families don't do anything." They looked out at the twinkling lights.

Bill said, "Imagine if everyone did a little."

They walked and talked for a little while more, but Susan had again worn out. So they headed back to the inn. Bill asked if they could get together tomorrow.

Susan said she'd like to, but needed to find out if her parents had anything in mind first. She said she'd ring his room after breakfast and let him know. She gave his hand a squeeze and said she was sure she'd see him sometime tomorrow.

That wouldn't come soon enough for Bill.

"One should always fill their heart

to the maximum capacity with their love."

Nicholas Kristopher Kringle, Santa Claus

Chapter One

The next morning everyone felt more refreshed. Many had turned in early and slept soundly. Most were raring to go and had called in an early breakfast. Having been through this more times than could be counted over the last century, the elves were ready for the onslaught of orders and varieties of food.

And with their usual efficiency the elves had everyone settled and eating in what would be record breaking time at any other hotel or resort. When the majority of the guests had finished breakfast they exploded into the lobby like an invasion force. Young and old seemed ready to make a full day of exploring this numinous land.

Jared and Julie finally caught up to Susan and Marshall and they exchanged stories and adventures over breakfast together. Susan talked about Bill, and Marshall told them about George. They were happy to see the kids having so much fun and that they'd found friends towith which to explore the North Pole. Susan asked if they had any special plans for the day that she needed to be a part of. Jared said it might be nice if they had dinner together tonight, but other than that, he didn't see any problems.

Julie agreed and they all planned to hook up together in the lobby at 6:00 pm. Jared and Julie were the first ones out this morning, as Susan said she wanted to call

Bill, and Marshall was moving a little slower than yesterday. It was already almost 9:00 in the morning according to Jared's watch.

As they reached the lobby area, Jared and Julie saw Fergie Keepitneet with his magic hologram on display. He had a full audience this time as people were crowding around to see the three-dimensional rendition of their vacation fantasyland.

As Jared and Julie approached the crowd, Fergie was saying, "Now the next few days might be considered educational days, and our elves, even though extraordinarily busy during the Christmas rush, have been asked to take time to explain some of the finer intricacies of the North Pole operations to you. However, we ask that you honor their busy schedules and attend the question and answer periods as posted on the board over by the door."

Fergie continued, "Similarly, Santa will also be available on a more limited schedule as he prepares for his flight to Australia and New Zealand in just two days. His schedule is also posted. There are names assigned to certain times and he has requested that you keep your appointments as he has laid them out for you. He wants to make certain he meets with each of you."

The Gradys had moved over to the two lists as Fergie was explaining on his map, "Now the administrative center is located…"

Jared and Julie were looking at the first sheet that listed various places in the village along with times listed underneath. They looked to see what things they may want to learn about "the Pole" as the elves called it.

The list read:

> Post Office and Letters to/from Santa
> 09:30
> 11:30
> 14:30   (2:30 pm)
> Polar Power Center
> 10:30
> 13:00   (1:00 pm)
> 15:30   (3:30 pm)
> Naughty or Nice Record Hall
> 12:00   (noon)
> 14:00   (2:00 pm)
> The Polar Times Newspaper
> 09:00
> 11:00
> 15:00   (3:00 pm)

At the bottom of the list it read: *All Q&A sessions will last approximately 30 minutes. Please do not be late, as due to time constraints, we are unable to answer questions more than once in the same session.*

They looked at the next list and saw the times posted for visits with Santa Claus. As Fergie had said, it stated that it was very important to keep the posted time. They looked down and were surprised to see **their** names listed at the following days and time:

> Wednesday:
> 2:30   Marshall Grady
> 3:15   Susan Grady

Thursday:
    9:30   Julie Grady
    9:45   Jared Grady

"Well, I guess we have an appointment," echoed Julie rather amused at the idea.

Jared almost felt as he was being summoned to the principal's office. He turned to Julie and asked "What do you say to Santa after all these years?"

She looked at him and said, "I guess whatever's on your mind."

She wondered if the kids would see their appointed times and whether she should call them. She thought Susan might, but knew Marshall didn't always pay attention to details. He was a more typical teenager, and Julie thought again, about how much she loved them both, but Susan spoiled them.

They went back to the other list and were looking to see what centers they might wish to visit when they heard Fergie say the following, "All times and schedules are also posted in The Polar Times as well. Tonight will be a special fireworks spectacular at 8:00 pm and tomorrow will be a special treat, as the Northern Lights will be in full force all during that afternoon and night from somewhere around 3:00 pm on."

Someone in the group asked how they could see the Northern Lights under a dome. Fergie responded, "Oh, we'll make the dome transparent and dim the street lights for better viewing."

The momentary silence of the crowd declared the surprise and awe perfectly.

After a few seconds, Julie recovered from Fergie's last statement and turned to Jared asking, "Where to?" Jared said he wouldn't mind hearing many of the secrets of the North Pole, but he professed a major interest in how Santa knows whose naughty and who's nice at noon.

Julie said she would like to get a copy of The Polar Times and wondered out loud if they would be allowed to leave with it as a souvenir? They decided to do a little shopping and go to *The Polar Times* building at 11:00, and the Naughty Or Nice Record Hall following that.

That decided, she went over to the counter and picked up the phone. She thought it'd be better to alert the kids than not.

Chapter Two

"Sure that would be great. See you in half an hour."
Bill hung up the phone. He was already dressed and
ready to go, but decided he could easily wait a half hour
for Susan.

He went back to his parents who were still eating
breakfast. Hailey already finished and was in her room
playing with the handheld game she brought with her.
She was going to go down later with another boy and
girl elf that she had met yesterday. The boy elf was a
year older at twelve but the girl elf was Hailey's age.
She had met them when she and her parents were
shopping yesterday.

Her parents, Clark and Jillian Fredrick, also told the
kids they would like to dine with them later. They had
heard from one of the elves in the village that tonight
marked the beginning of several festivities, and they
thought it might be nice to attend a couple of these as a
family.

Bill almost started to object, and then thought better
of it. Later in the week, depending on how things
progressed with Susan might be a better time to try and
argue for extended freedoms. It was still too early to tell.

Jared and Julie wandered into an antique toy store

next to Reindeer Inn, called "Bygone Days." They quickly were enraptured with all the old toys and doodads in the store.

Jared found a top that you had to wrap a string around and pull quickly to make it work. Julie had found a couple antique "Raggedy Ann and Andy" dolls that quickly brought her back to her childhood. They spoke with the elf that ran the store for quite a time. She was telling them that as far as history went; it was only in recent times that they produced toys at all.

"Actually, there was very little 'playtime' for children if you go back more than 75 years ago," acknowledged the proprietor, Stacey Buttons. She looked somewhat like an old fashioned librarian, with large round spectacles and wearing her grayish-brown hair in a tight bun on her head. She wore an old style apron over a dress that while it looked new it also looked like it came from the same period as many of the toys. She went on, "Before then, most children had far too many chores and too much work to do. There was little free time for them to do much of anything else. Santa was really about clothing and food gifts back then. He snuck a few toys into stockings around the turn of the twentieth century, but it wasn't until the 1950s that much of the world had any free time for leisure activities. In terms of 'real' toys, everything was developed for kids primarily in the last half century."

Julie picked up an old 'jumping jack' pull-toy puppet. "When did these come available?"

"Those were mostly introduced in the Netherlands around 1920s and 1930s," replied Stacey.

As they walked around they saw many things from their childhood and well before. Besides the usual dolls, yo-yo's and the like, there were dozens of pull toys like the old Pokey Little Puppy, a large Graf Zeppelin, a French paper-Mache dog made around 1800, early See 'N Say toys, Thumbelina dolls you wound up and watched as they wriggled around, and spring pull toys like old Slinky's, including the old Slinky caterpillar, and a Slinky dog.

Everything looked as if it were made yesterday rather than yesteryear. There were even vintage games from the 1960s in boxes that were never opened. "How do you keep them looking so new?" asked Jared.

"That's because they **are** new Mr. Grady. These have never been played with," responded Stacey. "You see in the beginning of the 'toy era' Santa had the elves make many more toys than we needed, so we had - shall we call them 'extras' - that we warehoused. Over the years we have sold many of them. Thank goodness eBay was finally developed!"

The Gradys laughed and said they wondered how some people hung on to things so long before selling them. Of course all these items contained the usual price tags of the North Pole rather than asking a monetary value.

Jared thought to himself, *Too bad, they might mean more to people if they had to do something more than click and send a PayPal payment.*

The O'Reillys were also on the move. Jim and Maureen had their appointments with Santa at 10:00 and 10:15, respectively. They were on their way over to the Visiting Cottage and wondered why they had appointments at all, let alone before the girls.

Their three daughters were scheduled this afternoon between 2:45 and 3:00 right in between the two Grady kids. Fergie suggested to the O'Reillys that they let the elves take care of the girls so that they could go over alone. Instantly, two elves appeared and said they would gladly take the girls shopping for their parents' Christmas presents.

Like Jared and Julie, they wondered what would take place and whether they should ask questions, or if Santa had something to say to them. They had seen other parents on the list, so they knew they hadn't been singled out. They were both excited and apprehensive at the same time. Imagine – the real, live, one and only Santa Claus. Well maybe not the one and only, but the true current Santa.

As they were walking over they discussed what kind of questions to ask. They knew even before they came here that every year there was something that each of the girls got. Jim and Mo would swear they weren't holding out on each other. Although they figured the other was pretending or fibbing, though they couldn't find evidence to the contrary. Each figured the other stole away a little cash for that rainy day.

They now knew it had to be **him**. *He* had gotten that pretty dress Renee wanted so badly, and the play stove last year for Ellen, and the special doll Annie practically cried over. They thought the first thing they should do was to thank him for his help and generosity.

Chapter Three

As Bill came down the stairs he saw Susan was already there. A good sign he thought."Good morning."

Susan responded with a smile saying. "You have a big day planned ahead of you."

He looked perplexed and asked, "I do?"

She nodded and pointed him to the two posters. He saw then his scheduled appointment with Santa at 3:30, following Susan's of 3:15. Susan then remarked how she would really like to know some of the inner workings of the North Pole so she suggested going to one or two of the Q&A's.

"I also understand there is a fireworks show tonight, and I'm hoping I have a date for that."

Bill wondered if that was one of the 'family outings' his parents wanted him to attend and hoped it wasn't. If so, he would ask if he could invite Susan along. He thought things were progressing very nicely indeed.

They discussed which things to go see and Susan also asked to go to the Naughty Or Nice Center at noon. He could pick any other interesting thing he wanted.

Bill thought the Post Office would be fascinating. He wanted to know how all those letters **did** get here, and if Santa really read every one? He wasn't sure, however, if they would be out in time to get to the Q&A Susan wanted.

He suggested that maybe they could save the Post

Office until tomorrow. She said that would be fine and
they could hit a couple stores before noon today, or just
hang out.

"Well we made it," said Jim O'Reilly slightly out of
breadth. It took longer than they remembered to get to
the Visiting Cottage. As they came through the front
door into the receiving room, one of the elves came in
from the parlor and said Santa would be with them
shortly. Like Jared, Jim felt akin to waiting to have a
father/son talk that he wouldn't mind putting off a
while longer.

A few moments later, Fred Wu came out looking
astonished and a little shaken. He was accompanied by
an elf, who was steadying him as he came out. Fred
looked as if he had been told a fabulous fortune from a
fortune teller and didn't know whether to believe it or
laugh out loud at the absurdity of it.

This did nothing to relieve Jim and Maureen's state
of uneasiness. After the elf escorted Fred Wu to the
walkway, he motioned to the O'Riellys. After receiving
them into the foyer he asked Maureen to have a seat and
took Jim into the parlor. Jim did not have the slightest
clue what to expect.

The Gradys were leaving the antique store about the
time the O'Reillys were entering the visiting cottage.

They still had an hour to kill before the Q&A at *The Times*, so they walked around and window-shopped. Again, they were amazed at how temperate it felt in the Pole, while at the same time feeling comfortably cold. They hadn't felt the need as yet to seek shelter or come in from the frigid temperatures, in spite of them both being from Southern California.

The most Julie had done so far was to zip her jacket up to her neck last night. She thought she might ask for a blanket though when they go to the fireworks display. She wondered where that was going to take place and if there was any danger of hitting the dome. She decided that it wasn't probable that Santa would risk fire or injury to the North Pole or its guests and residents and figured it was more than safe.

While she was musing to herself and looking at the display windows Julie suddenly realized that everything was going to be alright. It was as if someone had approached her with special news that would solve their ills.

She grabbed Jared's arm and pulled him closer and squeezed him tight. "Are you okay?" he asked, being a little taken by surprise.

"Better than okay, I feel great," she said with a grin.

He asked, "What's going on in that pretty little head of yours?" She really had his curiosity up now.

"Oh, nothing for sure, a hunch or a feeling if you will," she said, "I suddenly know things are going to work out for us."

Jared almost laughed; he had gotten the same exact feeling a moment ago.

FAITH HOPE & REINDEER

Marshall and George had finally left after conferring with Fergie about what was available on the upper level. George had said to Marshall that they should take the balloon ride to scout out the area.

"You're not still trying to figure some ways into the unauthorized areas are you?" asked Marshall.

George looked dejected, "No I guess not. It's just that so many things I'm hearing about this place that has got my curiosity on overload."

Marshall said, "Yeah, well you know what curiosity did to the cat."

George laughed and retorted, "Yeah, but satisfaction brought him back!"

Marshall did want to take the balloon ride, however, especially after hearing about the experience from his parents. His Mom talked about the flying sled and all the reindeer, and the odd-shaped vehicles that floated like a hovercraft. Even his Dad had seen more animated, and Marshall hoped he was finally having a good time for a change.

He had been worrying a lot about his Dad lately, not because of financial reasons, though he knew that seemed to be the root cause of the problem, but because he seemed like he had trouble getting out of his sad moods. Marshall had tried cheering him up and challenging him to do things with him, but his Dad was unresponsive at best.

He had heard how some people got so depressed that they couldn't come out of it by themselves. It made

Marshall sick thinking this could be happening to his father.

Marshall already knew what he was going to ask Santa for this afternoon. He wanted his Dad back.

Chapter Four

"Welcome Jim, it is an honor to meet you!" Santa
Claus said as Jim O'Reilly walked into the room. Santa
took Jim's hand and shook it with vigor and firmness.
He motioned Jim to a big overstuffed chair directly
across from his. "Please have a seat," Santa said.

Jim finally found his voice. "The honor is all mine St.
Nicholas."

"Please Jim, call me Santa or Nicholas. I am not a
saint, that honor is reserved for my illustrious ancestor."

His voice was an octave higher than Jim had guessed
it would be. It was a very pleasant speaking voice, but
not the big booming voice he had envisioned. Santa
wasn't obese as he is often pictured, either. He was a big
man to be sure. But Jim guessed him around 200 to 215
pounds, not tipping the scales at 300+ as often depicted.
He stood about Jim's height, which was 5'10".
However, one thing that was true to form – he was a
jolly man and had a warm, sincere demeanor.

"How have things been going for you?" Santa asked.

Jim shrugged. "I'm pretty happy, I have a great wife,
our three wonderful girls, an okay job and a roof over
our heads."

Santa said, "I've seen your girls, beautiful children.
You and Mo have done a wonderful job bringing them
back from the brink of a disastrous beginning in their
lives. You should both be very proud."

Jim blushed at the compliment. "It's easy when you love someone as much as we love them. I only wish I could do more."

Santa beamed. "And I intend to grant that wish to you…and Mo."

Other than himself no one had ever referred to Maureen by Jim's nickname.

He continued. "You both have a large capacity for love. and you enjoy sharing that. I have a proposition for you both. If you don't mind I would like to invite Maureen in and discuss it with the two of you."

Exactly twenty-five minutes later, the O'Reillys were leaving the room still dabbing their eyes. What they had heard was beyond their deepest dreams. They didn't know how they were going to hold in their emotions in check until they got home. And while they couldn't wait to tell the girls.

Santa made them promise not to say anything until Christmas Day. It was his present to the two of them and it couldn't be unwrapped until then.

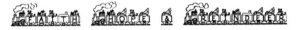

Bill asked Susan what she thought she might want to ask from Santa Claus.

She hesitated and said "It's kind of personal."

Bill nudged her. "Come on you can tell me. I won't ask for it first. In fact, since you're going before me you get first dibs."

She said it wasn't like that. She wanted to ask something to help her parents and her. Bill felt a little clumsy making a joke regarding a personal wish and apologized.

"No problem." and asked him, "What do you want from Santa?"

"Since it's too late to ask for double 800 on my SAT's, so I guess I'll have to reach for a new laptop."

Susan tried to smile at his joke. She was too wrapped up wondering if Santa could grant her wish, and praying to herself that he not only could, but also would.

FAITH HOPE & REINDEER

The Gradys were approaching *The Polar Times* building. It looked more like another cottage, than what you might call a building. It was crowded when they walked in, even though there were only a few people in there besides the workers.

All the elves were smiling and running back and forth with copies of the latest edition and any changes for the next issue. They handed out the last press run to the visitors coming in through the door.

A round little elf came down from the upper floor. He carried an air of authority and announced himself as Newbee Blotonpaper, the Editor-In-Chief of *The Polar Times*. He said it was the duty of *The Times* to keep up with all the activities that took place at the Pole, and that he would be happy to entertain questions.

A gentleman in the back that Jared hadn't seen before asked if they also printed world news in the paper.

Newbee said that while they received international news they rarely printed it unless it had a direct effect on the North Pole or its population. "There is sufficient news right here in our little corner of the world to keep our small staff plenty busy," puffed Blotonpaper. "For instance did you know that we have developed a better styrene plastic that is virtually indestructible? You can throw it, smash it and even run over it and it will not break or crack."

Everyone seemed impressed so he went on, "In fact there are more new inventions and discoveries made here every month than throughout the whole world in a full year."

Julie asked, "What about medical advancements, does the Pole work on those too?"

Newbee un-puffed himself and said, "Er, no. Because of the unusual climate up here nobody gets ill like they do in other parts of the world. We are very blessed in that. However, a good many of our discoveries are later used in the medical field."

One of the younger visitors asked if they interviewed different elves. Again Newbee puffed up and said, "Why of course, we have many fascinating operations taking place in the North Pole and everyone likes to hear stories about the different goings-on.

Julie asked, "What can you tell us about the fireworks display scheduled for tonight?"

Blotonpaper filled himself up to his full 4' 3" frame, and sounding much more like a ringmaster than an editor exclaimed, "This will positively be one of the most incredible displays of aerial pyrotechnics you will ever witness. The display will take place right outside the hotel and can be seen virtually anywhere throughout the North Pole."

Someone beat Jared to the next question, "What about the dome? Is it safe?"

The round elve's eyes sparkled, "Oh yes, it is quite safe. And I dare say you will be in for a major surprise when you see this tonight."

A few more questions were asked of no great importance and then the Editor thanked everyone for their attention and interest and dismissed them all. The Q&A only lasted twenty-two minutes, but answered all their questions.

The Gradys enjoyed the visit and hoped the next one would be just as interesting.

Chapter Five

Bill and Susan came from one side of the Naughty Or Nice Center and Jared and Julie approached from the other. They met at the front door. The Gradys surprised to see their daughter, laughed as they saw her expression as well..

Jared teased Susan that she was checking to see which list she made this year.

Julie turned and said, "You must be Bill" and Susan quickly apologized and introduced her parents to him."

Bill asked if they had seen anything of interest in the Polar Times and both shrugged.

"It was somewhat interesting," said Jared. "I believe this will be more so. Shall we?" He motioned them to go in.

They asked Bill where he was from, what grade he was in, etc. Forgetting what Susan had said earlier, Bill asked what they each did for a living.

The obvious awkwardness of Jared's answer reminded Bill that was a mistake in the asking.

Susan said, "My Dad's a financial manager in between positions right now." She had handled the situation with more grace and tact than Jared ever had, and once again he was proud of his daughter.

The Naughty Or Nice Record Hall was a large government style building. It had a dome in the center and halls at either end. The eddifice contained a good many elves and records, but had few windows throughout the structure and looked rather austere inside.

As they walked in, the occupants in the building were instantly viewed on screens around the room. Nearly everyone commented on how poor the video quality was.

Each person had a thick green shadow surrounding him or her. So much so it made their features hard to distinguish.

Bill said, "I think they need a serious upgrade to their video technology."

They could see several satellite dishes in the dome. They faced every direction on the compass. These were linked into two main cables that went into both sides of the halls. There was a second story and with a balcony overlooking the main floor from where the visitors stood.

Several elves walked onto the balcony. They looked at the monitors and nodded to each other with big smiles. The people below could not begin to imagine why.

The room was crowded as there were a good many more people here for this Q&A than at the last. Jared thought, *"Morbid curiosity. They probably all want assurance they're on the right list."*

At noon on the dot the elves held up their hands to quiet everyone down. An elf standing in the center moved forward. He resembled a science teacher that Jared had when he was young. His hair stood up slightly in the middle and was laid flat and long on the sides. He wore glasses, the kind you look over, as if you would use them for reading only.

He introduced himself as Earle Tellitall, Senior

Control Manager or SCM for the Naughty Or Nice
Record Hall. He also introduced his staff using only
their first names. He said he didn't want their last
names known to the outside world to prevent threats.
Everyone laughed at this, except the elves. Apparently
they were serious.

Then Earle kicked off the program saying,

**"One of the greatest buzzes around the
world is how does Santa know who you are and
whether you are naughty or nice. This has
puzzled people for many years. In the
beginning it was very laborious work. We had
to keep meticulous records and even then a
few people never made into our records when
they were born.**

**"We are now proud to report that since
1954 we have been hardwired into every
hospital and birthing facility in the known
world. As soon as there is a record of
someone's birth we have it stored in our
database."**

Everyone nodded saying that made perfect sense.

**"What is really amazing is how we track
whether you are good or bad after that. We use
two methods, one more general and the other
very specific. We can show you the general
method. In fact, you are already looking at it.
On the screens above you, you can see your**

image and the spectral ghost attached to it.

Ladies and gentlemen, if you were naughty your shadow would be red. The higher you are on the good or bad scale the more shadow you have. As you can see your image is almost completely blurred because you have so much 'green' or good in you. If any of you were fell in the other direction you would see red, literally."

Everyone started buzzing and talking about what a wonderful way to identify dangerous citizens and how they knew a couple people who wouldn't be 'green', and why police don't have this technology. Earle Tellitall held up his hands.

"The problem comes is that this scanning technology only measures a person at that instant. This is why we don't use it exclusively. A person might take a newspaper from a stand without paying because they have no change, or be thinking badly about someone because of something that person said to them and at that moment and they might have less 'green' shadowing or even cast a red hue.

"So we have a backup scanner that we use to identify a persons true nature and character. It assigns a number value to that person as either positive, negative or with rare exception, zero. The scale runs from +25 to −25. As examples, Mother Teresa always measured a plus 24. She was in the running for sainthood and with good reason. However, Osama Bin Laden on the couple times we were able to catch him on a scanner came out minus 22. A very bad character, indeed.

"In order to receive an invitation to the North Pole each member of the family must receive a plus 15 or better rating for more than a year. Infants, of course are excluded even though they begin life with a perfect +25.

"To give you an idea how this compares to average people. If you score a plus five and above, you are pretty well guaranteed you will receive a gift from Santa. If you are a minus five or below, well let's say you can be glad he no longer gives out coal. So each of you can be very proud you are here. You have done some extraordinary things in your life and it has been weighed and measured favorably. Questions?"

Hands shot up at once. The first one called on was Bill.

"Since we are all good individuals, can you show us a scanner that assigns a number?"

Earle was quick to answer, "We did that a couple times before, and it caused hurt feelings because each person wanted to know why a person was higher or lower than they were. So we no longer show the number scale, we only demonstrate the shadow scanners since they are more general.

He paused. "Next? Yes the young woman in the

back."

It was Katy Peters he called on standing next to Corey; the Gradys hadn't seen them slip in. "If the number scanner is so accurate why not let the authorities use this technology."

He nodded as if he expected this question before it was asked. "The problem with scanner technology, even ours, is that it also shows the *propensity* and history of someone to do good or bad things. It doesn't catch them 'in the act'. It would be similar to accusing someone of wrongdoing because they had done it before or were likely to do it again. This brings up another problem. If they have done nasty things in the past it can affect their scale.

If they were incarcerated and had done their time, it would still register. It is similar to getting a speeding ticket and having it stay 'on your record' for your lifetime. Yes, you sir." He pointed to Jared.

"Does the number change often?" Jared asked. He was sure his number had slid down over the last year.

"Very rarely," said Earle, "You see we also are programmed to see various intangibles such as your future tendency to do good or bad as well as your past. If you have had a tendency to do good all your life, it is doubtful, and even improbable, that you will suddenly revert to an evil person. While it can happen, those are extremely rare cases."

He took a couple more questions like how many scanners there where around the world (thousands of both types), and how often does one get scanned (depends on the region in the world) and finally, how likely is it that they scan everyone (extremely).

Then Earle said unfortunately their time had expired. He thanked them all for coming and he bade them a good day.

Chapter Six

Jared and Julie invited Susan and Bill to eat lunch
with them after the Record Hall demonstration. They
found a little restaurant up the street decorated with
flags from all around the world on the inside.

Inside were sayings written in various languages
written on the walls. It looked like a wild kind of graffiti
with all the different symbols. They found a few written
in English and discovered they were quotes of famous
individuals.

"I might have thought they are different ways to say
'Merry Christmas' or something," commented Bill.

A younger waiter-elf came over to the table wearing a
red, green and white stocking cap. He had a long, thin
moustache that ended in a full curl. He said with a
French accent, "Oui, dear guests, how may I help you?"

Julie said, "Do you have the same menu as the other
facilities in the North Pole?"

The waiter smiled, "And this distresses you, non?"

Julie laughed, "No, it does not distress me. It makes
me think harder is all."

The waiter said, "Perhaps you would like a beverage
while you are doing your thinking, oui?"

Julie said that would be fine and ordered a mint
julep. The others ordered different flavors of cocoa.

"Mint Julep?" laughed Jared, "You really are putting
these guys to the test aren't you?"

Julie looked hurt at the accusation. "Well, I don't really feel that way. I am only doing what they expect. I believe completely that if I ordered a Brontosaurus burger, they'd somehow bring me one."

Bill said excitedly, "Wow, you totally gave me an idea!"

Susan glared at him. "You wouldn't really, would you?"

Bill laughed at the thought. "No, nothing quite that bizarre, but I have always wanted to try a Buffalo burger and no place I've been to in Michigan has them. I can finally try one!"

"That's right you said you live in Michigan. What part?" asked Jared.

"Around Grand Rapids, on the Western side of the state," answered Bill.

"I'm more familiar with Ann Arbor," Jared smiled wistfully.

Bill grinned, "Let me guess, you're a Wolverine?"

Now Jared grinned. "Yep, dyed in the wool blue and gold!"

The waiter returned and asked for their lunch order. Julie said she was in the mood for something Thai, and asked the waiter to decide for her along those lines. The waiter studied her for a moment as if looking for a telltale mark, and then he smiled and scribbled.

Susan said she wasn't that hungry, but that she would like a piece of French Apple pie with some vanilla ice cream. The elf nodded and scribbled.

Bill ordered his medium rare Buffalo burger and onion rings without so much as a raised eyebrow from the waiter.

Lastly Jared requested an Italian sausage sandwich with grilled onions and mozzarella cheese.

Julie looked at him and said in a teasing tone, "Don't tell me you're catching on?"

Jared shrugged and said, "When in Rome...or wherever."

FAITH HOPE & REINDEER

"Wow, look at that!" George exclaimed. He and Marshall were floating across the Manufacturing Center in the balloon. George had spotted a very sophisticated looking robot guiding a squibble into the docking station.

"That's no R2D2 unit!" How advanced is that guy from us right now?" he asked Rory. Rory and Ben were the two elves flying the balloon. Ben was the pilot and Rory the tour guide. Both elves looked younger than the pair Marshall's parents and the Conners had. They were enjoying the two boys' curious nature and were answering all their questions. "You're just a few years off," replied Rory.

Marshall was beginning to catch George's enthusiasm for learning about the future. He was keeping pace with George asking question after question. They had learned everything so far that Marshall's parents had and quite a bit more.

Even concerning the naughty and nice scanners. They found out for instance, that because technology is so advanced at the Pole, the elves can run a long distance scan on you using a pinpoint scanner to determine your naughty or nice number. And that people pass stationery scanners every day, are rated and never know it.

Some of the scanners are hidden in telephone poles and street lamps, and most are no larger than a pocket calculator or PDA. Everything was being sent to the Pole via satellite.

And speaking of satellites the Pole has a full array of them in space. And they are so small that radar can't even pick them up. If they did, they would identify them as 'space junk' and ignore them.

The boys were told that most of this information would be considered classified once they left, but these elves had no problem sharing it with them.

After all, Ben told the boys, "You obviously carry the highest trust of the big guy, since he invited you here."

The other remaining members of George's family namely his brother, Hunter who was nine and his mother, Deb, were out and about the village themselves. Deb had been enjoying the North Pole as much as either of her sons. She was definitely glad she listened to her boys and took the chance to come here.

Deb was a nurse practitioner, meaning she was almost a doctor and could prescribe medications and do minor surgeries. She was proud of her job and her license, but she had problems since the medical group where she worked drastically cut back her hours.

So much so, that she didn't scarcely needed to ask time off to go on her trip. She received social security and had received a large insurance payment from her late husband's company, but she was trying to maintain a good portion of that money for the long haul. She knew as her two sons got bigger, so too, would be their financial needs for high school and college. Besides George's trumpet lessons and equipment, there was Hunter's hockey equipment and his training and so on.

Deb had loved her husband very much, and when he died in the car crash she wasn't sure if she would ever get over it. She had problems accepting it some days, but she took great solace in having George and Hunter.

They brought her tremendous pride, and she often cried the hardest because her late husband couldn't see what wonderful young men they were growing up to be.

Hunter was her athlete. He had gotten into playing hockey, and according to his coach, had a natural love and talent for the sport. Moreover, his coach had never seen such a sportsmanlike player.

Hunter never got mad or upset on the ice. He always listened to what the coach had taught him, and anxious to try new things to enhance his game. Though it was a rough game, Hunter played it with a finesse that was normally seen by much older players, some ready for college.

His coach really thought the best thing for Hunter would be to attend the USA Hockey camp and tryout for their team. He said he had done all he could to develop Hunter's natural ability. But the one covering his Oshkosh home was in Vernon Hills, Illinois, right outside of Chicago.

The cost was too much for his mother to part with in their financial state. She desperately wanted to see Hunter continue, but felt he would have to do so at a pace that made monetary sense for the remaining family.

They were out looking at some of the computer games, trying to figure out what George might like best. Deb kidded her sons saying that Hunter was her physical and George her technical, warriors. George could play computer games for hours on end while Hunter did the same with hockey.

They were talking with Ion Crosswire, and he was showing them all the different games that George would enjoy. He wasn't being as much help as Deb had hoped because he kept pulling out different games faster than she could figure out what he was showing her. Before she could even look at the package for one, he would stop and say he might have a different version George would like better.

Ion hated confusing the poor woman, but after all, he was under orders.

Chapter Seven

It was getting late when they landed the balloon, and Marshall knew he had to really move to get to the Visiting Cottage on time. It was two o'clock and he only had a half hour to get there. He didn't want to miss his opportunity to see Santa.

As soon as they touched down, Marshall bid a hasty goodbye to George and said he'd catch him later. He ran down the Aviation Center hall and secured a spot with a few elves in a horse drawn sleigh heading toward the gondolas.

"You look rushed," said one of the elves.

"Time got away from me and I'm worried about missing my appointment with Santa," he said.

The elves looked at each other and giggled. "Oh, I wouldn't worry too terribly much," chuckled a second, younger girl elf.

"Won't he be upset if I'm late?" Marshall asked. "The sign was very exact about not missing your time."

They giggled some more and a third elf said, "Yeah, they always say that. 'Gotta keep to the schedule' they're always sayin'. But truth is you can't throw Santa off schedule."

Looking more concerned Marshall asked, "Is that because he'll skip your time?"

The girl elf's eyes narrowed and she moved closer to Marshall. "No – It's because he'll *stop* your time!"

Marshall stared at her, confused.

She sat back on the sleigh and explained, "The time continuum factor is one of the advancements known at the North Pole. Santa and a few of us can control, and move in or out of the time vortex, as needed. It allows Santa to stop time throughout most of the world, while it moves at the same pace where he is. It can even give the illusion of appearing and disappearing at will. In the North Pole, he uses it to slow or nearly stop time until events can catch up with him. So if you're late he'll hold time until you get there."

Marshall was trying to grasp what the elf was telling him. "So," he asked still confused, "Santa can control time wherever he goes or wherever he is? Don't people notice they aren't moving anymore?"

"Not if everyone is moving the same speed. He could be slowing you to a crawl right now and you wouldn't feel it because around you everyone is still moving like you are," replied the first elf.

Though it was obvious to the elves, Marshall didn't get it. The third elf gave another try, "Look, imagine a movie. Now you know that a movie is so many still pictures played at a speed which plays out action, right?"

Marshall nodded.

"Okay, so if you slowed the images down and <u>you</u> stayed at the same speed..."

Marshall's eyes got wide as he said, "The movie would be going in slow motion!"

"Right," said the third elf, "Similarly, if you sped it up and stayed at the same speed, it would look like it was going faster than you. But, if you could adjust your speed to match the movies…"

Marshall's jaw dropped as he said, "*You can do that?*"

"Some of the elves have for many a year," said elf two. "Now, we don't like to see Santa have to do that, but as long as he knows you're on your way…"

FAITH HOPE & REINDEER

After lunch, the Gradys parted company with their daughter and her new beau.

After they were out of earshot Jared asked Julie. "Did you see the way he looks at her?"

"Well Susan wasn't exactly repulsed by him, either."

Jared shook his head. "It will never work you know," he sighed. "Long distance relationships and all."

Julie poked him in the ribs and tittered. "Yeah, like ours, huh?"

Jared had met Julie while he was a junior in college at a friend's party at UCLA. Julie was a freshman there, and they hit it off at once. They managed to keep a relationship going steadily while Jared finished at Michigan. They got engaged after he graduated, and married after she graduated. With the exception of occasional business trips, they were never apart since.

"Besides, he is applying to western colleges. He may wind up in L.A."

Jared looked at her. "What if they both end up at USC or UCLA?"

Julie winked at him. "What will be, will be, my love. Besides, he seems like a nice-enough guy."

Jared joked, "Well if he's good enough for Santa Claus..."

Julie smiled widely. "Now that's the spirit!"

Bill said to Susan, "Your parents are really nice."

Susan looked at him with a wide smile. "Yeah, as far as parents go, I have a pretty good pair. You said you get along with yours?"

Bill didn't hesitate at all. "Absolutely, actually, I am amazed at how well our family gets along. Especially after I see how other kids and their folks go at it. Even my Dad said he never got along with his parents. My grandpa died on his side of the family, but I love my Grandma. Dad said she mellowed quite a bit since he was a kid."

Julie asked, "What about your Mom's side?"

Bill twitched. "Oh, they don't speak about them at all. They're a forbidden topic. Apparently something happened a long time ago. I don't know anything about them."

"I'm sorry for you," brightened Susan. "So, what would you like to do now?"

Bill looked at his watch. "It's almost 2:15 and you and I have an appointment in about an hour. Perhaps we should start making our way towards Santa's house."

Susan nodded. They walked toward the main street and saw a horse drawn sleigh go by. It's passengers were Marshall and several elves.

The O'Reillys had been walking aimlessly around the village ever since they left Santa's Cottage. They talked in hushed but excited tones, careful not to let anyone hear. It was as if someone else heard they would lose their special gift from Santa. But this could not wait for Christmas Day to work out all the logistics. They especially wondered what their girls would say and how they will react?

So many plans, so many changes to all their lives.

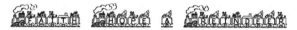

Fred Wu was in his room writing feverishly. He was not even allowed to tell Kaileen about what Santa gave him. Santa had laid out a specific timetable and Fred was still trying to get it all written down. It was the most incredible thing he had ever seen.

Kaileen wouldn't believe the incredible gift he had been given. Santa Claus had told him that since he had done so much for so many, it was time to do something for himself and his wife. Fred ran a small dry cleaning operation. Most of the proceeds he made he sent to China to assist several members of his family there.

They also gave quite a bit to their church, which had several mission programs that he and Kaileen believed strongly in. Santa felt his gift would be put to very good use.

Kaileen also received wonderful news from Santa, but was also not allowed to tell Fred just yet. It was something they both wanted and prayed for. Santa said he couldn't really give her the gift, as it wasn't his to give, he could only verify it.

Chapter Eight

Marshall caught the gondola as it was about to leave the station. It seemed to take forever to get to the base of the village, and time certainly hadn't slowed on his watch! It was fast approaching 2:30. He jumped out of the gondola as a reindeer sleigh pulled up to let some visitors off at the gondola.

Marshall asked the driver if he could help him get to the Visiting Cottage quickly. "Running a tad tight?" asked the elven driver with a decidedly British accent. Marshall said he had less than five minutes. The elf gave Marshall the same knowing smile that the other elves had, and told Marshall to hop in.

As they headed over, the elf named Winston asked Marshall if he knew what he wanted to discuss with Santa. Marshall said he had a pretty good idea, and then he questioned Winston about his accent.

"Oh, I did a time in London for a spell," he replied, "I was in charge of one o' the distribution points there."

Marshall asked him for how long.

"Oh, not too long, 'bout 60 years."

Marshall gasped, "Sixty years! That would be an age and a half to me!" exclaimed Marshall.

"Well I'm very glad to be back 'ere now. Wet and dreary city it were. Ne'er could get used to the weather there."

They talked about the differences between the

weather in California and Britain and about how different the cultures are. They also discussed the different meanings of the same words between the two countries.

Suddenly Winston said, "Well, 'ere you are." Marshall couldn't believe it. Only a couple minutes had ticked off his watch. It read 2:29.

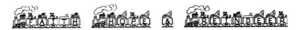

George was walking around the top level and came upon the arch that led into the Manufacturing Center. This time he didn't try to enter, having seen the large red and green nutcracker guards from the balloon. Except for the colors and the fact that they carried swords instead of guns, they looked equally as formidable. George knew he couldn't talk his way around them, so he waited.

About the time Marshall hopped into the sleigh with Winston. A wagon came through the arch with an elf heading for the Post Office to get another load of mail.

George hailed the wagon and the elf stopped. "How may I help you young man?" inquired the elf.

George wasn't exactly sure how to ask, but decided honesty was the best policy as the elf might have inklings to the contrary.

George fired off his request. "I really feel it is vitally important that I learn all that I can concerning the North Pole, and I'd like to ask if there was any chance of getting into the center behind you...I mean is there no exception to the rule on that score?"

The elf looked long and hard at George as if studying
the possibility. He stroked the little beard on his chin
and said in careful tones to George. "No one has ever
received permission to go into the Manufacturing or
Woodland area. One overly curious lad had managed to
make it in, but I warn you the consequences of such an
action will change your life forever."

George looked at the elf as if he had threatened him
and asked, "Why did you enslave the last one?"

George thought maybe Marshall had been correct all
along in his joking.

The elf gave a hearty laugh. "Good heavens, no! It's
only that after he saw some of the things that went on
in there, his life took a decidedly different turn than the
one he had planned. Plus his visit with Santa took on a
much more serious discussion."

George imagined that would be the case. He also
realized that the elf hadn't really answered his question.
"So you're saying there is a way in there?"

The elf laughed again. "Not that I can tell you
about, or help you with. Good luck figuring that one out
on your own."

He snapped the reigns and the reindeer began pulling
the wagon again.

Patrick and John were having more fun than they
could remember in their young lives. They stood in a
large circular area that marked the center of the village.
They entered a snowman contest with some of the other

kids that had come up with them, including the O'Reilly's girls and Hailey Fredrick, Bill's sister.

They challenged two teams of elves and all three teams were working, packing and shaping the snow as if the prize was the entire North Pole. Hailey, Renee and John were rolling the balls packing them solidly and making them as large as they could.

Ellen, Patrick and Annie were shaping the snow once placed into its proper position. Each team had a box of items including carrots, buttons, scarves, hats and the like to finish their creations.

The judge was standing nearby. The creations were all being placed under the town center maypole for all elves and visitors to see and admire. The judge was laughing and teasing and taunting both, the elves and the kids.

She loved this activity almost more than all the others. She loved making the kids feel that this was as much their home as hers. As in a way it was. Later, she would invite the girls back to her kitchen and have them help her mix up and bake a batch of her cookies to take to the inn. She would catch up with the boys tomorrow taking them to the campfire ring to tell them some of her best stories about Santa Claus and the North Pole.

Yes, Mrs. Mary Claus was indeed happiest when surrounded by children. But now it was time for the judging.

Chapter Nine

Jared and Julie decided to save the Polar Power Center for tomorrow. They thought it might be better to catch that Q&A after their visit with Santa. They felt more like relaxing and hanging around the Reindeer Inn for the afternoon. They wanted to feel more refreshed and relaxed to watch the fireworks tonight.

Jared figured to do a little reading in the lobby and watch the comings and goings of the others. Julie thought it would be nice if they could catch Jim and Maureen and chat with them a while to see how their vacation was going so far.

Jared finally dropped his insecurities and began enjoying himself. He also thought that if all this was possible, what wouldn't be? Like Julie, he quit asking questions in his mind and enjoyed the various things he learned about the North Pole.

He was determined to renew his faith and trust that things would work out. More out of curiosity, than doubt, he wanted to learn more of the history of this incredible place and its inhabitants.

As they were walking into the inn the Peters were coming out. The Gradys stopped to say hello and see how they were doing.

Katy beamed, "Oh, we're wonderful! We have been having a lazy day. A delightful elf named Annabelle came by this morning and said she would like to take

Todd off our hands before breakfast. She said this was our day to relax and be by ourselves. She said she would bring Todd home after dinner."

Cory said, "This is the first time the two of us have really been alone since he was born. It really feels strange."

The Gradys could relate. They remembered the days of having no time to themselves and needing to be available all the time for their kids. They were pleased for the Peters and told them to make the most of it.

Marshall was escorted immediately into the room where Santa stood with an outstretched hand. Marshall took it and said what a pleasure it was to meet him.

Santa bowed slightly, "You did an outstanding job with your team last year at the Relay For Life. I understand you raised $6,000 by yourself. That's quite impressive."

Marshall was surprised at him knowing this detail. "Thank you, sir, I had a lot of help."

"You have done many good things in your life, so far. I wish to see you continue. Giving of yourself to help others is the greatest gift a man or woman can give. And before I tell you what I'd like to give you, there is something I know you want to talk to me about."

Marshall didn't need another prod to begin telling Santa of his hope to have his Dad, and of course his Mom, happy again. He told Santa of his concern and worries about his Dad becoming depressed and unable to function.

Santa assured him that this would not happen and that his Dad was going to be fine. He advised Marshall that before his parents left the North Pole they would be as happy as at any time Marshall could remember.

Marshall was visibly releived and his entire demeanor relaxed at hearing this.

Santa said, "Okay now that we have addressed your concern on that, what might I do for you?"

Marshall hemmed and hawed and said, "I really haven't given that much thought."

Santa laughed, "That doesn't surprise me. You always think of others. It's what makes you and your sister so special. Luckily for you I have been thinking for you. I think I have a gift you'll appreciate. First, I want you to take the saxophone in your room home with you. I would like to see you to play it as much as you can. You know, music is one of the most important ways you can impact people's lives. By the mere playing of notes you can influence people's moods, lift their spirits, or allow them to slow down and relax. You can make them dance, forget their cares and enjoy life while they listen to your God given talent."

Marshall was thrilled and amazed at what the jolly old elf told him. He knew the moods he went through while playing music, but never gave much thought to how greatly it impacted others. He thought this was the best Christmas present ever.

But Santa wasn't finished...

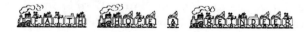

"Congratulations!" Mary Claus said to the children, "You have done a marvelous job!" The kids made a rendition of Sherlock Holmes complete with pipe, hat, monacle and shawl for the snow sleuth. It was well done and looked better than the two elven team's renditions of a circus clown and a fireman.

She placed the blue ribbon on the snowman and reminded the O'Reilly girls that it was about time to get moving in order to see her husband at the Visiting Cottage. She told them that later they would get together again, if they'd like. The girls said absolutely, it would be a great pleasure.

One of the elves came over and said, "I'll lead you over to the cottage, we best get going."

Mary turned to Hailey and said, "And you, my dear, are more than welcome to join them." Hailey said that would be great and asked what time. As soon as you are finished with Santa you can come over to the house next door and we'll be in the kitchen.

Hailey knew her appointment was right after Bill's at 3:45 today and she was very nervous about it. It was already 2:30 pm.

"What about us?" John asked.

She turned with a big smile and said, "Tomorrow I will take you, Patrick and a couple of the other boys over to the campsite area and I'll tell you stories of Christmas and Santa. I'll even answer questions you might have."

"Way cool." said John.

Patrick asked excitedly, "Even how he gets up and down the chimney?"

Mary nodded and said, "Even that."

Chapter Ten

"I'll never be able to keep quiet about this until Sunday!" said Marshall out loud to himself. "There's no way!"

He almost flew out of the cottage and thought this must be how reindeer fly. Santa gives them the most important thing their minds can imagine and they take off! He felt he could give them a run for their money right about now.

How the heck was he supposed to not say anything to his parents, Susan, or even George! He was busting out all over. "Okay," he said to himself, "Get a grip. It's real and you've got it, so take a few deep breaths and calm down."

While he said it, he knew he wasn't able to do it. He thought about the next seven years and what they would mean.

He passed the elf leading the O'Reilly girls up the path and was grinning like the Cheshire Cat. He looked at them and wondered what Santa could possibly be anywhere near as great as what he had received. He practically wanted to shout it out to them, like the way they came yelling at him about flying on a reindeer. He was still smiling as he headed for the inn.

He wasn't in the mood to go exploring anymore. He felt like playing his new Christmas present.

FAITH   HOPE   &   REINDEER

Bill and Susan got off the gondola as Marshall was leaving the Visiting Cottage.

They had stopped in front of "Crackin' Up", the nutcracker store. Bill said his Mom loved nutcrackers and had quite a few. He asked Susan if they could stop in and look around for a Christmas present for her.

She said that was fine they were only a few minutes from the Cottage and they had about thirty minutes to spare.

They walked into the store and Bill wondered if his mother had been there yet. He thought she might have fainted if she had. Like many of the shops they had visited, there were more sizes, shapes and styles of nutcracker than Bill ever imagined.

A whispery old elf approached them and said, "Looking for something in particular young folk?"

Bill said more to himself than the elf, "Where do you start?"

The old elf chuckled and said, "Perhaps a certain character or theme might be a beginning."

Bill was trying to take it all in when he suddenly realized the elf was talking to him. He stumbled around his words and said, "...Oh I'm sorry, were you asking me something?"

Susan had wandered toward the back of the shop. She was looking at all the knights the shop carried, some standing, some on horses, even one by a catapult.

She was wondering if maybe Bill might be her knight. He seemed the perfect gentlemen. She had gone out on several dates in the last couple years, but none of the guys struck a chord with her, or at least not a strong one.

She felt drawn to Bill. He seemed considerate, funny but not silly, grounded and responsible. All qualities she admired and not seen in that many boys at her high school.

Bill thought his mother would enjoy a reminder of this place and chose a particularly detailed Santa Claus Nutcracker. The piece showed Santa holding his bag behind him and a tree in his other hand.

It was meticulously done and while Bill hadn't met him yet, was sure that it was as accurate a depiction of the head elf as one would have in a nutcracker.

The elf seemed pleased with Bill's choice and advised him that it would be wrapped and taken to his room. Bill wondered if this service might ever catch on in the outside world.

Only in your dreams, he laughed to himself.

George was drifting around the upper level. He had stopped at a corner where the ice walls overlooked the other side of the village. He was directly above the train station. The station was quiet. He wondered if any other trains would be coming with more passengers before the one came to take them back to the real world.

From where he stood he could see the ice skating rink in the woodland area. He laughed to himself when he remembered Fred Wu pointing to the elves and commenting on 'the size of the people'. They knew so little as they approached the village in that train.

Then George had an epiphany. He knew how to get into the Manufacturing Center.

As Santa waited for the O'Reilly girls he suddenly had an epiphany of his own. He realized that George had figured out a secret, and that he found a way into the manufacturing center. Santa could prevent it of course. He thought about whether he should allow it or not.

The last person that 'snuck' in had made major inroads to the cultures of developed countries. He not only provided many new innovations to the world, but he had kept his promise to support the operations of the Pole and paid the Pole handsome royalties for the privilege of developing some of the ideas he'd learned from here.

But Santa had already given Fred Wu a major innovation that would be introduced in a year or so.

George was only fifteen, and of course it might be several years before he could develop any new projects. Unfortunately the world would lose a potentially great trumpet player in the exchange. After all, he had specifically told Ion not to let his family buy George any electronic gadgets for Christmas.

He really wanted to point George toward music. Like Marshall Grady, he had a natural aptitude, even if he hadn't realized it yet. Santa always promoted musical talent above another electronic wizard.

But George seemed fixated on the future. He supposed he might allow this risk once more. After all, it had taken the other young man more than six years to invent his first products of note.

And he thought that George Mendez and William Henry Gates were a great deal alike when Bill was George's age back in 1971.

He really had hoped Marshall could have talked George out of it.

Well once every 40 years or so isn't too bad.

Chapter Eleven

As the girls came into the room Santa dropped to one knee. All three girls ran without hesitation into Santa's arms. He was able to gather all three of them in his grasp and said how happy he was to get a chance to visit with them.

They all remained comfortably in his embrace, as he spoke warmly about what wonderful young ladies they all were, and how proud he was of each of them.

Almost as practiced speech, Ellen thanked Santa for her play oven and said how much she really enjoyed it, as did many of her friends. Santa smiled and said she was quite welcome, knowing he had a bigger surprise in store for them.

Santa sat in his chair, and as tradition dictated, all three girls sat on his lap and they talked about many things.

He told them how pleased he was that they had all remained true believers and thanked them in return for never giving up the Christmas spirit. Renee suddenly became quiet and pensive. Santa knew it was time for her "question".

He looked directly at Renee and said, "You have something you want to ask me, don't you?"

Renee nodded her head and a tear formed in her right eye. The other girls looked at her in surprise. She looked at Santa and said in a halting voice, "I really love my foster parents, and they are w-wonderful to me, but why did God have to take my r-r-real parents away from me, and w-will I ever see them again?"

The tear fell away from her eye and down her cheek.

It was early, and George thought about going right away, but he really wanted to bring Marshall along. Since he wasn't sure how long it would take him, or how many hours he might have to explore, he thought it best to wait until tomorrow morning.

He then wondered about going tonight, but felt that would be more obvious than during the hustle and bustle of daytime. Besides he wasn't too confident he could talk Marshall into a night raid.

Plus what if they closed everything up? He wanted to see what was going to take place in the future. He wasn't breaking in to steal anything! It wouldn't do him much good if they shut everything down and put it away.

He knew he would have right up until 4:00 in the afternoon. Then he was supposed to meet Santa. He promised his mother that he would have breakfast with her and Hunter, but he knew he could be out by 8:00 am.

He thought Marshall would be game for that time as well. Especially since Marshall met Santa today.

Speaking of which, Marshall was long past seeing Santa by now, and he wondered where he was.

George went to look for him to lay out his plan.

FAITH HOPE & REINDEER

Bill and Susan were coming out of the nutcracker store when they saw Marshall. She called to him and he practically bounded over.

Marshall was all smiles and Susan said, "What's up, you look like the cat that ate the canary."

Marshall could barely contain himself, and tried to say blandly, "Nothing really, are you heading over to meet Santa?"

He wanted to yell out, "WAIT TILL YOU DO – I HOPE HE GIVES YOU SOMETHING HALF AS COOL AS I GOT!"

Instead he said through a grin. "He's really cool."

Susan said they were heading over there now.

Bill told Marshall that his appointment was right after hers.

Marshall suddenly stopped his musing long enough to see the two of them with the same eyes his parents had. Yep, there was something brewing here. Like his parents, Marshall thought Bill seemed like a pretty good guy. He had no complaints.

Bill said, "You looked like you were heading off at a pretty good clip, something up?"

"Not really, actually I was heading back to the room. Thought I'd kick back a while."

Susan looked at him strangely. Marshall wasn't the type of person to 'kick back a while'. He was always on the go somewhere. "Are you feeling okay?" she asked.

"Yeah, I'm fine. I kinda got tired after running around all morning with George."

He said the next more to Susan than Bill, "Hey, have you done the balloon ride, yet? Mom and Dad were right - it's amazing. You should go."

Bill said speaking of going they had best start walking. It was getting late and they didn't want to keep Santa waiting.

Marshall said nothing. With a wave he said, "Later." and walked off grinning again.

Chapter Twelve

"It's as your new parents told you. Sometimes
terrible things happen, but that doesn't make it
anyone's fault, not even God's. But, there is very good
news in the middle of all that sadness. First, you should
know that except maybe when you were born, your first
parents are happier than they ever could be on earth.
They get to live with God now, and that is the very best
present we will ever get. And they get to be with Him
forever and ever. And the second is that they get to
watch you grow and experience all your joys. They will
also help you through your sadness. And yes Renee, you
will get to see them again. As will you Ellen, and you
little Annie. And they will tell you things about yourself
that even you didn't know! Like many families now, you
have two sets of parents. The one that watches over you
here on Earth and the one that watches over you in
Heaven.

Annie said, "But won't our Mom and Dad here go to
heaven, too?"

Santa smiled at her. "Of course they will and then
they will get to thank your first parents for giving the
gift of you to them. And with grace that won't happen
until you are all grown up and have children of your
own, and they're grown up."

Santa wished he could guarantee this, but knew that
was not in his power. But he felt reasonably certain that

such hardship wouldn't so cruelly strike these children twice.

They were quiet, but he could sense that they were feeling better about things. Not because he explained them, but because he verified they already knew this in their hearts and heard it before from Jim and Maureen.

It was now time to cheer them.

"Well now, I've been thinking about what to give you for Christmas. And because you are all so very special, I think you should each get something special as well. I happen to know what you all love almost more than anything.

Ellen looked at him with wide eyes. There was only one thing that the three of them shared a special love for. Other than that, they each had their own ideas about things.

But that wasn't possible...they couldn't where they lived.

Santa smiled as if reading Ellen's thoughts, nodded his head and said, "You're each getting your very own pony!"

All three girls screamed.

Santa threw back his head and roared a "Ho, ho, ho!"

Ellen, afraid to have the gift taken before they got it said, "But Mom and Dad said we couldn't have a horse where we lived, that they didn't allow them there. Also, they said horses are very expensive and they can't afford to feed and keep them healthy."

Santa laughed again and said that he was taking care of those problems and more. But they had to keep this secret until Christmas Day. They couldn't even tell their parents.

"That's not fair!" cried Renee, "How can we keep quiet about this! Especially Annie, she'll blab to the first person out there."

Santa said, "Well I suppose you could tell your Mom and Dad. Then you can ask them to talk to me if they have any concerns. But I don't think they will. No one else though! I mean that."

They promised and gave Santa another huge hug. He laughed again and said, "Remember to share all your gifts with others. Do this for all your lives."

He wished them a very Merry Christmas and sent them on their way.

Susan and Bill were approaching the front door of the Visiting Cottage as the three girls were coming out of the room that held Santa.

Annie saw them and yelled out at the top of her voice, "GUESS WHAT!"

Ellen and Renee grabbed their sister and immediately put their hands over her mouth. They mumbled something to Bill and Susan on the order of 'have a nice day,' then left still holding their wriggling sibling with her mouth covered.

Chapter Thirteen

"For instance, even with all the things we produce in the North Pole, there is still not enough resources to take care of every family member needing assistance or a present. That's why Santa and Mrs. Claus make appeals to local charities and churches. Today a great many toys are donated from other families and given to Santa to help distribute through local fire departments and other charitable collection points. You've seen the various signs for 'Toys For Tots' and 'Sparks of Love' campaigns as well as Chamber of Commerce gift drives, "Angel Trees" and other charity sponsors.

"They all help Santa spread the spirit of Christmas and use his Ambassadors to bring joy to those who may not get as much as others."

Julie and Jared were listening to the various elves as they told stories and other items of note about the North Pole. They were learning a great deal of how things work from elves that would come by to bring them something to eat or drink or come by to visit.

The occupants seemed anxious to give information and none of their questions went unanswered. They had been listening to an elf that looked around forty years old, but he told the Gradys he would be 238 next February.

He was explaining the many ways gifts were distributed in addition to the all-important Christmas

Eve trip.

Jared asked, "Excuse me - Ambassadors?"

The elf nodded his head and said, "Of course, you see them all the time right about now. They are all the "Santa Look-alikes" that are throughout the various shopping malls, charities, senior citizen centers, hospitals, and many even make home visits to girls and boys."

Julie was gaping at the elf and said, "You mean all the Santas we see are connected to the North Pole?"

"Many of them, yes. We try to train as many as we can. We offer classes and schools in various countries, but we need a bigger school so we can reach as many who want to help as we can. Once they have done their 'training', we set them up so that any request given them is automatically tracked at the North Pole, whether we can fulfill the request or not."

Jared looked puzzled, "You mean there are requests you can't do?"

"Naturally. People come to us and ask to be cured of illnesses, or children ask us to get their families back together, or to return their Mom or Dad from military service, and of course the pleas to return family members who have passed away."

The elf shook his head. "We have a great many things asked that we cannot do. That is left for God alone to handle, as we are only mortal. Long-living to be sure, magical as well, but we haven't figured out the answers to most of those problems, and we never will. Some things are best left to the Creator."

The Gradys had never given a thought to how tough

it could be to be Santa before.

"Wow," said Julie, "What do the Ambassadors and Santa say?"

The elf shrugged and said, "We tell them the truth. We will pray for them, and with them, and encourage them to do the same, but some things are not in our power. Sometimes Santa can catch a glimpse of their future, but most often he can only hope for some outcomes. Also, if some people got their wish, it would affect others adversely."

Jared said "Oh you mean like to wish for one team to win over another. They may both deserve to win, but one has to lose."

"Exactly. But even tougher are the ones where to grant one person's wish would cause a major life change for someone else. As an example, say you have a job but you want to be promoted into your supervisors' position. Then say that supervisor has advanced as far as they might in that company. The only way to attain that job is for the supervisor to lose the position or quit. But someone will ask Santa for that job anyway. How do you grant that knowing it could hurt the other person and their family?"

Jared shook his head and said, "Yeah, I guess there are quite a few tough calls."

The elf brightened and said, "But Santa can grant far more than he turns away, and we still do a tremendous amount of good to be sure."

The Gradys agreed immediately thinking of the millions of children who believe and meet with Santa and his Ambassadors every year.

FAITH HOPE & REINDEER

Marshall was in his room playing his golden-toned instrument when he heard a knock on the room's door. He placed the saxophone on the bed and went toward it. As he began to open it he almost got knocked to the floor as George pushed it open.

"I keep forgetting there're no locks on the door and I can check if you're here." said George.

Marshall regained his balance and said tersely, "Yeah well, knocking and waiting to be let in is still more polite." He wasn't happy about the intrusion or George's lack of sensitivity that maybe he didn't *want* to be interrupted.

George gave a wave of his hand and said, "Yeah, well I thought I heard the sax and figured it had to be you. Besides this really can't wait. I thought you'd come back up top. I wanted to show you something."

George was practically crowing now, he gave a huge smile to Marshall and said, "I figured it out. I know how we can get in the center!"

FAITH HOPE & REINDEER

Susan was escorted inside the main room where again Santa was standing with an outstretched hand. "So good of you to visit me. I am very pleased to meet you personally and spend a few minutes together."

Susan felt flush, but responded, "I am very pleased you invited me and my family. This has been a wonderful trip, and it couldn't have come at a more needed time."

Santa nodded in complete understanding. He said to her, "You know, I've been meaning to get you Gradys up here for a while. But unfortunately you kept getting bumped by someone with a more immediate need."

Susan listened to him and tried to understand his comment, "More need?"

Santa smiled and motioned to the two chairs. As he settled in he explained, "Yes, you see there are many families and even individuals that are on our list to visit the North Pole. But because we can only bring a limited number in any year, we have to constantly review the need in their lives for a visit. The Grady family has been on our list for years, since you were eight and Marshall five."

Susan gave a surprised look. Santa continued. "I'm sorry it took so long, but we recognized it was a more critical time for you to come now."

Susan said in rather a flat tone, "Is that because we are in trouble?"

Santa laughed, "No my child, you only need a booster shot of faith. Plus as you so accurately asked, how many more opportunities will you have to all be together?"

Susan said shocked, "You heard that?"

Santa said, "Not from your lips, but I see the question in your heart. And you're right to ask it. We all get involved in our lives, and yours will be taking a major new turn. You are beginning college next year and many new things will be placed before you."

Susan asked, "Can you see the future? Do you have any idea what is going to happen?" She was certain if he could read her heart, he could foresee events.

Santa shook his head, "Only rarely. But many things I do know intuitively. For instance, I know you are a good girl and that you will do many wonderful things in your life, because you have paid attention to your parents and other adults in their teachings. This has given you a solid platform to build a strong life. I also know that you are very intelligent and care for others, especially Marshall. And by the way, you can place that concern to rest as well."

Susan stared at Santa. "You know?"

Santa said, "Of course I do! And you needn't worry anymore. Marshall is fine. Looking at you is like taking different pieces of a puzzle and putting them together until you are able to see the picture clearly. I'm happy to say that yours is a beautiful picture, Susan."

She smiled brightly, and almost chidingly asked, "Do I have your word on it?"

Santa laughed hard, "I think I can even do better than that. I will help you shape that future…"

Chapter Fourteen

"I can't and I won't," said Marshall.

George looked at him incredulously.

"But why?" George complained, "It's foolproof. And we'll be in and out and no one will ever know."

Marshall shook his head and said, "I'll know. Besides I received a wonderful gift from Santa Claus, and if you were smart, you might consider the consequences if HE finds out what you're up to, and the effect it may have on you."

He thought again at how different his life was going to be, now knowing what was in store. Marshall wasn't about to jeopardize that for any reason. He tried to reason with George. "You know, he may even realize what you're up to before you do it. Remember what they said about the scanners? They can predict your actions almost before you do them."

George seemed undeterred. "Look I am not going to let some little gift prevent me from getting a glimpse of the future, and what kind of things might be in front of us. What if we saw things that could help other people out? Sure Santa may not think were ready, but I've heard that argument before. If we saw certain things, we might be able to figure out what we're supposed to do in the future."

Marshall said a little too quickly, "I already know what I am supposed to do." He regretted the comment as soon as he said it.

George glared at him, "OH, and I suppose Santa Claus told you that, too?"

Marshall tried to recover. "Not entirely, but I have some pretty good ideas of my own. Look all I'm saying is they gave us only a couple rules, and I don't want to break any of them. It's not that important to me."

George shrugged. "Well I'm going anyway, with or without you. It's that important to me. I'm leaving at 8:00 tomorrow morning, before too many people are out and about. I hope you change your mind, but if you don't, please don't tell anyone."

Marshall looked hurt. "You know I wouldn't do that! I just don't want to be an accomplice in this." He tried to change the tension between them and said, "C'mon let's go get something to drink. I feel like a soda and there isn't much in here."

George said, "No thanks, I think I want to go back to my room and read for a while."

Marshall knew both were lying, but decided not to push it. Besides he really wanted to get back to playing his new sax.

"Suit yourself," he feigned. "But while you're reading, you might do some more thinking."

George gave him a wicked look and said, "Oh, I plan on it." Then George left the room.

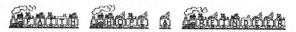

Susan was agape. She couldn't say anything even though her mouh was moving. She suddenly jumped onto Santa and gave him a huge hug and a kiss on his cheek. He laughed his laugh and said, "Your very welcome, now continue to do good things for others, so I can stay proud of you."

Through the well-formed tears in her eyes, she nodded and said weakly, "I promise."

He gave her a minute to pull herself together, especially since he knew Bill was right outside and would be concerned if he saw her like this.

He handed her a tissue, which appeared from nowhere, and she dried her eyes. She sniffed a little and thanked him again.

As she turned to go she stopped and asked, "Will I ever get to see you again? I mean maybe later, when I have my own children?"

Santa stood to walk her out, "You never know. I obviously make visits to homes you know, and while very rare, there have been a couple return visits over history. As I said before, I'm not that good a fortuneteller. But I have a strong sense that, yes – we will see each other again."

As Santa escorted Susan out he saw Bill look at her.

In a concerned voice Bill asked, "Are you alright?"

Susan nodded and Santa said laughing. "Yes, I have that effect on many people. Let's see what I can do to you!"

Susan assured Bill that everything was wonderful. She swore to Santa she would not tell anyone until Christmas Day, but she also hoped that Bill would have similar news.

As Santa ushered Bill into the other room, Bill saw

there were two comfortable chairs facing each other.
Santa motioned him to have a seat.

As he did so often, he instantly put Bill at ease telling
him about all the wonderful things Bill has done over his
years. Bill asked him how he knew so many details.

Santa chuckled and said he could easily find out that
answer with a trip to the records room at the Naughty
Or Nice Center.

Bill quipped that even though he had been, he would
have to check that place out more carefully, to which
Santa gave a hardy laugh.

They talked for a while and Santa asked him his
plans for the future.

Bill told him about wanting to become an Electrical
Engineer, and the schools he applied to.

Santa remarked, "An Electrical Engineer, eh? Well
that's wonderful. We can always use good minds like
yours in that field. Have you checked into financial
assistance to any of these schools?"

Bill said with a sigh, "Well, my parents aren't that
well off, and we discussed it. I have applied for a
National Merit Scholarship that I hope to get, but
nothing too large has been offfered yet. I am also
looking into a student loan and work during school and
in the summer."

Santa nodded his head and grinned like he had a
secret, which of course he did.

Bill was one of those few individuals that Santa could
actually see what the future held in store for him. There
was something in Bill's aura that he could tap into. He
knew he could help Bill shape his future, as he had

already done by bringing him here. He looked deep inside and saw a happy family man with two daughters and a son. He smiled wider as he saw that he knew the mother. She had just left moments ago.

He mused to himself and thought, *Well Susan, it looks like indeed you will see me again, and with Bill.*

He saw that Bill would live his dream becoming a successful engineer, and would be one of the very rare families that would earn a return trip to the Pole. He also knew how he was going to help Bill accomplish this dream.

The O'Reillys saw their daughters after they came out of Santa's Visiting Cottage, escorted by the two elves that met them this morning.

Maureen called to them.

As soon as they saw their parents they screamed and ran over to them. Jim and Maureen were laughing at the sight. It was as if they hadn't seen each other for days.

Ellen and Annie reached them first with Annie falling into Jim's arms and Ellen grabbing her mother. "Daddy, Daddy you'll never guess," Annie was overflowing with excitement, "We're getting PONIES!"

Annie screamed and again, Ellen and Renee who had came up behind and both shushed their little sister and Renee said sternly, "You heard Santa. He said we could tell Mom and Dad, not the whole Arctic Circle!"

Jim and Maureen looked at each other. Ellen was waiting for them to give the arguments of the past including how they weren't allowed in the neighborhood, but her parents said, "Oh, that's wonderful! What you girls have always wanted!"

Suddenly Ellen felt that she was on the outside of an inside joke.

The elves advised Jim and Maureen that they were on their way to Mrs. Claus' Village home so that the girls could help her bake cookies, and that Jim and Maureen were welcome to accompany them.

Maureen looked at her husband and said, "Jim?"

He nodded and took little Annie by the hand and teased her saying, "Okay but you guys will have to make a special batch just for me. I'm very hungry you know!"

They all giggled and shouted, "No way!" as they headed over to see Mary.

The O'Reillys stood at the door with the two elves. Mary Claus opened the door and said with joy, "Oh good, you found each other! I'm so glad you decided to join the girls and visit me, too. Come in, come in."

They walked in and she led them back to the kitchen. She had already put on her apron, and she began setting out the baking needs for the cookies. The two-story house was spacious and smelled of cinnamon and apples, *exactly as it should*, thought Maureen.

Mary was dressed in comfortable slacks and a chenille shirt under her apron. She wore her light silver and auburn hair long and it fell to the center of her back. She looked to be in her late forties or early fifties, and while she wasn't a small woman, she hardly fit the depictions of the Mrs. Claus' they had seen before.

Jim said what he and Maureen were both thinking.

"Ah, I don't want to sound rude, but you don't look a lot like the pictures I've seen depicting Santa Claus' wife. Obviously you are younger and, ah, smaller than your pictures."

Mary laughed heartily and Maureen wondered if she learned that from the master. She was still chuckling. "Oh Jim, you're so sweet. It has always amazed me how the rest of the world thinks we are so 'round' and depict us as so old. I'm only seventy-eight next May! I'm not even considered middle-aged up here."

Ellen yelled out, "Seventy-eight!"

Renee let out a low whistle.

Maureen stood aghast at her children's exclamations. "I'm so very sorry for the girl's outbursts. You really don't look a day over forty."

Mary laughed again, and finished answering Jim's question. "You see very few people over the years have come up here and met me. Nick's Mom, Marie who is Father Christmas' wife, was a little 'plumper', and it is she who wears those awful mop hats and loose dresses. I wouldn't wear them anymore than Mo."

They liked her instantly. Mary was very candid and warm. She did not stand on ceremony, and it was not hard to imagine her as the wife of the current Santa Claus. She kidded about how there were some things that she did do like the other Santa's wives, such as make cookies and run the horticulture center and village.

Maureen said, "You run the Village?"

Mary looked at her with kind eyes. "Actually, I'm the CEO, Chief Elf Organizer of the North Pole, but all the credit goes to Nick. We joke about it all the time. I keep threatening to let the world know who really runs this place. But he kids me back saying the world would never believe or accept it. Of course, the old coot's right. But someday…" She held a threatening fist and laughed.

Jim thought this was truly delicious and wondered what people would think if they did learn the truth. He asked gingerly. "Well no offense meant to Santa, but if you run the North Pole, what is he in charge of?"

She grinned. "He runs the manufacturing and woodland areas, and of course handles all R&D."

Annie asked her, "What's are-an-dee?"

Mary lifted her up on the counter and said into her big brown eyes, "Research and Development my dear. That means he helps make new games and toys. And he is very good at that!"

"Now," she said turning to the others. "Who's going to help me bake some cookies?" Everyone's hand shot up except Jim's. Mary looked at him. "You won't help?"

Jim gave her a wink. "Oh, I'll know when my part comes along. I'll guard the cooling rack!"

FAITH   HOPE & REINDEER

Marshall was right about George. As soon as he'd left, he came down the steps and straight out of the lodge. As he passed the elves busily scurrying around him, they gave him a smile and a nod.

They were smiling as much to themselves as to George. Each had been told to not interfere with the young boy's actions. It had been a long time since they received that order. Santa's assistant at the cottage had come forth and put the word out.

More often than not Santa would put the word out to block the possibility of the person or persons trying to get over to the center. They looked at George and wondered what Santa knew about this one and that set him apart. He had certainly been right about the last one. And of course they all trusted the head elf completely.

So they watched. Curiously trying to figure out when he'd make his move and from where. They all knew the weak spot. They also knew few people would ever see it or figure it out.

Chapter Fifteen

Susan met Hailey as she was waiting for Bill to exit
the cottage. Hailey's appointment followed her
brother's.

Susan told her that Bill had spoken kindly of her.

Hailey giggled and said, "Well I know there are times
when I get on his nerves. But then he can be a big jerk
sometimes himself." She relayed a story of how Bill and
his friends told ghost stories one night in his room and
purposely talked loud enough to make sure she heard. "I
couldn't sleep for like the next three nights. Mom and
Dad were ready to shoot him by the end of it. And they
told him that if he and his friends ever did that again,
they'd have to stay up with me."

Hailey was 11, and was about to start middle school.

Susan had hated those years the most. People change
so much during that time. She really liked Hailey.
"Listen, there are a lot of not so nice things coming your
way in school. You probably won't like it much more
than I did. Try to stay ahead of it, and stay out of
trouble. It's not worth it if you don't."

She felt a little preachy so she changed the subject
back to Bill. She asked what he liked and didn't, when
was his birthday (April 10th) and anything else his sister
might offer.

Bill came out soon after and said, "Hey squirt, better
get in there or you may get coal."

Hailey retorted, "Shows how little you know, he doesn't give coal anymore." She marched off with a superior air to see Santa.

Bill looked at Susan and shrugged. "Well there's another threat down the drain."

Susan thought he seemed calm considering just moments ago he left Santa. She couldn't resist and asked him. "WELL? Did you get something good, or did you get something you deserve for tormenting that poor sweet child with horror stories?"

Bill chortled but didn't answer Susan's question.. "Oh is she still on about that? I think she was five when I did that. That girl never gives up on some things."

She pushed him further and he finally said, "Now listen here Susan Grady, you know the rule. No telling until Christmas Day. I won't even give you a hint. Though he did say a few odd things to me while I was in there, not the least of which when I was leaving. He said to tell you he'll definitely see us both later."

Susan almost fainted.

Mary pulled out a tablet not much bigger than a small book. She punched a few keys and said more to herself. "Now let's see. Chocolate Snowballs? Lemony Snickerdoodles? Ah here we go...Decadent Cocoa Drop Cookies."

Jim thought that sounded promising. Mary showed the recipe to the girls and said, "Okay, your Mom and I will supervise while you young ladies mix up the batter."

She asked Maureen if she'd like some coffee and she nodded and said that would be great.

After Mary got the coffee made, she turned back to the girls and told Renee to get the cocoa mix out of the pantry, and pointed to a door.

Renee opened the door and exclaimed, "Oh my gosh!"

Mary walked over and asked what was wrong.

Renee said, "Nothing really, it'd just I never saw a pantry so huge!" The pantry was about twelve feet long, six feet wide and ten feet high with shelves on both sides and a ladder on a roller that went in a long U-shape around it.. There was nearly every type of shelf stable food or ingredient one could imagine.

Renee asked staring at the massive closet, "Where do I start?"

Mary pointed to about the halfway point on the left side and said "Third shelf about midway down in the C's." After Renee found it she looked at the variety and sizes of some of the jars, cans and bottles.

"Wow," she said, "You've got everything in here!"

Mary said, "Well if you run out of things up here you can't run to the corner store and get more."

Jim and Maureen imagined there wasn't a truer statement they'd heard so far.

Jim asked Mary, "Which reminds me, how does the North Pole manage to have every kind of food and know ahead of time what it is we will want?"

Mary looked at him faking surprise. "Why Mr. O'Reilly, whatever do you mean? We try to be prepared is all."

Jim said, "And I suppose you learned that from a boy scout?"

Mary grinned. "Actually, we taught that to them. But to answer your question, we may have a little insight into what you might want and we plan accordingly."

Jim looked at her. "Honey walnut shrimp? Ring necked pheasant? You plan that?"

She teased him. "No dear, you did. We prepared it."

Maureen jumped in. "So you're saying you know what we are going to order before we do?"

Mary said, "Not entirely. We know you have preferences. We can't predict the order. As I said, we try to be well prepared when you do."

FAITH HOPE & REINDEER

Jared and Julie went up to their room and decided to rest for a while and try to ingest all the information they had gleaned from the elves. When they came in they heard Marshall in his room practicing "Greensleeves" on his saxophone.

They went quietly to their room not wanting to disturb him or vice versa. Julie said, "How much of this place do you think they'll let us pass on?"

Jared shook his head. "Well it promises to be an interesting debriefing. I mean how do you stop some of the kids from talking about the things they've seen and heard? Heck even the adults are going to have a hard time."

Julie smirked. "Maybe when we get back we will all wake up with no memory of this place. Like out of one of those Sci-Fi movies."

Jared hoped that wouldn't be true. "It would be nice to hang on to these memories for a while." He lay down on the bed and Julie came and laid next to him.

"We'll know soon enough," she said. "But for now I want to soak this place in like a sponge."

FAITH HOPE & REINDEER

Brian and Heather also were returning to their room. They had been out all day shopping and visiting different areas. They had the boys with them when they found an area that caught them completely off guard.

There was a petting zoo in the North Pole! Only this one didn't have your usual goats and a few deer. This one included reindeer, arctic foxes, arctic hares, seals and seal pups, polar bears and penguins.

Brian informed the elves that if he remembered correctly penguins were South Pole inhabitants. They told him he was quite right, but Mary Claus thought they were so wonderful that she asked Santa to bring a few up with him one year and they had flourished. Now they were a popular attraction.

Heather was more concerned about her children petting a polar bear. She knew they were not the friendliest creatures to man, or any other species, for that matter.

She was assured that this was the North Pole and that nothing could, or would, happen here. She was told that the same thinking didn't hold true as in the rest of the world, and that while it's a good idea to avoid them under any *other* circumstance, here it was perfectly safe.

And it was already too late for worry - both Patrick and John had their arms wrapped as tightly around two of the bears.

Heather was in store for an even bigger surprise. As she was petting an arctic fox one of the elves called her and came walking up to her with a full grown female arctic wolf on a lead.

It was almost a comical scene as the wolf stood as high as the elf. She was the most beautiful thing Heather had ever seen. She threw as much caution away as the boys and ran up and hugged the beautiful creature.

Heather had always loved wolves and had studied them in books since she was a little girl. She thought to herself, *I can now die a happy and satisfied woman.* She spent over thirty minutes with the wolf. The animal was as gentle as any she'd ever known.

After a time Brian wanted to go and look at some other places. Heather reluctantly pulled herself away, but the boys wanted to stay.

One of the elves approached and said they would be happy to watch over the boys and bring them back later. Brian gave in to his boy's pleadings and Heather's casual nature about it.

As the first cookies came out of the oven a voice came from the other room. "Is that Cocoa Drops I smell?" said Santa in a big booming voice.

"In here, dear," said Mary Claus, "The O'Reillys are helping me bake them."

The big man walked in and said hello to the O'Reillys like they were his next-door neighbors. He walked over to Mary and gave her a quick kiss. Annie giggled at the sight. Santa looked down at her and pretended to be stern saying, "What? I can't kiss my own wife?"

She giggled more and gave Santa's leg a hug.

He grabbed a cookie off the rack and juggled it saying, "Oooooh, they're still hot!" Mary laughed at him and said, "Serves you right for taking before our guests!"

Santa winked at Jim and Maureen and feigned disbelief. "Guests?" he said, "I don't see any guests, only our friends in here."

Jim and Maureen had been in a state of disbelief themselves ever since he strode into the room. They weren't quite sure how to react. Their minds had been spinning since their last meeting with him.

And here he was again, acting as if he hadn't done anything unusual earlier. Maureen felt as if she got pushed on stage of some play and was expected to adlib her lines.

Jim was in shock, period.

The girls however were acting as if the man was a long lost uncle. They were teasing him and saying how they couldn't make enough cookies for everyone especially if he ate them all. He kidded back and said that little girls didn't need cookies, as they were quite sweet enough. The five of them bantered this way back and forth.

Jim and Maureen watched the play unfold before

them.

Neither of the Clauses took any offense to the O'Reillys actions or lack of. They could guess what was going through their minds.

The poor dears, thought Mary, *They probably can't make heads or tails of the situation.*

Mary put a few cookies on a plate and passed them to Jim and Maureen saying, "You better not wait on ceremony or Nick will eat them all."

That seemed to finally break the spell and they came out of their stupor.

It was beginning to get late and everyone once again gathered back to the Reindeer Inn. Many of the families asked their members to meet up so they could dine together. There was much commotion and excited conversation about where everyone had been and what they saw and learned.

Bill and Susan strolled in. Susan was still attempting to figure out if what Santa said to her and Bill is what she understood him to mean.

She obviously couldn't say anything to Bill, even though he had reacted to her swooning earlier. She said she got a little light-headed for a moment, but she was fine. She tried to imagine the reaction of her parents if she told them. "You know that guy you met at lunch today? He's your son-in-law-to-be. And we'll get to come back here again someday. What do you think?"

She tried to look at Bill with the eyes she saw him

with earlier today, but it was no use. She looked at him in an entirely new, and not unpleasant, light.

The Conners came in and asked Susan how her parents were. They said they were going to call them and ask if they wanted to join them for the fireworks later. She said she was sure they'd enjoy that.

Chapter Sixteen

Later that night everyone gathered again in the lobby. The fireworks display was scheduled for 9:00 pm so the stores could close and everyone could see them. The visitors were told anywhere in the village was fine to see the fireworks.

Some wanted to go to the upper level. The Conners were among them and they suggested the same cocoa shack that the O'Reillys had learned of earlier. That was fine with the Gradys. So Jared, Julie, Brian and Heather all took the gondola up to the upper level.

Marshall found George and though he was still miffed at Marshall for not wanting to go with him, he got over it long enough to hang out with him for the fireworks. They decided to go to the Snow Cone Shack and get another treat and watch them from the tables there.

Bill's parents thought it would indeed be nice for all the Fredricks to watch the display together. Bill asked, and got permission, to bring Susan with him.

They were enchanted with Susan and spent more time talking to her than Bill and asking her about life in Southern California.

That was certainly okay with him.

Hailey was still in a daze from her visit with Santa. So much so that she had entirely forgot the invitation of Mary Claus to come and help bake cookies.

As they all settled in to watch the fireworks, the

lights around the Pole dimmed as if on a giant switch. At the same time the lights of the buildings grew dark.

They heard it before they saw it, in the distance, down by the woodland area. They heard the bells ringing. They grew louder and louder. Then suddenly they saw him.

It was Santa Claus in his sleigh pulled by nine reindeer. He flew all around the Village and after several passes he landed atop his house by the Visiting Cottage.

He bounded out of the sleigh and with a mighty, "Ho, ho, ho!" said, "In celebration of all of your lives and the great things you have done, and will do in the future, we of the North Pole dedicate this fireworks celebration to you. In fact, you are in for a double treat. Tonight you will see manmade fireworks and tomorrow you will see God-made fireworks. We hope you enjoy both shows. Merry Christmas and God bless you all."

He bounded back in the sleigh and with a quick snap of the reigns, was off into the sky. As he pulled closer to the top of the dome fireworks suddenly shot out of the back of the sleigh where his toy bag would normally have been.

That 'fired up' the show. For the next thirty minutes aerial displays bigger and more spectacular than anyone had ever seen exploded above them. There were so many 'special effects' fireworks that every time the people thought they'd seen the best, a new one even more incredible would detonate before their eyes.

The 'Grand Finale' lasted a full ten minutes at least. Then the most unbelievable thing of all happened. The fireworks actually went right through the top of the dome as if it were transparent. The last rocket ignited high above the dome and filled the sky as far as the eye could take in with a beautiful full faced Santa Claus of red and white sparkling showers.

"All journeys have secret destinations

of which the traveler is unaware."

**Martin Buber,
Philosopher and Hasidic Theologian**

Chapter One

George couldn't eat his breakfast. He picked at a couple things and told his mother he was off.

Deb asked, "Where are you going so early? The stores aren't even open yet."

When he told her nowhere special. She asked, "Then why don't you take Hunter along if you're not going anywhere in particular?"

George said, "Well I'm meeting up with someone and I'm not sure where they want to go. It might not be very fun for Hunter." He looked down at his brother shrugged. "Sorry, bro, maybe later."

When he was out of the inn he made a beeline straight for his destination. There was little movement about and scarcely anyone was in the village. Precisely as he expected. He reached the train station and saw there was absolutely no one about.

He walked behind the station and then silently, but quickly, dashed onto the railroad tracks and into the tunnel.

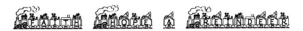

"She is a lovely girl. It's a shame she lives so far away from us," said Jillian Fredrick.

Her husband Clark agreed.

Bill said, "You never know. I may wind up going to

school out there."

Clark furrowed his brow. "Now son, we had this discussion. Out of state tuition is too expensive at those schools. We told you that would be too much for us. And I don't want to see you buried with a student loan that big, even if you could secure it."

Bill smiled at his Dad and said, "Really Dad, I wouldn't worry about that right now. That won't be a problem."

Clark thought of pushing the issue, but Jillian placed her hand on his arm and shook her head slightly. She thought there was a time and place for this discussion and this wasn't it. Nothing would get resolved this week, especially here. She couldn't have been more wrong on both counts.

Clark Fredrick was a school principal at a grade school. He always loved his job, but right about now he was wishing he had gone into something that would have provided a larger salary.

They were still in their early forties. But neither his, nor Jillian's third grade teacher income, could keep up with the mounting cost of colleges. They had a nice modest lifestyle and were active in their community. They had traded their love and nurturing of children for larger paychecks. It had weighed very heavily on Clark's mind as of late about how he might have done more.

Jillian asked, "What do Susan's parents do?"

Bill explained that Susan's Dad was out of work and her Mom was a part time accountant.

After that, the Fredrick's didn't feel so low on the totem.

The Gradys were getting ready for their big appointment. Jared went back and forth between feeling silly and excited. Julie wasn't much better. She had asked her husband what he thought Santa might say to them.

Jared couldn't guess. But he said it was a good bet Santa knew how upset he'd been recently. He kidded with Julie saying, "I'll bet lately I have sent a few of those scanners into the red with sirens to boot."

Julie came up and squeezed him from behind. "You're a good man and you know it. We all have our 'days'. Particularly with what you've been through. Who knows, maybe Santa will make you an elf and you could work here!"

Jared snickered. "I think I'm above the height requirement."

Meanwhile Julie had changed sweaters three times and Jared kidded her about acting like she was going on a first date. She chided back saying that she wanted to look good so he might give her a nice new toy to take home.

Jared said the heck with toys, he wanted a new plasma screen television with a matching surround sound system.

At breakfast, neither of them ate much. It didn't help when they asked the kids how their visit with Santa went. Susan and Marshall looked at each other and started cackling like hens.

They tried to cover up their outburst and each said,

"Fine."

Jared pressed Marshall, but he told his Dad that he couldn't say much right now. His parents would understand later.

Julie asked Susan, "Why all the mystery?"

Susan shook her head. "No mystery, merely a request that I intend to honor."

Neither would say any more on the subject. This left Jared and Julie even less in the know than before they asked the kids.

They finally came out of their room a few minutes before nine. As they put on their coats Marshall chuckled. "Have a good time!"

After his parents left, Marshall said to Susan he'd like to see them when they were through with their visit. He asked her if she wanted to stroll down toward the cottage in a little while.

Susan thought about it and said, "Yeah, let me call Bill and tell him to meet me later today. Are you getting together with George?"

Marshall muttered that he didn't think he'd be seeing George today. He said George had other things he wanted to get done.

Chapter Two

The first hundred yards into the tunnel were fine for George. There was sufficient light from the village for him to see, but as the tunnel took a curve it got darker. Now where he was walking was nearly black. He could barely see his hand before his face. He wondered if he had made the right choice.

He knew the tunnel opened at the woodland area of the Pole. He remembered from the train ride to the North Pole how everyone saw all the trees, and some of the buildings before entering the tunnel and arriving at the Village.

He also guessed that there wouldn't be any guards, nutcracker or otherwise, preventing him from getting into the manufacturing center from the woodland side.

What he hadn't figured out yet was how he was going to move around the two areas without being noticed. While George was only five foot two, he still towered over the elves by a good half-foot or more. Plus his clothes didn't match the more colorful outfits of the Pole either.

But he had more immediate concerns right now. The tunnel had become black as pitch. He couldn't see where he was going and stumbled on the rails and a couple of the ties. He wasn't sure how far he had gone, but it didn't seem he had gone as far in as he had left to go. He was thinking about turning back when he saw a small glimpse of light.

FAITH HOPE & REINDEER

Jared was thinking about how strange the events of the last week had been and said so to Julie.

She agreed and said to her husband, "Yeah, if you had told me that we'd be walking around the North Pole on our way to see Santa Claus, the genuine article no less, I would have thought the stress had finally cracked you. I would have called in some serious help."

The Gradys approached the door to the Visiting Cottage and an elf opened it for them before they could reach for the knob.

"Good morning!" the young girl exclaimed, "Santa is getting ready. Would you care for some cocoa or coffee?"

The Gradys mumbled no and Julie thought how she would probably spill it all over Santa if she had anything. She was that nervous.

Jared thought back to when he was a young boy and remembered his parents told him how scared he was to see Santa Claus and how he used to cry. He thought how bizarre it was that he felt that way now. He couldn't imagine what the exchange was going to be between the two men. He had been trying since yesterday to visualize how this was going to go. Every scenario he played out in his head was crazier than the last.

Suddenly the inner door opened. Santa Claus said, "I'm so very sorry to keep you both waiting like that. I got a little behind in my production meeting and the time flew by."

Julie chuckled as much from nervousness as humor and said, "Time gets away from Santa Claus? I thought that only happened to us mortals."

Santa laughed hard at Julie's comment. "First my dear lady, let me advise you that I too, am mortal, just old. Second, while it is true that I can control time to some extent, it still marches on even for us up here."

He laughed again his familiar "Ho, ho, ho!" that they heard last night at the fireworks display.

Santa looked at Jared and softened his expression. With a low chuckle he looked into Jared's eyes. "You may quit doubting yourself, you are the same wonderful father, husband and person you have always been. You need not fear the future anymore."

With that Jared felt tears welling in his eyes and almost broke down.

Santa motioned them both into his other room, the little girl elf had completely vanished. Entering, they saw three chairs facing each other in close proximity.

Santa took one and the Gradys sat in the others. Julie looked gravely at the old man before her eyes. Only it wasn't whom she expected. Jared looked like he had aged twenty years.

Santa kicked off by saying, "I know you both have been under a lot of pressure. And you feel you have lost your faith. But you still have many reasons to give thanks and count your blessings. Your children are happy and healthy."

The Gradys looked as if he spoke a foreign language. "Marshall is in complete remission. You have an attractive home, money in the bank, food on the table,

and the love of your relatives, friends and church
family."

Julie stammered, "Ah Santa, how do you know about
Marshall?"

At four, Marshall showed signs of weakness and was
diagnosed with Leukemia. The Gradys wept for days at
the prognosis and what their little man was going to
have to face to try to save his life. And even then the
outcome was much less certain. The next year and a
half consisted of endless hospital and doctor visits,
radical chemotherapy and radiation treatments. An
incredible belief in medicine and prayer got them
through it all. Marshall had survived. The only sign of
the turmoil and illness was that Marshall's growth was
stunted from the chemo and he would never come close
to his Dad's six-foot stature. They almost never talked
about the experience.

"You'll have to trust me on this, but the point is
there are so many things that a vast majority of people
don't have that you still do. You can lose a great many
more things and still have more than ninety percent of
the world."

Jared felt guilty and rather sheepish over how much
he fretted. He knew that Santa was right and was
suddenly ashamed for his carrying on. However, he still
wanted his life back to the way it was before.

Julie looked between the two men as if a father was
having a heart-to-heart with his son.

Jared started to say something but it sort of fizzled
out.

Santa said, "Alright, enough of that, you may know

your Christmas gifts now, and I am delighted to give
them to both of you."

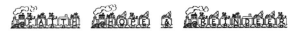

George noticed the light was growing even though he
wasn't moving very fast at all. Then he heard a low
rumbling sound. He finally realized what it was. There
was a train coming from the other direction. He couldn't
see too well, but he could see there was no place to
escape. The tunnel was very narrow. Not much room for
the train to get by, maybe a foot or two on either side.
George knew at once this wasn't big enough for even his
small frame to fit.

He also knew he couldn't outrun the train by the way
the light was growing. It was still around the corner, but
it was definitely getting louder with each passing
moment. He started to panic. The walls were solid ice.
There were no handholds or places to scurry up. Instinct
moved him away from the approaching train.

Then he saw it.

There was a little alcove on his left as he was heading
back. Not large, and certainly not tall, but if he could
wedge his body into it the train might pass safely
without killing him in the process.

He could see the train now as it came around the
bend. It was a huge freight train with an engine much
larger than the one they arrived on. He squeezed as
much of his frame as he possibly could into the alcove.
As the engine approached, he pushed himself harder
against the icy cut out. The roar was deafening in the

cramped space. Then it happened...

George pushed harder against the ice at his side. It was then he felt the wall move slightly. He wasn't sure he actually believed what he felt so he shoved again. The wall moved more.

He gave as much of a shove as he could since he couldn't step out of the niche. As the train met up with him the wall gave way and he fell through the other side.

Chapter Three

Marshall and Susan pretended to be out looking for their parents' Christmas present.

Bill told Susan he would join them around lunch as he had a couple things he'd like to do as well.

Susan wanted to tell Marshall so many things and knew he felt the same. She desired to tell him about the fabulous present, her budding relationship with Bill, her guessed promise from Santa that she would return.

She thought to ask Marshall how his visit went, but didn't want to bait him, and ask if he thought everyone was getting such wonderful gifts. She would begin to say something, stutter and stop.

Marshall wasn't upset at this, as he was in the same situation. He was also willing to bet the same problem was happening throughout the Pole right about now. He was especially interested to know what his parents would think of the jolly old elf.

They walked from place to place doing a little chit-chatting. They would talk only about what their parents might like and what places they had or hadn't visited, yet.

As they were walking toward yet another shop they saw him coming. They thought they had seen him last night, but there was certainly no doubt as he approached them now.

He was absolutely beautiful. He moved with a grace

and style they couldn't imagine possible. And his bright red nose lit everything around him.

George had fallen into the opposite side of the woodland area. He had the manufacturing buildings on his right and the woodland area on his left. Apparently he had found a service entrance to the tunnel. He looked out toward the woodland area and saw a large structure before him.

Reindeer were roaming around it and he surmised that he was looking at the Reindeer Stable he and Marshall saw from the air yesterday. It looked much bigger now. He saw movement around the stalls and thought he better get out of sight.

He ran quietly behind a tall pine tree that he felt covered him well. He looked over to the manufacturing center and thought how lucky he had been to find that exit. He also thought how close he had come to losing his life. He sat down, suddenly feeling a little woozy and rested for a few minutes.

George wasn't the only one feeling a little off balance. The Gradys were getting the shock of their lives.

Santa nodded and focused on Jared. "I suppose you know that due to a very industrious elf, the North Pole has a major stake in Mattel?"

Julie said that Marshall had told them about the

various entrepreneurial enterprises of the North Pole.

Santa nodded and looked at Jared. "Well it so happens that after twenty-three years our Vice President of Finance is retiring at the end of the year, and I would like you to take his place."

Jared thought Santa was pulling his leg, until he looked into his eyes, which were very serious indeed. "But...but what about the board, and the President and others? How can you decide this and what am I supposed to do...walk in and say '*Hi, here I am, Santa sent me!*'" He thought this whole conversation was surreal.

Santa was smiling now. "We had secured your resume online. The board and the President have already approved your appointment. We still have some clout here, but overall they thought you were an excellent candidate and the President looks forward to meeting you right after the holidays. You begin on January 3rd.

Santa turned his attention toward Julie. "And now for you my dear."

She was still sitting stunned, trying to contemplate what had happened. She wasn't even thinking about herself at this point because of the unbelievable news concerning Jared.

She shook off her amazement and looked at Santa. "I think you already gave your gift to me," she said very shaken.

He laughed quietly. "Well maybe part of it, but I have another part I want to give you. Now that Jared and the kids are taken care of, I'd like to do something for all the juggling you do between your volunteer

organizations and work. Someone you do not know
needs your part time position far worse than you do
right now. I'd like to ask you to resign your position, so
it will open up for her. In your spare time I want to see
you begin writing the book you've been carrying inside
you the last three years."

Julie looked thunderstruck. "How did you know
that!"

Jared looked at her in surprise. "What book?"

She looked at Jared. "I have been thinking about this
story that involves a little girl who moves to the city and
is really lonely until this stray dog comes into her life.
They have the most marvelous adventures together, but
I've never said a word about it to anyone!"

Santa looked at her. "And now that Jared will be
making sufficient money it will free up time for you to
begin writing it at long last. I also have a person I want
you to contact. She is expecting your call, I'll give you
her phone number and email address on Christmas day."

Santa looked at both of them. "A very Merry
Christmas to you both. Make sure you continue to share
your extraordinary gifts with the world as much as you
can. Jared, I know you will never doubt yourself again,
and there is much you can teach other. I look forward to
seeing you do exactly that."

Suddenly the door behind them opened.

As they rose to leave, Santa made one request, asking
them to keep this information secret until Christmas
day, even from their children. That was going to be quite
a day, they thought.

Chapter Four

George surveyed his surroundings and got his bearings. He could see that like the village, there were two levels to the manufacturing center. He thought about which level might be best to start. He wondered which would be more progressive in its features. He thought he might have a difficult time getting up the ramp he saw without arousing suspicion or being seen.

He could barely make out some of the factories. One looked to be exclusively building trains and their components. That didn't interest him. He saw an elf pushing a cart of dolls out of another. Definitely not. Next to that was what looked like a remote control factory? Now that might be interesting. It was the first one on the upper level. There were other ones further out, but he couldn't see what they might contain.

He made his move toward the ramp. It looked clear at the moment. As he got to the bottom of the walkway, he spotted an elf resting against the base with his hat pulled low over his eyes. George thought maybe the best way to get by him was to act as normal as possible and maybe he wouldn't even notice him. He headed up the ramp.

From under his hat the elf said, "Geez George, I didn't think you were ever going to get here. I've been waiting for you for almost a half hour."

George froze. He couldn't believe he was busted so

soon.

"Well," said the elf as he tipped his hat up and looked at George. "Ready to get going?"

George slumped, "So do we go back the way I came or do I get a more direct route?"

The elf tilted his head and looked at him. "My name is Cedric Rekinstuff. I was asked to accompany you on your tour of the manufacturing center and make sure you're safely returned in time for your appointment this afternoon with Santa Claus."

George thought he was hallucinating. "You mean I'm allowed to tour the manufacturing area?"

Cedric laughed. "I guess Santa figured you going to find a way in here one way or another and didn't want you to get hurt. You could have walked right passed the nutcrackers today. But Santa knew you'd come through the tunnel. I guess that's why he's got the big job. But just in case…"

Cedric tapped his watch and spoke into it saying, "Okay guys, I've got him. You can leave the other entrances."

George said, "There were others expecting me?"

Cedric shrugged. "Never know for sure, best to be prepared." George felt downright silly thinking he could sneak around without the residents knowing exactly what he was up to. Marshall was right about that.

"So?" asked Cedric, "Upper or lower to start?"

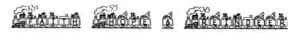

All three O'Reilly girls came running up out of nowhere as Marshall and Susan approached the red hosed reindeer. They were shrieking with glee and saying how beautiful he was. Marshall asked the elf leading the reindeer exactly what caused the bright nose. The elf whose name was Forrest Hedemup said that it was strictly hereditary.

Forrest explained. "Many people think it is a fungus or a skin condition, but truth is there is only one in hundreds of thousands that are born with it. It is highly prized and sought after in the North Pole. It is called luciferins. If anything happened to Torch here, we don't know what Santa would do. The last reindeer born in the North Pole itself was with a nose like this was Starlight back in '94. We only have four total with Torch bein' the youngest.

Marshall laughed. "That's not so long ago. And I thought his name was..."

Forrest stopped him at once. "Shhh, don't say it. He is sensitive to being called that name, and uh, that was 1794. Starlight only lived until the 1950's. Torch came much later and Rudy was born in 1936. We keep hoping one of Torch, Flash, Strobe or Rudy's offspring is born with a nose soon. But many times it skips several generations."

Susan said, "You have four?"

Forrest just nodded.

Marshall said, "I suppose Pocatello didn't have one?"

The elf looked impressed with Marshall and replied. "No, but he is a great reindeer all the same."

Marshall looked surprised. "You mean he's still alive?"

Forrest laughed. "Why of course. He only turned two

hundred this last year! They generally live to between two hundred twenty-five to two hundred fifty years. Torch here is abouty 60. Pocatello is too old now to draw the sleigh. They retired him many years back. He hangs out down in the woodlands."

The girls were fussing over Torch and brushing and stroking his neck and flanks. He wasn't the least bit bothered by the attention and was obviously enjoying it. Even Susan kept stroking his muzzle, but she had to face away from the bright beacon at the end of it.

She said to Forrest, "I could see why they were the brunt of so many jokes. That's quite a flashbulb on the end there."

Forrest laughed again. "Oh that's a fairy tale. They are never picked on. In fact there is a great celebration when one is born. The reindeer are always pleased to have another RN in the fold."

Susan looked bewildered. "A nurse?"

Forrest shook his head. "No a Red Nose. They almost started training them before they can they stand. The stories were made up by others of your world who thought since were different, they must have been outcasts." He looked at Torch's eyes and lowered his head slightly. The reindeer dimmed to about twenty percent of the brightness it was a moment ago.

"That's amazing!" said Susan. "How does he do that?"

Forrest looked at them. "He can control it like you can control which direction your eyes are looking. There are receptors that lead into the nasal area. Not unlike a firefly or the Black Dragonfish."

FAITH HOPE & REINDEER

The Gradys drifted aimlessly much as the Wus, O'Reillys and their own kids had done the day before. Jared felt giddy and kept chortling to himself. He knew beyond any doubt that what Santa had told him was 100% true and that sure enough his new job was waiting for him in El Segundo, CA. Their kids missed the opportunity to catch them off guard, as they were still hanging around Torch and Forrest.

Almost the instant they had left the cottage, Jared asked his wife questions about the book. What gave her the idea, why hadn't she began writing, was she planning a series of books or only the one.

Julie admitted that she wasn't sure she could write, and there always seemed to be other things to do, and she hadn't begun writing it yet so it was difficult to tell whether there would be one book or twenty.

"Well obviously you have at least two fans for your writing already – me and St. Nick," he said.

She shook her head. "I still can't understand how he knew what was in my head like that. I really don't remember breathing it to another soul."

Jared looked at her. "Good thing. I'd be sorely disappointed if I was the only one who didn't know."

Julie jabbed him. "Well I know now I'm supposed to do this. I hope Santa threw a little writing talent into that Christmas present he gave me."

Jared smiled at his wife. "Don't need to give what already exists."

They decided to go back to their room and have some

cocoa and truly relax for the first time in over a year.

Chapter Five

George went with what he had thought about before, and asked to see the remote control factory.

Cedric shook his head. "Oh it's a lot more than RC stuff. That's also where we build…well I'll explain when we get there." The elf asked George all kinds of questions trying to figure out what made this young man so exceptional in Santa's eyes. He was likeable, true – but there had to be more than that. They had stopped hundreds of attempted trespassers over the years. Even some pretty determined characters. Well he guessed he had time to try and figure it out. He'd be with George for hours.

As they crested the top of the ramp, George could see more clearly the shop they were heading for. They had racing tracks running in and out of the building and cars were flying faster than George remembered seeing them do in any of the stores he visited.

As they walked into the factory, he saw numerous elves with what looked like wireless controllers in their hands. George wasn't surprised they were wireless, but he was disappointed they were only playing with RC cars.

When he expressed this to Cedric he looked at George and shook his head. Then he walked toward the nearest elf and said, "Hey Indy, could you show my new friend here what you guys are really working on?"

The elf chidingly called 'Indy' looked a little perturbed. "Can it wait? I've almost got Taylor beat again."

Cedric pointed to his watch and Indy gave a resigned look.

Indy brought his car around and it stopped in front of him. With the controller still moving in his hands, the left car door opened and suddenly the driver stepped out from behind the wheel and gave a bow. The driver turned and waved at George. All the while Indy was pushing buttons. "They aren't racing cars, they're racing miniature robots racing cars," said Cedric.

George decided right there he best not take anything at face value here.

In addition to the miniature robots racing cars there were also aviation robots flying planes and having incredible dogfights above their heads. Then in a different area he saw cars that were changing all by themselves. They were manifesting into multiple shapes and attacking one another with the click of a button.

The idea apparently was to outmaneuver your opponent by changing into a more suitable shape with which to gain the advantage.

"Kind of an automated transformer, that's cool," said George.

The next building they went into was run almost entirely by robots. It looked like several scenes right out of Star Wars. There were robots of every style and design. From the more customary assembly line type that could be found in many manufacturing companies, to ones that made C3PO look like the Tinman from the

Wizard of Oz. They were all performing different duties and George couldn't quite figure out what they were supposed to be making.

"Making?" said Cedric. "They aren't 'making' anything. We are testing the dexterity and program functions of the various types of robots. We have over two hundred different models and this is the testing and proving ground to make sure they can perform their programs and live up to expectations."

George approached a couple to gain closer inspection. One of them was putting a computer together and moving with unbelievable speed doing so. He had the entire unit assembled before George figured out what he was doing.

"This is amazing," George said. "How far into the future is this guy?"

Cedric guessed that was about thirty years out.

George said that Christel told them that there were things here that were more than sixty years in the future. Cedric nodded. As they headed for another building he explained, "We have rockets that don't need explosive elements to break the earth's gravity. We can create water from molecular fusion, and our satellites are no bigger than your smallest tablet, but thirty-seven times more powerful. The dome that protects us from the weather and prying eyes is, as you saw last night, totally translucent. You can walk right through it and walk right back, but it will stop weather forces from permeating it. We can also program it to deflect a crashing meteor at 28,000 miles per hour if we need to."

They were entering a very busy and bustling place.

This looked more like what George had expected to see.
Toys, and dolls, and trains, and games, and even
computers were being brought in by the freight-sized
squibble full.

Cedric said, "This is the main distribution center.
They are staging everything for Santa's flight
tomorrow."

George corrected him saying that tomorrow was only
the 23rd, not the 24th. Cedric shook his head and said
"It's already the 23rd, in Australia and New Zealand.
Tomorrow is their Christmas Eve."

George looked at everything around him and
wondered how Santa got everything in his sleigh for
even one country let alone all of them.

Cedric explained about the distribution centers where
Santa stops. Then he said to George, "But the best trick
is right through those doors." And he proceeded to lead
the way for George.

As they went through the doors George couldn't
believe what he saw. There was a giant conveyer belt
that all the toys were being placed on in the other room.
As they came into the room where George was standing
they passed under a large machine and disappeared.

George gasped. "They're gone!"

Cedric said, "No, no, they're not gone, they're
miniaturized. Here I'll show you." They walked over to
the end of the belt and sure enough, there were the
items, but now no bigger than an average thumbnail.

"So that's how he does it!" exclaimed George. "But
how do they become full size again?"

Cedric said, "This is a 'temp-min' or temporary

miniaturizer. When Santa sets out the items he presses a button and they return to normal size. We also have a "perm-min" or permanent miniaturizer, but there's no button for that. Much of that is used to reduce our technology to workable size. Like our satellites I was telling you about. We make them 'full-scale' if we need to and then reduce them.

"Is that how the robots work, too? You make them full size and shrink them?"

Cedric shook his head. "Actually no, some things don't quite miniaturize as well as others. Especially if they have a large number of moving parts, we think they don't all miniaturize exactly at the same time, so we are still working those bugs out today. So those are made that size."

Cedric looked at his watch and told George it was time to move on.

Chapter Six

Nicholas Kristopher Kringle XI was having a good day. There were many things to be done before tomorrow, but he trusted his associates at the North Pole beyond question to get everything accomplished. He always thought how strange it seemed that no matter how many years passed, the excitement of Christmas and the big trip always filled him and everyone else at the Pole with joy beyond measure.

Each year a special elf was chosen out of all the North Pole residents to accompany Santa on his trips around the globe. It was done by secret ballot and this year one of his personal favorites had been chosen.

That elf would be announced tonight. He was pleased with the choice, as he loved this elf and thought how she went out of her way to please others. This trip would be her time, and Santa was anxious to get going. He looked at his list again.

~~Jared Grady~~
~~Julie Grady~~
Cory Peters
Katy Peters
George Mendez
Deborah Mendez
Hunter Mendez

He knew it was time for the Peters' visit. They were an extremely attractive couple. Katie had long platinum hair that she wore to the middle of her back with blue green eyes and high cheekbones. When she smiled her whole face lit up. Santa felt she didn't do enough smiling.

Cory was tall and lean well built from his time in the Navy. Being over six feet tall, one wouldn't want to pick a fight with Cory unless they had no other choice. But his look deied the gentle nature of his soul, and Santa knew his soul well.

Todd was too little to do much of anything for, being that he was just three, but he would get a beautiful fishing kit on Christmas Day. He knew Todd would like fishing and have ample opportunity for it in his life. He heard the outer door open.

He opened the inner door and welcomed the Peters to his cottage. He told Cory and Katy how proud he was of the work they had done for abused children and spouses. It always broke his heart how some people could treat others with such intolerable cruelty. In particular, people that they should love more than anyone else.

Katy had studied to become a paralegal in order to help families wade through the legal maze and protect themselves. She also worked to assist two others, a woman and a man, as they got their own degrees in law. She turned most of the operation over to them once Todd was born.

Cory, after getting out of the Navy, was helping build shelters and helping Katy do fundraising and special projects. He always wanted to teach Adult Education,

but never received his formal degree. He had applied to
several schools, but was told without a proper degree or
license he couldn't teach.

Santa turned to the Peters' and asked how they were
enjoying their stay. Although Santa knew the answer
already, he always enjoyed hearing how well his guests
were treated. They chatted about many different things
first. Santa wanted them at ease and listening carefully,
as he verbally unwrapped their gift to them. He first
looked at Cory. "I understand you would really enjoy
teaching?"

Cory espoused how he had always wanted to teach,
but joined the Navy right out of high school. Once he
was out and married Katy, he really never had a chance
to use the college incentives offered by the armed forces
to return. And now with Todd, it became even harder to
find time.

Santa listened attentively, though he had known all
of this. "I think I might have a solution for you. In the
Northwoods of Wisconsin, outside of a place called
Eagle River, I have a school for Ambassadors that is in
need of a new administrator and teacher. I would like to
ask you to take it over for us." Cory sat in stunned
silence for a time. Katy didn't say anything either.

Finally, Cory asked what he needed to do.

Santa told him, "Teach the program we have laid out
for the various men and women who work as Santa and
Mrs. Claus around the world. Make sure they are
registered with us and that they become hard wired into
our system so that the requests of those they see are
directed to us at the Pole. Also you need to be certain

they understand the ethics and professionalism of the role they undertake. You will need to help them acquire the right supplies and clothing. We will provide you with everything you need, including the students."

Santa turned to Katy. "I understand you've always wanted to run a Bed & Breakfast Inn?"

Katy was as surprised as Julie Grady had been earlier. "There is a lovely B&B that is attached to the school. I would like you to run it. You will have plenty of help, as there are half-dozen elves that help handle all the usual goings-on. You only need to direct their activities."

The Peters' now experienced what nearly every visitor to the Pole had faced at this moment. Their reaction was usual. They cried with joy and gratitude.

Brian and Heather Conner headed to the Post Office to send off letters, including ones posted to themselves. They were concerned that once they left this place, things might fade from memory. So they had spent a good deal of time writing what they could in great detail and would mail it to their house.

Of course they knew the post office could censor the letter and not deliver it, but they thought that was a little over the top. This wasn't a military state and they weren't sending this to the *New York Times*,though they doubted they'd believe it, let alone print it, anyway.

They wanted the promised postmark from this post office. They thought one more souvenir, although they had already received numerous gifts. Brian not only got his locomotive from Santa, but also got several cars and houses from that same period. The total worth of everything he got was into the thousands. He had priced out the locomotive before and it was over $1,200 alone, and had been over a year ago. The cars were priced all over the board, but Brian knew the ones he got were rare with many animated parts. These were more pricey than not, *if* you could find them at all.

But that was the icing on his cake. He couldn't wait to tell Heather and the boys his "real" gift. Even though he doubted the boys would understand until they were older.

Heather had received, or rather would receive, as her gift was being shipped directly to her home as promised by Santa, an entire new set of cookware and appliances. For the last several years the Conners had been doing more and more entertaining. Heather loved to cook and prepare for large groups, and often kidded Brian that she'd like to establish a catering business.

Santa gave her that as her "true" gift. He told her of a catering company that had a large and successful clientele. The owner was looking for a partner, as the company had grown so much recently. Santa submitted her name to the caterer who had been a previous visitor to the North Pole. She could barely hold the secret back from her husband.

John and Patrick, their boys were going to receive new computers each geared to their own age. For instance, Patrick was getting a new 'Leapster' system with all the programs geared for the next three years. John got a more sophisticated gaming computer. Both were wrapped and awaiting Christmas Eve delivery.

The Conners talked to the elf at the other side of the counter in the Post Office and asked about how best to send their letters. The elf told them there was no charge but they needed a stamp to identify it with the U.S. Postal Service.

As they talked, a large cart was pushed out onto the floor by two other elves. The cart looked to be six feet high, five feet long and over three feet wide.

"What's that?" questioned Heather.

The elf said nonchalantly. "That's one of the carts of Santa letters."

Brian looked at the size of it and asked. "Tell me, how does that work. I mean how do all the letters get here? Or does the U.S. Postal Service send the ones marked only 'North Pole'?"

The elf looked at Brian. "Heavens, no! They send everything up here. To not do so would be interfering with the mail."

Brian said, "Okay, but I was wondering how does it work? I mean suppose I address a letter to Santa at the North Pole. How does it arrive?"

The elf looked had answered this question a thousand times and went into a monotone voice saying, "Letters, faxes and emails arrive at the Pole from a method similar to a protected email box. In other words, for some companies, if you send an email using their dot-com address it automatically arrives at an established administrator's mailbox, no matter what name you use. If it doesn't recognize the recipient it goes to them. This is similar to what we do, but we can also incorporate this to printed pages like letters, telegrams and faxes as well."

"So no matter where we mail it in the world it ends wind up here?" asked Heather.

"We could never lose a request, whether we can grant it or not. It wouldn't be right to not know about it, and see if we can't do something for that individual," said the clerk.

He stamped the letter with the coveted postmark and sent both the letter and the Conners politely, but firmly, on their way.

Chapter Seven

George and Cedric wandered through some of the other shops. George found everything from known manufacturing processes to types of manufacturing he couldn't grasp or explain. He told Cedric he couldn't wait to talk to Santa about a lot of what he saw. Cedric knew George still didn't grasp the gravity of his situation.

They stopped for some lunch. Cedric actually took George to Mount Elfish and the Ski Resort. George was looking at all the beautiful ice sculptures. He had seen a couple in the village, and his parents said that one of their balloonists had been sculpting for decades. He admitted to Cedric he thought they were quite beautiful. The way the ice was carved acted like a prism and broke light into all the different spectrums of color, each one reflected rainbow upon rainbow.

As they were eating, George asked Cedric if he had ever been outside the Pole. Cedric said that he had been out a few times and didn't care for it much. George could understand why.

After lunch they ventured to the lower level. George was right in his assumption that it wasn't as technically interesting as some of the other things he had seen, but told Cedric he admired the masterful ways in which everything was made. He called it 'art in motion'.

He was also mistaken about the train factory. It was

fascinating as multiple robots assembled the trains without a single flaw. Even the painting of the railroad cars and buildings took on an art form with artificial life.

By now, they were nearly running through the factories, as there was still too much to see, but their time became short.

Cedric saw that George was intelligent, inquisitive and enormously curious. He was beginning to like George, and felt that maybe he *could* see the beauty and poetry in things. He showed more interest beyond the high tech machinery and secrets he came for initially.

As George was touring the Manufacturing Area, his mother, Deb Mendez had her younger son, Hunter, in the Visitor's Center. They just came out of "Deck The Halls", a wonderful shop filled with every kind of Christmas decoration imaginable.

Deb, who loved to work with crafts, created incredible displays with porcelain houses. Every year she created winter wonderlands with dozens of houses along with trees, snow and loads of accessories. Deb's creation was large in scale and greatly admired by everyone who saw it. That was before they'd lost Bruce.

She missed doing things around the house like that, almost as much as she missed him. It already seemed like a lifetime ago. Looking through the store she thought, *maybe it was time to resurrect some of the traditions that they had begun as a family.*

They were heading over to Santa's Visiting Cottage for their appointment. As they crossed the square something started to happen. The lights across the village dimmed again, exactly as they had last night. The dome also became dark above them. No wait, not dark. It's transparent, she thought. There was almost no light from the outside world coming through the protective covering.

Then it began.

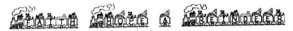

Jared noticed the darkness through his window. The Conners stopped before getting on the Gondola to come to the lower level and walked toward the wall, instead. Marshall, Susan and Bill, who joined them after lunch, sat down on a bench under the maypole where the snowman contest had taken place. The contestant's entries and the ribbons were still as they had left them. Everyone looked around and were confused.

Cedric and George paused after coming out of another in their whirlwind tour of the factories. George asked Cedric what was going on.

Cedric said, "It's already beginning. We'll have to skip the last ones. Sorry George, we are out of time. The Northern Lights are beginning."

A moment later the sky was filled with swirling, dancing lights. Jared Grady watched through his window and then called to his wife to grab her coat that they were going outside. He thought to himself, *Another wish fulfilled.*

Except for George and Cedric, everyone else stopped whatever they were doing. Few words were exchanged. Bill put his arm around Susan and pulled her close. The hues were glorious. They floated over the village like a dream that had come to life.

Bill saw them before with his parents in Michigan. But these were infinitely richer and the colors deeper. He guessed it was because he was so much farther north. He certainly didn't remember them being quite so beautiful.

Clark and Jillian Fredrick couldn't agree more. They were even closer, as they were floating in a balloon. They were almost getting dizzy trying to look both up and down. The elves suggested they might wish to return and take the tour another time.

Clark asked how long were they expected to continue, and the elves shrugged.

"One time," their pilot said, "they went on for more than four weeks. Other times they last only a few minutes, but I think I heard these are expected to go through the night."

After a quick look to his wife, Clark said, "Okay, let's head back, please."

Deb and Hunter also stopped where they were, and Deb's breath caught in her throat. She felt this was a sign from Bruce, since she had just told herself she should get back to her life with the boys.

Hunter kept going, "Oooooooo," much as he did last night with the fireworks. For the first time today, Deb wondered where George had gotten off to.

Except for the elves, everyone stayed frozen in place

for several minutes. Slowly some of the people began to move again.

The elves wanted to stop and watch, too. This was something they never tired of seeing. At other times the whole North Pole would freeze in place when the Aurora Borealis begun.

But tomorrow was a very big day. There was still much to finish before Santa took flight.

Chapter Eight

As his mother and brother inched toward the Visiting Cottage, George and Cedric had reached the lower level gate with the two giant nutcrackers. Cedric turned to George and proffered his hand. George took it and thanked Cedric for showing him all the wonders of the area. George was anxious to find Marshall and share all he had seen.

Boy, he thought, *is Marshall ever going to be sore he didn't come with me!*

Suddenly George felt a hand grab the back collar of his coat.

George tried to turn around but the grip was too strong.

Cedric looked up at the Nutcracker Guard and said, "You know your orders, straight to Santa with this one."

Cedric mocked a salute at George and headed back to the manufacturing area. George felt half marched and half carried back into the village.

He blushed bright red as he passed elves and visitors alike all pulling their eyes away from one spectacle to see this new one.

It was a tough choice in many of their minds to watch either the Northern Lights or a twelve foot giant Nutcracker manhandling a teenager through the street. More often than not, the Nutcracker won.

Bill was overcome with two beautiful things before him. The moment took over his senses and he turned and kissed Susan full on the lips.

Susan didn't fight it and returned his kiss.

Bill thought he could have created some lights of his own, and indeed was almost lost seeing the lights reflect in Susan's eyes. He felt a huge surge in his heart and kissed her again.

Marshall missed the first, but caught the second kiss. "Okay," he said embarrassed, "I guess I'll move on to another shop and see what else I can miss."

The three of them all blushed and mumbled some goodbyes mixed in with apologies. Then he left them alone. He already sensed he was going to be seeing a lot more of Bill after they left the North Pole. He felt stronger about this premonition, now.

Marshall wasn't the only one to witness Bill's actions. As they floated toward the Flight Center, Clark and Jillian had a birds-eye view of the couple. Clark looked at Jillian and shrugged his shoulders.

Jillian said, "Well if the magic of this place doesn't stir your emotions, I guess nothing could."

Jared and Julie were coming out of the hotel and also saw the couple. While he wasn't really surprised, interestingly enough Jared thought he wasn't bothered by this either.

Julie spotted Bill's parents hovering over their daughter and her new beau. They seemed to be smiling. She realized so was she.

The whole scene was suddenly and completely changed as all eyes moved to the Giant Nutcracker marching down the path with a young man held firmly in his grip.

Bill thought it looked like the nutcracker was taking out the trash. Julie and Jared saw where George was being led. They were thankful to have seen Marshall leave Bill and Susan moments before.

"At least," Jared said, "Marshall knew enough not to get caught in whatever act George tried to pull."

Julie nodded as she watched the pair march in front of the shocked face of George's mother and brother.

Deb was staring with obvious dismay. Hunter was giggling and sniggering until his mother gave him a mighty shove. She didn't mean to push Hunter quite so hard, but she was upset at the scene marching directly at her. Hunter fell in the snow still giggling.

As they approached within earshot, Deb scolded George. "What have you done? Do you see everybody's looking at you?"

She would have said more but the nutcracker marched right by her and up to Santa's Visiting Cottage with its young ward still tightly held in its mighty grip.

Chapter Nine

"Well, what have we here?" Santa Claus asked the young man as he was released at the front of the cottage.

George looked at the ground and mumbled in a shameful voice. "I believe you already know, sir."

Santa looked hard and sternly at the young man and said, "Yes. I believe I do. Well George, let's go into the room and talk about this." Santa turned and went inside while George thought briefly of running as fast and far as he could in the opposite direction.

Where exactly would I go? he thought to himself. Besides, he saw his mother and brother were heading straight toward the building where he was standing.

He resigned to face his fate no matter how bad it might get. Seems Marshall would have the last laugh. He walked through the door after Santa.

As Hunter and Deb reached the first entrance a very pleasant elf met them and bade them to sit down.

Deb didn't know what to say, as she was overcome by anguish and anger. She turned to the elf and asked. "Will we be sent home early for this?"

The elf patted her hand. "Of course not, dear. George broke a rule, yes. But Santa is not so hard as to destroy a whole family holiday over an infraction. He will definitely make George uncomfortable for a few minutes, but…well, you'll find out soon. Don't worry about it."

Deb wasn't sure if she felt relieved or even angrier at George's "infraction". She hoped Santa would indeed teach him what for, and if he didn't, she certainly would.

She looked at Hunter who now looked a little more concerned since his brother had been literally marched into Santa's private chambers. *Good*, she thought, *remember this*.

On the other side of the door, Santa had made himself comfortable in his chair. While a second chair was still in the room, he did not invite George to sit down, as he had his other guests. He looked at George but said nothing. Instead he waited for the boy to open up first. He didn't have to wait long.

"I'm very sorry, sir. Really I am. I guess my curiosity got the worst of me. Please don't send us back, I'll stay in the hotel if I have to, but please don't send my mom and brother back home yet. We haven't done anything together since my dad died, and they would hate me the rest of my life if..."

Santa held up his hand, and George stopped, though tears had already escaped his eyes.

"You know George," Santa said. "I had some very big plans for you as a musician."

George looked at him as if he had started a completely different conversation.

George said, "Well I wasn't all that good, and I get tired of all the practicing." He wondered what this had to do with his breaking 'the rule'.

Santa continued, "Oh, you would have been good. But I suppose we'll never see that now."

George started to get a little scared. *Oh my God, maybe he is gonna lock me up as a slave here,* he thought.

As if he read George's thought Santa sighed. "Well now that you've seen the Manufacturing Area, we have no choice…"

George thought, *Here it comes, slavery eternal!*

"…because you are forever changed by your experience. You may not know it today or even tomorrow, but soon you will begin thinking how you can recreate some of the things you witnessed. It will become an obsession that will take over your every waking thought. It's why we don't allow people in there."

George looked stunned. He couldn't understand what Santa was inferring. Was he going to go mad? Would he lock himself in a room for the rest of his life trying to invent the impossible? What did this have to do with him being a crackerjack musician?

Santa finally softened his eyes and offered George a chair. "You best sit down. I have much to say, and you need to listen to every word, very carefully."

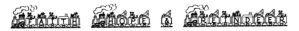

Marshall actually was one of the few who missed George being dragged through the street, as he beat a hasty retreat from the romantic shift between Bill and his sister. Instead he headed back toward the store with the electronic gadgets. He wasn't as impressed with all the software as he was in his last visit. He saw Ion Crosswire and nodded. Ion was distracted going over a list in his hand. "Well that's the last of those for this year," he said more to himself than Marshall.

Marshall asked what was going on.

"The last of Santa's list," he replied. "I'm gettin' the items they were out of at the warehouse. Well, I suppose you already know about George?"

Marshall's eyes got wide. He hadn't been thinking much of George and didn't know quite how to respond to the elf. He decided to play it cool. He looked at Ion saying, "No, what about him?"

"Well Santa let him sneak into the M.A., and now he's telling him what's in store for him."

Marshall figured 'M.A.' stood for the Manufacturing Area, but wasn't sure he heard right, "Let him sneak in?" he questioned.

Ion nodded.

He asked the elf. "So what is in store for him?"

Ion looked at Marshall. "I guess it's better he tell you in a couple days." He left Marshall and walked into the back storage area to fill the rest of the list. Marshall suddenly lost all interest in the trappings of the store and walked out to find George.

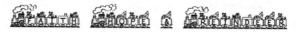

Jared and Julie walked over and sat down on the next bench by Bill and Susan.

They smiled and nodded to each other. Bill sat a little

straighter and felt his face get a lot warmer.

Susan thought, *"They might as well get used to seeing us together. They're going to see it for a long time."*

A little while later the Fredricks walked up and introduced themselves to the Gradys. After pleasantries were exchanged, they sat on the third and last bench around the maypole. All three couples watched the lights and were smiling.

At one point Jared suggested they all have dinner together a little later and they agreed that would be nice.

Chapter Ten

Before George could finish comprehending what Santa Claus had told him, Santa got up and opened the inner door, "Deb could you step in here? Hunter I'll be with you in a few moments."

Deb Mendez did as she was asked. Once she was in the room, she glared at George, still furious.

Santa closed the door and motioned to her to sit in the chair he had formerly occupied.

"First let me tell you that George is in no serious trouble. We discussed his little discretion, but it was actually me that let him into the Manufacturing Area. I told the elves to let him pass, though he found out firsthand how dangerous it is to sneak about."

Santa was thankful that George wasn't slower or the train quicker. Some things he couldn't control.

"Now let me tell you why I allowed him to 'break-in' to this area."

For the next ten minutes he told Deb Mendez about Bill Gates and his advancements that led from his tour of the North Pole. He also said that it was about time for another series of advancements. He explained that George had a musical aptitude, and he apologized that Ion Crosswire had been instructed to confuse her into not buying an electronic gadget for George, as he wanted George to focus more on that.

But, he admitted, George also had electronic aptitude

as well, and it was time to let *that* cat out of the bag, so to speak. However, this would have to be followed by strict plans and instructions regarding George's future. So he would be tutored in electronics and computer programming and theory by none other than Ion Crosswire.

This tutoring would take place over the summer breaks from high school and through college. It was further expected that upon completion of a master's degree from college, that George would be funded to begin his own company, and that a portion of the proceeds would be returned to the North Pole, as was done with Bill.

Santa continued looking directly at Deb, "And now for your Christmas gift. There is a hospital in your area that you need to go to work for."

Deb shifted uncomfortably. "I had applied there and they turned me down."

Santa grinned. "They are about to be bought out and the deal will be completed by the end of January. I have written down the name of the new administrator and he is expecting your call at that time. You will find your hours and pay very suitable to you and the boys. Secondly, regarding George's tuition for college...so long as he keeps up his end of the bargain we struck, and studies very hard, he will have a scholarship to help him all the way through completion of his master's degree."

He looked at George and George nodded fervently his agreement.

Suddenly an elf appeared and Santa Claus nodded.

The elf opened the door and invited Hunter in. As

Hunter moved into the room, the elf pulled another chair from nowhere and placed it by Santa. Santa sat down and motioned Hunter to join him. Even though he was nine, he hopped up on Santa's knee like he did when he was four.

Santa chuckled. "Now young man, I hear you are one exceptional hockey player. Is that true?"

Hunter nodded ecstatically. "I love hockey, it's the best game in the world! And yeah, my coach thinks I'm pretty darn good."

Santa ho, ho, hoed. "Well I have a special surprise for you then. I'm going to send you to the USA hockey camp in Vernon Hills for their summer program and we'll see how good you really can be!"

He winked at Deb and nodded with a knowing smile.

Hunter screamed out loud. "I'm going to hockey camp? Really?"

Santa laughed. "Absolutely! But you have to promise you will always help your other teammates, even if they're not as good as you, okay?"

"DEAL!" Hunter exclaimed. "See Mom, I told you this would be the best thing we could do together!"

Deb, who was dabbing her eyes with a tissue nodded at her son. "When you're right, you're right."

Santa gave the usual time for pulling it all back together before he wished them all a very Merry Christmas and bade them on their way.

Chapter Eleven

The Peters had returned to the petting zoo. Todd was having tremendous fun chasing the animals aroud the pens. Cory and Katy had completely lost their fear of young Todd getting hurt, even by the largest of the bears.

Besides the elves continual assurances that there had never been an incident at the North Pole, Santa had also said they should spend a little more time there today. Since Todd loved it so much, they didn't object.

One of the elves walked up to Katy who was petting one of the reindeer and said, "Mrs. Peters, would you and Mr. Peters follow me?"

Katy called Corey over and followed the elf to the back of the zoo's barn. The elf produced a bundle from inside the barn and held it up to her and said, "Santa said this goes with your other Christmas gift."

Wrapped in a blanket was the most beautiful Siberian Husky puppy she had ever seen. The puppy was caramel in color and had a thick reddish-brown mask about her eyes. Her fur was softer than the softest silk. She had piercing blue eyes. She whimpered low until Katy held her closer.

"You'll find a travel cage in your room," the elf beamed, "Of course you can name her any name you wish, but we call her Tasha."

Katy was in tears, and Tasha was eagerly licking

them from her face, "Tasha," she said, "What a perfectly exquisite name!"

FAITH   HOPE   &   REINDEER

The O'Reillys were checking out different stores and secretly getting Christmas gifts for the girls. This would be the best Christmas they ever had. With a wink and a nod to one of the elves, they would choose a special gift that one of the girls would swoon over.

The elf would slip it away after they left and send it to the wrap room. There it would receive its special coverings and be sent to the resort delivery area. This area was stacking up pretty high, but they were used to this and it certainly wasn't beyond what they were used to handling.

They were on their third haul over to the resort, today. They knew one more day and they could all take a nice long rest. At least until the first families of the New Year came in February.

Jim and Maureen were having more fun than the girls. For the first time they weren't fretting over how much they spent, or whether it was the right gift, or would one girl feel slighted. They saw that Ellen, and especially Renee had been changed by their visit with Santa.

They were happier than they ever remembered seeing them. It was as if they had laid a major burden down and were traveling lighter. They knew whatever Santa told them, that they were going to keep it with them, hopefully all of their lives.

They were at the last shop they had wanted to visit when the Northern Lights had appeared. Now they were all pretty worn out and were going back to the resort.

Fergie Keepitneet said he was going to have the girls "escorted" one last time for shopping for their parents for Christmas tomorrow. That would also give their parents one last day to relax and be by themselves. He insisted they should take advantage of it.

Marshall had wandered back to his room and wasn't there five minutes before there was a knock at the door. When he opened it he saw Christel Bunkinstyle on the other side. He invited her in.

She nodded and entered. "Fergie said he saw you come in. I have a request from Santa. He's asked if you would please be at the center of town at 7:30 pm this evening, and he also asked that you bring your Christmas present."

Chapter Twelve

By now, many of the visitors were filing back to the
resort looking more tired than not. Fergie stayed later
than usual to help Christel. He knew this was one of the
busiest days of the week with guests. He also didn't
want Christel to get too exhausted.

The Mendezes came in looking stunned more than
tired, except of course Hunter who was going on
incessantly about the hockey camp. The O'Reillys
followed suit, then came the Peters and their new family
member, Tasha. Katy was showing off the puppy to
everyone she saw. Little Todd was giving the puppy
plenty of attention by petting it every second.

Fergie bustled about asking guests their desires as
they marched or dragged in – Dinner? Babysitting? A
cup of coffee, cocoa, or…? The answers were as varied
as the questions. But after a little while they had
everyone settled in, fed and relaxed. In just a little over
an hour they would round them all up again. After all,
this was the big night.

He knew that the Gradys and the Fredricks were out
together. He recommended they try Conner O'Conlan's
Irish Bistro for a fine dining experience about an hour
before. Of course like in all places at the NP, you could
order whatever you felt like eating, but the ambience
was a little more spacious and special in an Irish kind of
way. Before he sent them off he had advised them that

they would need to be finished by around 7:15 pm, as there was a special assembly taking place at 7:30. He knew Connor would tell them the same.

Fergie remembered Marshall, and called up to his room to ask if he wanted anything. Marshall said no thanks as he was now nervous since Christel's brief visit.

It was now 6:32, less than an hour to go.

Chapter Thirteen

As instructed by the elves, everyone headed to the
Maypole tree in the center of town about 7:15. No one
knew much about what was going on. Marshall was
already there and he had begun warming up by playing
some of the Christmas carols he knew by heart. Some of
the elves had gathered around and begun singing to
Marshall's accompaniment.

The music put the other guests in a festive mood.
Some of the guests started singing with the elves.
George showed up with his trumpet joined Marshall and
played along. The music continued to build and soon
everyone was singing and the entirety of the North Pole
was filled with beautiful Christmas music.

When the town center was filled with guests and elves
alike, the entire area lit up. The maypole tree glowed so
intensely some had to shield their eyes. As quickly as it
brightened it dimmed and standing on a small stage
they swore wasn't there a moment ago was Santa and
Mary Claus – who also magically appeared.

Everyone applauded wildly. Santa and Mary took a
bow and Santa raised his hands. As the crowd died down
he looked around and smiled. Then he said, "Merry
Christmas, everyone."

The crowd responded "Merry Christmas, Santa".

He looked around checking the crowd and said, "God
bless you all as He has blessed us in the North Pole. I am

especially pleased that we have been able to spend precious time with new friends from around the world. I have felt great pride and comfort by your deeds to others. You have shown how good people can be to each other and I expect great things from all of you."

He looked over to George and said, "Even the more mischievous of you." Everyone looked at George and chuckled as he blushed a bright crimson.

Santa continued, "But like all things our time together is coming to an end. Tomorrow I leave on my annual mission to take gifts to families and children who have been good this year. And to let them know that God's love shines on them and that they are loved at Christmas and all the year through.

"And I won't be going alone. Every year I take a special helper with me. The elf that is chosen is elected through balloting across the entire elven network. They pick an elf to accompany me and represent all the thousands of elves that make everything Mary and I do possible. The elf chosen this year makes me very proud. And to introduce you to her is my wonderful wife, Mary."

Applause rose again as Mary stepped forward, waved and spoke to the crowd. "Each year the choice of a special elf is not taken lightly. This year's winner has done many unselfish and caring things and for many years. She makes everyone she meets feel special. And she provides incredible comfort and assistance to our special visitors. It is my distinct pleasure to give our Elf Of The Year Award to none other than our beloved Christel Bunkinstyle!"

Christel almost fainted. She had always hoped to take a trip with Santa, but had not been chosen as yet. She jumped up on the stage and gave the victory sign. She said thank you to the elves that picked her and promised to be a good representative.

Santa stepped back to the forefront and said, "I am so proud of all our citizens, friends and assistants around the world. You once more made the impossible look easy, and you have given hope to hundreds of millions of people around the world. Tomorrow at nine in the morning I will take off. And so my assistant, Christel, and I must bid you farewell. To send you all off I want to give one last Christmas gift to you. I will need the assistance of a future musician that you will all know someday soon."

Santa raised his hand backwards and another stage lit up and there stood an entire elven orchestra with Marshall standing in the center. Santa closed saying, "Okay Mr. Marshall Grady, let her rip."

Marshall played a jazz rendition of "Santa Claus Is Coming To Town" that had the whole area swinging and swaying to the music. When he finished the applause was deafening. He followed with a soulful solo of "Greensleeves" also known as "What Child Is This?" and after the first verse was completed, the elven choir joined in.

Before the end of the second verse, there wasn't a heart that wasn't moved and many had tears in their eyes. Two of these people were Jared and Julie. They were certain that they were prouder of their son than any parent had ever been.

As the song ended, everyone applauded the closing of another spectacular day at the North Pole.

Friday
December 23rd

"On Dasher, on Ginger, now Prancer and Cinnamon.

On Comet, on Blaze, now Donder and Blitzen!

Now lead on dear Rudolph and hasten with speed,

the whole world awaits – let's go fill the need!"

Nicholas Kristopher Kringle, Santa Claus

Chapter One

Everyone was outside to watch Santa and Christel depart at nine o'clock. Santa coasted his sleigh and reindeer over the village and blew one last kiss to Mary.

Then he stood on the sleigh and called out, "On Dasher, on Ginger, now Prancer and Cinnamon. On Comet, on Blaze, now Donder and Blitzen! Now lead on dear Torch and hasten with speed, the whole world awaits — let's go fill the need!"

He cracked the whip and off they flew. He circled only once and flew his team straight through the dome. A moment later they were gone from view.

Since most of the guests finished their shopping and had visited the various parts of the Village, many had a couple easy days prior to Christmas. So their visitors wouldn't become bored, Mary and Fergie planned several activities across the town and posted them in the lobby of the resort.

Like the orientations before, they were listed by chronological order:

Friday —
10:00	**Gift Wrapping Class** by Shelly Wrapitup	
11:30	**Wood Carving Class** by Rory Whitlesee	
1:30	**Ice Carving Class** by Ramsey Hampton	

3:00   **Snowball Throwing Contest** by Jolly
Havinfun

Saturday –
10:00   **Recreating The North Pole** (Crafts) by Frieda
Cutinglas
1:00   **Ornament Painting** with Pricilla Huffinpuff
2:30   **Tinsel Toss** with Frosty Foilenrap
3:30   **Reindeer Rodeo** Range Boss - Forrest
Hedemup

Fergie took charge of the sign ups and made the plans. He was enjoying being in charge of the resort and pleased that Christel finally got her chance to go with Santa. He wasn't the least bit jealous as he was only ninety-three years old and figured he had many years to get his opportunity.

Besides it was fun to plan all the activities and games for the guests. Plus for once, he had the most special day to plan. Everyone would be together in the resort for Christmas dinner.

That was the only day that guests weren't allowed to pick their own meal or time. But nobody had ever complained in the years they had done this. Most found the food so varied and scrumptious that they said they couldn't come up with a better decision on their own.

He called in Shelly Wrapitup and they cleared an area for her demonstration. She had invited various guests to bring down a difficult shaped gift to wrap. Shelly could wrap anything given paper and tape. Of course she also had a magic wand that most don't know about. It was actually a tool that melded paper to paper, similar to a glue gun only much smoother and with no heat.

But she couldn't pull that out for this demonstration, as the technology for this was still a dozen years away. So it was back to the old tape and glue guns. Well she thought, *it still is an art form, and they can learn quite a few tricks to make packages look beautiful.*

FAITH HOPE & REINDEER

Marshall and George were back to hanging around together. They were both dying to tell each other about their gift from Santa, but knew better than to even hint about it.

They agreed to get together right after Christmas breakfast so they could share what they had each received. Pacts like that were being made all over the village. Some couples even said they would set their clocks for one minute after midnight on Christmas Day, because they didn't think they would make it one minute more.

George said he wanted to see the carving demonstration and Marshall said that in Boy Scouts he had tried carving wood but couldn't quite get the hang of it, but he'd go along with George. They were told they would take a sleigh over to the demonstration area at around 11:00.

Shortly before 11:00 a few others started gathering for the demo including Cory Peters, Brian Conner and Bill's sister Hailey. Soon a large sleigh drawn by four

reindeer pulled up next to the resort. As they all got in
and pulled blankets over themselves, the sleigh pulled
out and headed through the village. It passed the now
dark visiting cottage and worked its way toward the
giant nutcrackers. George became visibly shaken. The
driver, named Thurmbull, said to his passengers that
there was nothing to fear, and he drove the sleigh right
past them without so much as a twitch from the guards.

"I thought this was 'off limits'," said Corey.

Thurmbull said, "As long as you are properly escorted
by an elf and don't go wandering off on your own [he
gave a smirk to George], you can go to certain places.
Besides all the manufacturing is done until the New
Year and the buildings are closed. Both carving lessons
are being given at the Mount Elfish Ski Resort & School,
and the only way to get there is through the
Manufacturing Area.

Marshall couldn't help but laugh at George. But
George knew he had seen more in only one of those now
closed, 'off limit' factories than all of them together
could see riding by. And he smiled to himself knowing
the secrets he would develop over the next few decades.

As Shelley showed Julie, Susan and several other
visitors the intricacies of creating the perfect bow from
ribbon and cloth, Jared went off to have a quiet cup of
coffee alone. He never knew he could feel so at peace. He
sat quietly and digested all the information of the last
several days. He looked around to see if anyone else was

nearby. When he saw no one in the area, he laid his face in his hands and sobbed.

He was overcome with gratitude and felt his remaining stress melt away being replaced by a deep sense of appreciation for everything he had been given in his life, including his beautiful wife, amazing daughter and talented and loving son.

Chapter Two

The rest of the day was spent at the various
demonstrations and lessons. Everyone had a good deal
of fun and interest and excitement was building for the
Snowball Throwing Contest. There were three divisions.
Men's. Women's and kids youmger than 15. Marshall
and George had to compete with Bill, Jared, Corey,
Brian. Jim and Clark.

An elf strolled over looking like the home plate
umpire in baseball. complete with chest guard. He said
to the crowd. "Good afternoon, my name is Basil
Pitchintoss, and I will be officiating the snowball
contest."

He pointed to a stack of gear to his left. "Over there
you will find the necessary gear. Men will go first. You'll
find special jackets and helmets that you need to wear.
These have sensors on them and will "mark" hits to
them. Five solid hits to the upper body or head will set
off an alarm and you're out. We will split into two sides
and play elimination."

After the men had strapped on their gear, they split
into two separate teams with Marshall, George, Clark
and Corey on one side and Bill, Jared, Brian and Jim on
the other. At the whistle, they pitched snowballs at each
other.

Jim was the first to be eliminated as Marshall and
Corey formed a lethal double-team concentrating on a

set target. Next they took Jared out. but lost George and Clark to the same tactic used by Brian and Bill.

The free-for-all that followed had all four running in circles after each other. The sideline spectators were howling at the melee. Finally, Brian and Marshall got tagged at the same moment with their fifth hit. Bill was a tad slower than Corey's military training and was the final person eliminated, leaving Cory victorious.

The women had a slightly harder time of it, but Katy had a strong edge over Julie, Maureen, Jillian, Susan and Heather. It turned out she was a softball pitcher for the last five years and her shots were extremely accurate.

Heather was also very good, having grown up in the Midwest with four brothers. It was down to her and Katy in no time. But, Heather only got two solid shots to Katy's five.

The kids were doing more "smashing" of snow on their opponents than throwing. Hailey, John and Hunter soon out flanked the other kids and it was down to John and Hailey against Hunter. Hunter tried valiantly, but finally lost with two straight shots to his helmet. Since they were on the same side Hailey and John were declared dual winners.

That activity sapped the last of the energy the guests had and they fairly limped into the lodge, even the kids looked beat.

That evening everyone stayed close to the resort and the meals were more along the line of light snacks and sandwiches. The appetite of most of the North Pole guests had shown a marked decrease since their individual meetings with Santa Claus.

Although nobody could seem to resist Mary Claus' cookies, which kept appearing by the tray full in the resort lobby. She had sent a variety and each one seemed better than the last.

Like Santa himself the cookies disappeared.

Saturday
December 24th

"Never let us forget that even when surrounded by miracles all around us, the greatest miracle resides in an infant whose birth we should celebrate every day."

Reverend Goinpeace, Pastor of the North Pole

Chapter One

The day before Christmas brought great excitement. There were still many things to do, and so much to prepare. It also meant that all the secrets that had been held would soon be able to be spilled like a load of gravel from an overly full dump truck.

Bill was trying to bend the rules, asking Fergie. "Would it be so wrong to tell my parents?" He was exasperated. "What's one more day, anyway?" Bill had been following him around like an errant child.

Fergie was looking a little exasperated himself. "Look, all I can tell you is that's the rule, and if you say anything before Christmas then a memory charm takes effect and you forget EVERYTHING!"

Bill looked as if he had been punched in the stomach. "No way!" he exclaimed, though he felt Fergie was telling the truth.

Fergie just stared at him.

Bill conceded the point and decided he could wait one more day, after all.

After Bill left, Fergie smirked and spoke quietly to himself. "Works every time."

Deb Mendez was more than excited this morning. The moment she saw the class on "Recreating the North

Pole" by Frieda Cutinglas she couldn't sign up quickly enough. She was at the door at 9:45 waiting for Frieda to usher her in.

Ever since she saw the 'Deck The Halls' shop, she had been thinking and planning to rebuild her North Pole display. Now she was going to get tips from an expert.

She hardly ate anything that morning. After receiving her gifts from Santa, she had wanted to recreate some of the traditions she had started while Bruce was still alive. She was as happy as could be and knew after talking to Santa that Bruce was still watching over all of them.

Her display was already a good size and she had nearly thirty buildings, several dozen elves, and of course Santa and Mrs. Claus. Though she felt they looked quite different from the genuine articles.

Frieda was a few minutes early and opened the door on a North Pole Fantasyland that was nothing like Deb's humble display. Frieda laughed at the look on Deb's face and said that she had always wanted to take before and after shots. One when they walked in, and another afterward, when they knew so much more.

As she was coming through the door at the Reindeer Inn with Frieda, George had burst past the door at 'Deck The Halls', as he had it 'on good authority' that they knew exactly what his mother wanted for Christmas.

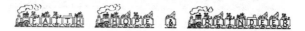

The O'Reillys decided to head back to the petting

zoo. The girls couldn't seem to get enough of polar bears and reindeer. When they got there they saw Patrick Conner, Hailey Fredrick and Katy Peters with her son, Todd, already there.

Katy was leading her puppy, Tasha, around while Todd was surrounded by penguins and Patrick was feeding a baby polar bear. Jim O'Reilly still thought how this would be the only place in the world where it would be safe to feed any baby bear while the mother was alive, let alone in her presence.

Other reindeer had come by the petting zoo, now that the Christmas rush was over. The whole mood of the North Pole had taken on a more relaxed atmosphere. There was still plenty to do and to get done, but it didn't have the same urgency as before. The reindeer were mingling around and Forrest Hedemup walked over to the girls with a reindeer in tow.

He came up to Hailey, Renee and Ellen and asked. "Do you know who I have here?" The girls shook their head.

"This is Vixen. One of Santa's most famous reindeer!"

Ellen asked, "Is he retired?"

Forrest shook his head. "Actually, she's pregnant, so Santa didn't want her on an exclusive alfalfa diet."

Ellen said, "Hey wait a minute, I thought Vixen was a boy! How come she's a girl?"

Forrest laughed, "A lot of our reindeer are girls. Actually, Santa uses many girls on his team, such as Ginger, Vixen, Dancer and Cinnamon to name a few."

Renee asked, "Dancer is a girl, too?"

Forrest replied. "Sure is, and one of the fastest reindeer we've ever seen. Even at her age, the old gal can outrun the fastest reindeer we've got."

Maureen overheard the conversation and asked, "*Does Santa ever retire the reindeer?*"

Forrest turned around and said, "Of course, though many don't like it much. They have to give in to nature sooner or later, even up here. Santa has faster or stronger reindeer, and they take over. But they all have places of honor and we treat them like royalty, as they should be."

Suddenly, the large wolf that Katy fell in love with came sauntering over.

It startled Maureen and Jim but Forrest walked over and said "Hello, Silver, ready for your morning treats are you?" He put his hand in his jacket and though the wolf was the same height as the elf, she took the treats from his hand in an almost dainty manner.

Jim came up. "No one is ever going to believe half the tales from this place, but it sure will be fun to tell them!

Chapter Two

Again, most of the day was spent wandering in and out of shops, and trying different crafts. For the ornament decorating, most of the participants were children – both guests and elven kids, including many that were at the petting zoo earlier. Same with the tinsel toss.

While everyone was eagerly waiting to tell and hear about all the fabulous gifts, they were also saddened that their time in the North Pole was rapidly coming to an end. They were all returning to their realities, and while many had new realities to be sure, it was still different than the world they had found here.

Julie was one of these, and while anxious for Jared to begin his new position, she had found a peace and a joy she had not experienced since she was a young girl. She was almost melancholy at the thought of leaving. She was out walking through the village rather aimlessly.

She heard her name and laughed when she saw Susan and Bill in a balloon high above yelling to her. Well this had come full circle; it was her yelling at Susan from a balloon when she literally ran into Bill.

She still had a little shopping to do and went into Electrons For Protons to get Jared what she thought he would really need for the new year.

Ion Crosswire greeted her promptly and said with a large grin. "I have what you need for Mr. Grady, right

here, Mrs. Grady." This caught Julie by surprise since
she had yet to tell him what she had come in for.

Ion continued. "This little machine has everything
Mr. Grady will need, a huge terra hard drive, the latest
full DRAM available today, media cards, all the
peripheral devices and all the programs that are on your
desktop, plus a few more that he will find useful at his
new position."

Julie Grady looked at Ion. "Does everyone know
what happens up here?"

Ion shuffled his feet at the comment. "Well, we are
updated on certain critical changes so we can help you
prepare properly, if we can be of any service at all." Ion
told Julie he would have it properly wrapped and placed
under their tree.

"You mean the one at our home?" Julie asked.

Ion grinned. "No, the one in your room."

Julie said, "But we don't have one in our room."

Ion beamed. "Oh but you will!"

He explained that this afternoon, Whitey Slippenfall,
our Master Forest Manager, would be placing a tree in
each guest's room and either decorating it, or in the case
of the Gradys, leaving sufficient adornments for Susan
and Marshall to decorate it themselves.

"Then, you can place all the gifts under the tree to be
opened tomorrow morning."

Julie smiled. "Some gifts are too big to be opened."

"There's always a way to show a gift through
symbolism and a little imagination," Ion replied.

She knew that was probably true.

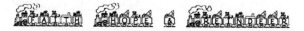

Susan and Bill were in awe of the complexity and size of the North Pole. They were heading back to the landing zone, and were still commenting to each other about how much there was to this marvelous land.

Bill was particularly animated about the woodland area and commented about how thick the forest was, and how many animals were coursing through the woods.

Susan couldn't help wonder how much of the Pole would change, if it all, when they eventually returned. She asked her balloon tour guides the question on her mind.

Ferdinand the pilot answered her, "Some things about the North Pole change constantly. We come up with new methods of manufacturing, new ideas for gifts, and of course your cultures dictate to a large extent what we make the most of in any given year. But the general architecture and overall look of the Pole changes, or has changed, very little."

Susan was glad to hear it. She wanted to remember everything and show it to her and Bill's children, when they had them. She had already decided that they would raise their children with all the imagination and magic that life had to offer.

She now knew that magic was everywhere around them and she wanted to make sure to pass on that wonder and knowledge. She snuggled up to Bill and gave him a big hug.

Marshall and George were giving thought to their return to home as well.

George said to his new friend. "Listen Marshall Grady, I don't care how far we go or whether either of us becomes famous or not, though I suspect we both will, I insist we stay in touch with each other."

Marshall looked long and hard at George, and though he tried to say it with a straight face, the corners of his mouth turned up into a smirk. "Naw, you're too damn annoying for me, and a rule breaker besides."

George saw the smirk. "Yeah, and now that I think about it, why the heck would I want to hang around with a goodie-goodie like you, anyway."

Marshall laughed. "Okay, deal."

George replied. "Deal."

Marshall got up. "Hey let's head over to the lodge, they're gonna have that rodeo and it might be fun to watch."

George shrugged his shoulders. "Yeah, okay."

Chapter Three

A large arena was erected during the day for the Reindeer Rodeo. The elves were still busy putting up pens and bleachers. Others were herding animals toward the area. Of course these weren't your typical barnyard animals. There were several polar bears, dozens of reindeer, and a slew of penguins. There were also three large sleighs sitting right outside the ring.

Some of the elves were waiting for the festivities to start and many were wearing western garb including cowboy hats, vests and coveralls. There were even rodeo clowns in attendance with painted faces and wild colored wigs and clothing.

Several of the guests had already congregated around the arena. They wondered what would be in store at this unusual rodeo, but guessed whatever it was, it would be entertaining.

A rather large bodied elf wearing a ten gallon hat came to the center of the ring with a wireless microphone worn like a scarf around his collar. His hat looked as big as him and the sight made the clowns look less comical.

The elf announced to the guests to please be seated on the bleachers, as it was almost time for the rodeo to begin.

As the guests discovered, not only were these bleachers padded, but they were heated as well. And not only the seats, but the footboards, too. They were comfortable beyond reason. There are so many things to remember about this place, where would they ever begin?

The elf introduced himself as Forrest Hedemup, the range boss for the North Pole. While many guests couldn't tell it was him under his hat at first, they soon recognized him as the elf in charge of the all reindeer and the Petting Zoo.

Forrest said, "We have a spectacular show for you. Many of the elves here are going for the Annual Championship and have been in competition all year for this coveted award." At that the elves and guests hooted and hollered in true rodeo style.

"Our first event of the afternoon," Forrest continued after the crowd noise subsided, "will be the reindeer roundup. Henry Stuffinsuch is our current reigning leader and could take it all with a win tonight. But first up is Etheleen Chocochip who is out to change the standings. Etheleen is riding Snowbound. The judges ready? Let the games begin!"

Out of a pen shot two reindeer, with Etheleen atop one of them. She and Snowbound were chasing the first reindeer. She pulled a rope from her side and twirled it guiding the front running reindeer. She managed to cut off the reindeer and chase it back to its pen. As soon as the lone reindeer was behind the gate a buzzer rang out.

Forrest yelled out, "Official time is 23.37 seconds! Very well done, Etheleen! Henry has some serious competition on that time.

And so it went on. Henry did manage to hang on to

his lead with his trusty steed, Thunderclap and beat Etheleen by .05 seconds to claim first place.

Following the reindeer round up came the gift stacking event. The three large sleighs were pulled into the center and squibbles filled with wrapped presents of all sizes and shapes were ushered in and unloaded by the sleighs. There were three teams of three elves each. At the sound of the buzzer, the elves commenced stacking gifts atop the sleighs. One elf would stand atop the presents and continue stacking as the other two would toss or pass each other the presents. The winning team got every present stacked and the pile stood roughly 25 feet high and looked solid. The two other teams had more difficulty and the presents went toppling down on one of the teams, and were precariously balanced and looked to go any second with the other. The whole event took about five minutes as the presents went up at a lightning pace.

The next event really got the crowd going. It was polar bear riding. Much like bull riding, an elf rode on the back of a very strong and bucking polar bear. Of course one thing a polar bear can do, that a bull can't, is stand upright.

So when the bears thought they had carried their charges long enough they stood upright which knocked every rider off except one who hung on the rope while the bear danced about. That elf was declared the winner, though his grip finally slipped at the end and he fell onto one of the rodeo clowns.

One event involved the guests. All guests wishing to participate had to stand in the center of the ring while

thirty-six penguins were released into the arena. At the
buzzer the guests had to round up as many penguins as
they could and put them into a pen with their number
on it. Shortly after the buzzer, the people in the stands
were nearly on the ground rolling in laughter. It seems
penguins are quicker than most expected and a whole
lot smarter.

Hailey was coaxing several to her and then suddenly
they all switched direction on her as she tried grabbing a
few without success. Katy Peters was doing the best at
first with four penguins, but when she ran off to get
more, one managed to jump the fence, which made her
even with her husband, Cory.

Jim O'Reilly was looking rather flustered and red in
the face after trying to scoop up three penguins and
having one nip him on the nose making him drop all
three. His daughter Ellen wasn't doing much better and
actually chased one penguin right into the pen of
Kaileen Wu.

Hailey got the idea of coaxing the penguins by acting
like she had food. She soon got sixteen of the penguins
into her number seven pen and won by a healthy
margin.

The last episode really took the guests breath away.
The Cowboy elves wore more than padding for this
event. They wore large backpacks over their shirts. As
they mounted their reindeer for the bucking reindeer
encounter, they flew out of the chute, *literally*!

The reindeer started flying and bucking at the same
time. The elves held on as long as possible and when
they were thrown from a great height they opened their

parachutes and floated back to the ground. One of these elves floated right onto the stands and nearly knocked Jared off the bleacher.

Three had actually hung on until the reindeer wore out and landed again although, one was thrown upon hitting the ground. She still got a standing ovation from the crowd. In fact, they all got thundering ovations because of the heart-stopping nature of the event.

When the last event was over, everyone returned to the hotel. They found a giant banquet table in the lobby where some of the overstuffed sofas had been before. The guests were told that Christmas dinner would be served in the lobby tomorrow, and that this was the only time they wouldn't be able to order what they wanted.

When the Gradys returned to their room, there it stood. A perfect 12 foot Christmas tree.

Susan shrieked with joy.

Marshall beamed. "Oh great, here we go again!"

This time Julie and Jared also pitched in and the four of them found they had all they could want to create a stunning Christmas tree.

The same scene was recreated in the other rooms, and everyone from the Wus to the O'Reillys spent that evening decorating their trees for Christmas in different themes and traditions.

Later everyone settled in and a few families did their traditional Christmas Eve dinner as they would have at home. After dinner, it was suggested by the staff that they attend the midnight Christmas service at the Chapel. It would begin at 11:00 pm and end at midnight.

As 10:45 approached, every family came into the lobby where teams of horse and reindeer drawn sleighs awaited.

Fergie noted that all the guests were in attendance and felt good about it. He knew that Reverend Goenpiece would bring the genuine message of Christmas back to each of them.

Even though it was officially Christmas everyone was too tired to expound on their Christmas present to others.

Late that night, as the last eyes closed a common last fleeting thought was universal — the best Christmas ever was finally upon them.

"Step forward into your life

as you did when you were a child,

when you believed anything was possible "

Vince Gowmon,
Founder of Remembering to Play Events

Chapter One

They sprang from their beds. Adult or child, each had an excitement that would not be contained any further. Some woke in the wee hours of the morning and some waited until a more usual time, but each held all the excitement like they had never known.

Fred Wu got up at 3:30 in the morning. He knew upon opening his eyes he would sleep no more this night. He walked into the kitchen and turned on the light over the sink. He decided to make a pot of coffee. As he filled the reservoir he heard the toilet flush in the bathroom attached to their bedroom suite.

Kaileen came in, shuffling her feet and asked, "Not sleeping anymore tonight?"

Fred tried to look nonchalant and shrugged his shoulders. "I really don't think I am able."

Kaileen knew her husband was busting at the seams. "Okay, I'll light the tree and then let's hear it. C'mon give."

Fred said she better have some coffee with him and pulled out two mugs from the cabinet. He poured some coffee into each mug while it was still brewing. He said, "Before I start, maybe you should tell me yours first."

Kaileen shook her head and said she could wait a little longer.

Fred Wu said, "Santa has given me an invention and the seed money through a grant for developing the product. I need to form a company and also I need to apply for the patent under my name. He told me that in two years, and before I take the company public, that I have to sell 25% of the company back to the North Pole through an organization that is already established and recognized by the IRS.

Kaileen asked what the product was. Fred went into the bedroom and pulled out a small box. He opened it. Kaileen looked inside and gave a stunned look to her husband.

She said breathlessly, "You're going to be famous!"

He smiled back at her, "Yeah, and rich, too."

It was now Kaileen's turn, "Well it's a good thing, too, especially since you're going to have another mouth to feed!" She told her husband that Santa confirmed what she suspected, that she was finally pregnant after almost a year of trying.

Her gift from Santa was taking place while they were up at the Pole, as they were getting one of their bedrooms redone into a nursery complete with all the furnishings, and the other spare room was being made into an art studio, so Kaileen could pick up where she had left off several years ago, and begin painting again.

Santa told her she would be able to stay home and take care of their new baby and paint. After her husband's news she knew this to be fact rather than a premonition.

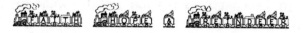

As the Wus were finishing their second cup of coffee,

the O'Reillys were on the move. Maureen had made a big batch of cocoa for everyone and then they tore into the gifts under the tree. Somehow Shelly Wrapitup even managed to beautifully wrap the rocking horse for Annie.

There was a rather large square package under the tree addressed to Jim and Maureen. Ellen pushed it over to them and told them to open it. Renee also urged them. She too, wanted to see what her parents got.

Maureen ripped the paper and opened the box inside. She pulled out a large doll house structure and began crying. Jim read the attached note and explained to his daughters, "This is the new home in the country that Santa is giving us. You are going to have plenty of brothers and sisters to help look after."

The girls almost fell over.

"We're moving to the country?" asked Renee, "Will I have my own bedroom?" Maureen answered through her tears. "Yes. and it will be much bigger. And we will have more bathrooms and a huge yard and a barn..."

"...For our horses?" Ellen interrupted.

Jim nodded his head.

Next to the large box that contained the house were three other boxes addressed to each girl.

They ripped them opened and each held a horse with a note. Renee screamed. "I got a Palomino like this one!"

Ellen called out, "I'm getting an Arabian!"

Annie's was to be a Shetland pony that looked quite a bit like her new rocking horse.

In the Rudolph suite everyone was holding on to their news and presents until after they had finished breakfast. Jared said that he expected they all had extraordinary gifts from Santa, but he wanted to see and hear them on a full stomach and a wide awake head.

After breakfast they again looked at the beautifully decorated tree and the score of presents beneath it. Susan said it was almost too gorgeous to disturb.

Marshall looked at her and said, "Yeah, right." He dove into the stack looking at the names.

He produced a large box marked in calligraphy, *Jared*. He handed it to his father and told him to open it. Inside was a model of a high rise building with a single word at the top – Mattel.

Jared got to tell his tale first. The kids sat in stunned silence each with broad smiles.

Susan finally jumped up and hugged her Dad's neck. "I'm so very happy for you!"

Marshall finally came out of his spell and joked with his father. "Sure, you get this now! After I'm grown and wouldn't get caught playing with all those cool toys. Why didn't this happen say eight or ten years ago?"

Jared kidded back, "Probably because you would have bankrupted the company wearing out all the toys with your friends."

Marshall thought how good it was to have his Dad back to his normal humor.

The next gift was for Julie. It was the new laptop she thought she had gotten for her husband, the note simply said *To our Budding Author*. Also included in hers was a note from a popular author who happened to live

in Southern California and an invitation for tea to
discuss her new career. It included her phone number
and email address, just as Santa said.

Again her children stared in disbelief as she talked
about how for three years she really wanted to write the
book in her head.

Marshall shook his and said, "I wonder what they put
in the air under this dome?"

Jared opened the identical machine from his wife. He
laughed and said, "What do you know, his and her
notebooks! I sure hope I don't take your book to the
office by mistake when you're off having 'tea'."

Susan opened her package from the North Pole and
it was a sweater and a pennant both with the scarlet and
gold letters USC on them and a note that said, *Good
luck in college!* and was signed, *Love from Nick
and Mary.* Susan explained how Santa had not only
told her she would be accepted at USC, but he would see
to it that she got a full scholarship to attend!

Her parents reeled at the thought. They couldn't
believe their ears, but that wasn't all.

Marshall had a similar gift and note except the
pennant said "Julliard School of Music" and instead of
a sweater, he had a personal invitation to spend a week
with Kenny Gorelick to help with his particular
saxophone style.

Susan fairly screamed, "You're going to play with
Kenny G?"

He told them he also would be given a scholarship to
Julliard as Santa thought it was important he bring
music to the world. Marshall explained, "He said the

world needed more musicians and other artists. He said
I need to start making my own music as well as playing
other people's, but he thought Kenny could help me find
my 'voice'."

It was almost too much to take in. They sat and
talked for hours about the ramifications of their gifts.
Susan sat hanging on tightly to the Teddy bear she got
from her brother. She wondered while they talked if Bill
received a similar present to hers from Santa.

She wouldn't wonder too long, he had.

Bill would be going to the School of Engineering at
USC with his full scholarship. Bill's parents sat
dumbfounded listening to their son, and then Jillian
cried with joy and relief.

Bill said, "I told you a solution would present itself."

Clark Fredrick admired his son with Bill's faith and
optimism.

Hailey received a miniature bedroom set in a gift box
and was told the real deal would be waiting in her
bedroom when she got home. It was exactly the set she
pointed out to her mother. Her mother told her at the
time that the set cost too much for them right now.
Hailey guessed Santa may have put that thought in
their head, so he could give it to her.

Clark also had news. He was to be promoted to
Superintendent of his school district. Clark said, "Turns
out that Mr. Peabody is going to retire after fifteen years
at his post and "someone" had urged him to look at me

as his replacement. Santa told me it was all arranged. I will be taking over for the next term." Clark shook his head as he spoke still trying to believe the news, himself.

Going along with the need for more artists, Santa gave Jillian all new tools to develop her latent talent in sculpture. She would also have a new studio upon her arrival back home. It had been set-up in their rarely used spare bedroom while she was up in the North Pole, along with Hailey's bedroom set.

She loved the Santa Claus Nutcracker Bill gave her and said she hoped one of the first sculptures would be of the jolly old elf.

Brian was trying hard to explain the gift he received from Santa to his boys. while Heather sat with tears of joy streaming down her face. Santa gave Brian a new invention that would actually develop into an entire new sport. He explained to Brian that recently a new composite material was 'discovered' and that it was exceptionally good for personal aviation.

Especially as a new type of personal parasail that would have a very short and lightweight wingspan, while giving tremendous lift and agility. The result would make a product that needed almost no drop, and little space, unlike the ones today. It, and Brian, would revolutionize the parasail industry.

Brian was to develop the product and the sport, with help of course. of the North Pole.

His boys thought the train was the coolest gift.

And on and on it went throughout the Reindeer Inn. When they finally ran out of gifts to be opened and tired of telling the tales of the incredible presents from Santa to their families, they poured out into the halls to tell the others. Each person's story and gift seemed more fantastic than the last.

George finally got the chance to tell Marshall some of what he saw and the gift that he got from Santa. He had been briefed by Ion on just what he could share with his new friend and others.

Marshall was pleased for his friend, but he was also a little sad. He thought Santa had probably wanted to send George to Julliard as well. After all, he knew Susan and Bill would be going to USC together.

Cory Peters carried around the model of the Ambassador School and attached B&B all day. He even ate lunch in the main lobby with it sitting on the table in front of him. And the O'Reilly girls ran around to each guest they could and started every conversation with "Guess what?"

No one left the Inn during the day. Not that any of the shops were open anyway. And for this Christmas, no one would have any returns.

Chapter Two

Many of the guests were hanging around the lobby, and Fergie advised each of them that dinner would be served at 4:30 sharp that afternoon. The elves in the back were calling the other guests on the in-room phones to advise them of the same. The smells were already beginning to permeate the inn. The aromas of cinnamon, turkey, and more were wafting through every door jamb.

A couple more hours might be sheer torture for the now hungry guests.

When 4:00 came around, nearly everyone was hanging around the table. Punch and several other types of drinks were available, all nonalcoholic and quite tasty. The tables had seating cards and the families had been carefully placed together along both sides of the table. Little touches were noted, such as where the Grady family member ended on one side and a Fredrick family member began. Meaning Bill and Susan were seated next to each other.

As people moved to their assigned seat a voice they all recognized came from behind them.

"Merry Christmas!" Christel Bunkinstyle called out.

Everyone was surprised – not only to see her, but that

she looked as if she had all the rest she needed and was
still ready to take on the world. They all congratulated
her and asked about the journey and what was it like to
fly with Santa and how did he really get down the
chimneys and...

She held up her hands as she had done that first night
and the din finally quieted. "Thank you all for your kind
comments and enthusiasm. I will gladly share my
adventure, which right now I will just say was fabulous.
But it will have to wait until after dinner. I promise I
will make myself available by the fireplace around 6:30
tonight. If you will, please take your seats for dinner."

As they sat around the massive table they noticed
two empty seats at either end. Suddenly, Santa and
Mary Claus burst through the door and yelled "Merry
Christmas!"

Everyone jumped up when they came in and the kids
including Patrick, Todd and the O'Reilly girls screamed
at the sight of Santa joining them for dinner.

Santa took one end of the table after seating Mary at
the other. More than half of the guests were still
standing when Santa bade them all to sit down again.

When everyone was finally seated Santa addressed
the diners. "Please bow your heads and take an attitude
of prayer. Dearest Lord and God, we thank You for the
many blessings You have bestowed upon each of us. We
pray that the gifts You have given each of us will be best
used in Your service and under Your guidance. We thank
You for this feast and pray it will nourish us and make
us strong in Your name and service. Amen."

After the prayer, many of the patrons expressed

surprise at his presence.

He laughed. "What? You don't think I would miss one of Christel's feasts, do you?"

Mary said, "You haven't yet my dear. And your round shape shows it."

Mary Claus stood after she received a glass of punch from one of the elves. She tapped the glass with her fork to get everyone's attention. "Normally Nick gets to make the toast, but it has become tradition for me to do it at Christmas. Mostly because he's too tired to think clearly and because I talked him out of it."

The diners chuckled.

"So it is with great pride that I ask you to raise your glasses. We want to toast each and every one of you. Every person at this table is a credit to your families and to all humanity. You all have done, and will continue to do, many great deeds in your life and it is our honor and blessing to know each of you. We are thrilled to be able to serve you and to help you serve others. May each of you live very long, accomplished lives and may you rest in the palm of God's hand when you're work is finished."

Everyone looked red faced at the lavish praise they had received as they clinked their glasses with each other.

As if on cue the doors from inside the Reindeer Inn burst open and elves carrying numerous trays began a procession toward the table.

There was turkey, both fried and smoked, ham and prime rib. There were all manner of salads including pasta, potato and tomato salads, there were the traditional green bean casseroles, corn and yams, three different stuffings, mashed potatoes, apple sauce, rolls and breads of several varieties and garnishments of every type, right down to Julie's spiced apples, cored of course.

As the dishes were served there were several exclamations from the group. Most had said how much the individual dishes tasted wonderfully like their own treasured family recipes.

Santa and Mary winked at each other while trying to steal bites of food in between their guests unending questions and comments.

After a little over an hour and half, Santa and Mary pardoned themselves from the crowd and Santa said that he was going to retire for a few days and catch up on his rest.

He thanked them all again, told them they were most welcome for their gifts and that they should do everything in their power to spread the joy and feeling of Christmas the whole year through.

With a last smile and a wave, the Clauses instantly disappeared.

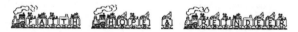

Some of the families hung around to hear about Christel's adventure, the remainder split between walking off the sumptuous feast around the village and going up to their rooms to take an after dinner nap from too much food.

The Gradys did all three. Susan decided to go for a

walk with Bill, and Marshall went back to the room. Jared and Julie said they wanted to hear all about the Christmas Eve trip.

Precisely at 6:30 according to the cuckoo, Christel marched out of the back and headed over to the fireplace. Besides Jared and Julie, there was Cory and Katy Peters, Maureen O'Reilly and Brian and Heather Conner waiting for Christel.

She started by saying, "First I have to tell you all, it was the most exciting time I've had in my 152 years! I knew about the process, but to see it in action is unbelievable, even for me!'"

Christel was more animated than any of the guests had seen her before and she spoke about the trip in broad strokes. She answered several questions about how Santa got up and down the chimneys (he touches his nose and he pops in and out, which is why he can go into homes and apartments without fireplaces), how he loads the sleigh at the different distribution points (he has hundreds of other elves throughout the world that do that for him), how he lands on roofs without snow (the sleigh operates more like a helicopter or harrier jet than a sleigh), what happens if he's seen, what is it like covering a good portion of the world in two nights, and how tired was she and was there any special spell or magic to keep them going (no, just pure adrenaline)?

Christel showed her usual stoic behavior in answering questions, but on the last question about how tired she was, she admitted that she had pretty well used up the aforementioned adrenaline. She said there wasn't any special spell or magic that she was aware of, other than the slowing of time that Santa is able to do.

She finished by saying that normally the feast alone would take it out of her, but she was so far beyond exhausted she was running on raw emotion, and that perhaps it really was time to hit the sack.

The group acquiesced to her wishes and let her head off to bed.

And while they all wished they too could slow time, they had to admit it was getting late and they had to pack for their return tomorrow.

When they got to their room each guest found a note from the staff of the inn that had instructions for their departure. They were to leave any gifts they would like shipped in their room.

They could even leave their luggage if they chose and take only what they thought they would need when they arrived home. The remainder of their belongings would arrive within one to two day's time.

They were instructed to please be in the lobby by 9:00 am for debriefing and final instructions including time of departure.

"As your faith is strengthened you will find that there is no longer the need to have a sense of control, that things will flow as they will, and that you will flow with them, to your great delight and benefit."

Emmanuel Teney, Doctor of Psychiatry

Chapter One

Everyone moved more slowly the next morning.
Many of the families took their hosts up on their offer
and took only the necessities they would need upon their
return.

Unfortunately for Jim O'Reilly, nearly all their
belongings were deemed necessary, and he looked like he
was moving rather than traveling. He had to finally hold
his ground with Annie's rocking horse and a few other
gifts that just wouldn't fit in their already bulging
suitcases.

Susan was up before 4:30 and ready and packed by
5:30. She and Bill had rendezvoused at that time to
spend a little more time together before they would head
off to their separate states.

They had begun making plans on getting together
during spring and summer break and when they would
arrive at USC.

Bill felt that truly the best gift he received from
Santa was Susan. Of course he was grateful for the other
things, but he was head over heels in love with Susan,
and could easily see spending the rest of his life with her.
Most importantly, Susan said she felt the same way
about him. He had always been confident about his
education and career, but before this trip he was less
certain about his love life.

The missing puzzle piece had been dropped neatly

into place.

At 9:00 everyone was gathered once more in the
lobby. Fergie Keepitneet actually did the debriefing as
Christel was "hibernating" for a few days. She had bid
everyone a very fond farewell.

Fergie reminded the guests that it was their duty to
let as many people as possible know that Christmas was
more than just a day. It was a state of mind and action.
They were able to tell people everything they had
learned about the North Pole and Santa with only a few
exceptions.

"As we have told you that for your own wellbeing, it is
better that you don't know too many futuristic
advances; it's also a good thing not to tell others about a
few things that you know about. The first is about the
naughty/nice scanners and monitors. Many people
might not understand the concept and the last thing we
need is more paranoia in the world."

The group laughed at the truth of that comment.

He continued. "The other item you must not mention
is anything about is our distribution system. We can't
have individuals trying to locate staging warehouses, or
trying to break into locations and disrupting deliveries,
especially since it takes us all year to get everything
ready and placed."

Brian asked, "What about your location up here?"

Fergie smiled. "For well over a century, people and
the most sophisticated equipment you have including,

but not limited to, satellites and metal detectors have been trying to find us. They have not. Some, like yourselves, have been here before and tried to find us again. They couldn't. We obviously don't want people to risk their lives trying to find us, but at the same time we are quite secure in our location."

"Is there any way for us to contact the North Pole again?" asked Kaileen Wu.

Fergie beamed. "Of Course! Just write us a letter, or send us an email, and we'll respond as soon as possible. We love hearing from our former visitors and some stay in touch with us for many, many years."

"Anything else?" Fergie questioned. "Okay then, your departure will be at 10:30 and you are asked to have everything you are taking with you, including yourselves, in the lobby at 10:15 sharp. You will have lunch on the train, and should have plenty of time to make your first connecting flight to Seattle from Fairbanks at 2:30 pm."

Everyone switched to departure mode now. While they were very sorry to leave, many were anxious to get started on their new lives. Maureen, Jim and even the girls would be packing up their own home as soon as they got back. Their foster home was waiting and Santa had already arranged the licensing and paperwork with the state.

Jim said there could be no doubt he was the genuine article, as only Santa could wade through a bureaucracy that would drive any normal person to distraction.

The Peters were also to begin packing as soon as they got back, there was much to do before the first classes in March at Eagle River, Wisconsin.

Marshall found George outside the lodge. It looked like he was having a very serious talk with Ion Crosswire, though it looked like Ion was doing all the talking.

As Marshall was getting closer, he heard Ion say, "That should about cover it. Make sure you get that class changed before the start of the next semester. Remember, I'll be there on June 21st to cover your summer training. Good luck and email me if you have any problems at that address I gave you. And lastly, remember not a word of any of this to anyone, not girlfriends or even best friends like this one." Ion was pointing at Marshall.

Marshall said, "I didn't want to know while I was here, and I still don't. I have my own life to live."

Ion smiled and took Marshall's hand saying, "And a good life it's going to be. No matter how good electronics will get, live music and its artists still can't be truly duplicated."

After Ion left, George and Marshall went for one last cocoa. Marshall joked about how if he ballooned up to three hundred pounds when he got back, he'd find this place alright, no matter how well they hid it.

George seemed quiet and alone in his thoughts. Marshall asked what was up with him.

"I guess I realized talking with Ion, the awesome responsibility I took on. I wasn't expecting that what I was doing might affect the whole world," said George.

"Well if anyone can handle it, I think you'll be the one. Don't let it get to you or overwhelm you. Stay focused on the moment, and don't get discouraged or depressed."

George looked at his friend and smiled saying, "Oh yeah? And how'd you get so smart?"

"Easy, I listened to my Mom and Dad. And speaking of them, I think I'd better head back."

When they came back to the inn, everyone was already gathered in the lobby for the last time. Fergie spoke loud enough to get everyone's attention. "On behalf of Christel, myself and all the elves of the North Pole, I would like to say it has been our honor and pleasure to serve you and get to know you. I echo the sentiments of Santa and Mary, when I say we will be watching with rapt interest the wonderful gifts you will bestow on so many others. We wish you the joy of this Christmas throughout your lives. Good bye and God's speed."

A few elves placed the luggage on a cart and led the guests back to the train station.

It was a short distance but a long walk to the train. They saw the Northern Express waiting in the depot for them. Conrad, Fred and the other traveling valet/waiters stepped off the train and loaded the luggage and their passengers. Each person took one long, last look at the North Pole, as if trying to burn the image in the front of their brain, so as to never forget it.

Susan asked to sit with Bill and his family in the next car and Julie told her of course she could. George had asked and received the same permission to sit with Marshall on the way back.

As the train pulled from the station not a word was spoken. Even the valets kept quiet for a time, and when they asked for lunch orders, very few passengers were hungry.

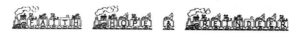

The rest of the trip home for the Gradys was uneventful. When they finally reached their driveway it was already the next day. They talked little on the flights or ride home. It seemed that they spent most of their time concentrating on every detail of the magical place they had left. Marshall did bring his saxophone with him, and Susan brought her new bear. Both were too precious to leave behind, even for a couple days.

As they entered the house they looked at the artificial tree they had decorated before leaving. It was still beautiful, but didn't look nearly as grand as the tree they left in Rudolph.

What little they did say to each other was to make a pack, that if any of them forgot how important their lives were to each other and those around them, that someone in the family was to firmly remind them.

As Dickens wrote so many years ago, "They would keep Christmas in their hearts forever." They would also talk about the true meaning of Christmas to others, but as Julie told the kids, the best way to change hearts was to lead by example.

Susan wondered once more when she would return to

"the Pole". She felt Santa Claus had told her she would through Bill.

Bill. She was already missing him, but knew she would have her whole life with him, so this memory was almost bittersweet.

As they tried to return to their lives, they knew that in a very good way, they would never be the same as before.

They hoped they would always affect others the same way.

The End.

Read an excerpt from the 1st Book

in The Santa Claus Trilogy

Believe Again,
The North Pole Chronicles

Believe Again

The North Pole Chronicles

1st in the Santa Claus Trilogy

Joe Moore

Chapter One

All the best things in the world

can be found in the eyes of a child.

- Forrest Hedemup

The Beginning

Long before Santa Claus moved to the North Pole and became world known, the North Pole began, and was run, by the elves. They had come to the top of the world after being treated poorly by bigger people. It was not so much that they were beaten or kicked, though occasionally that would happen, but because largely they were just ignored or dismissed. People didn't take them seriously, if they paid attention to them at all. Tallfolk thought that since they were small, they couldn't be very smart. Nothing could have been further from the truth.

So they had come from many lands, each hearing the promise of a better world. Elves came from every continent, and like the tallfolk they lived among, these elves were every shape, color, with pointed ears and round, some short and others taller. Unlike tallfolk, most of them were around four feet give or take a few inches. They spoke different languages, they had different stories and legends, and they brought various hopes and ambitions with each one. When things had become unbearable in the country where they lived, those elves would pack up their belongings, and hoping the stories they heard were all true, and the inner voices were not false, they would make the arduous trek to the frozen north.

Sincere speech needs to be spoken here, these elves

were, are remain far smarter than the people they had lived amongst. And once they banded together, they discovered that together they exceeded genius levels. As anyone knows, two people are smarter than one, and four are smarter than two, and so on. But with the elves, as they increased their numbers, their collective smarts geometrically progressed and became nothing shy of brilliance.

In addition to being much brighter than tallfolk, they have a very peaceable nature to themselves. Rarely do they ever have a disagreeable day. Each one finds great joy in working with each other elf. They have a strong sense of accomplishment in everything they do together. On the rare occasion elves disagree on something, they work it through with compromises, or when in doubt, they bring in a couple more opinions from other elves, until an agreement on a particular course is resolved.

Because the North Pole was inhospitable to others, they were not only left in peace, but were able to build quite a large settlement. Elves advanced their discoveries much faster than the outside world, and they began constructing marvelous inventions and ways to accomplish things to tame their new land. The developments they came up with would have given any other country pause. Soon they were centuries ahead of any other civilization.

Being friendly and forgiving by nature, the elves not only did not hold a grudge against bigger people, but found tallfolk children wonderful in their overall innocence and curious nature. This was something that always had been particularly endearing to every elf.

They enjoyed the fact that through play, many tallfolk children learned how to get along, and received good lessons from others. All of the elves wanted to encourage that playtime for children everywhere.

It was Carrow Chekitwice who first suggested that perhaps the elves might build some things for the children to play with and enjoy. Again, while the elves were genuinely not against tallfolk they still avoided them as much as possible. Of course even with their collective smarts, they had to deal with the tallfolk from time to time. They needed many goods and occasionally services from them, because even with all their advances, the North Pole could not provide all the raw materials that were sought after. But the elves had plenty to trade in order to get what was needed.

Not the least of these items were our wonderful toys that would often touch a heartstring of the tallfolk and cause them to remember, even if just for a moment, what it was like to be a child. And the tallfolk wanted to give these toys to their own children, which of course was what the elves wanted, too.

Because of their advances in tools, tallfolk often would be happy to trade for what the elves produced. Much of it had never been seen before, and often they were decades ahead of their own inventions and tools. Soon their products became in high demand. But problems developed as some of the inventions that were traded became used in ways that the elves had not intended.

Many products were constructed and used against other people and changed from their initial designs.

Wars came about because of our advances to the tallfolk and their misuse. So the Council of Elves decided that they needed to carefully trade only the tools and advances that the tallfolk could handle during a particular time in their development. Many products and innovations would have to wait until the Council thought the tallfolk would not use them for destructive, rather than constructive purposes.

Meanwhile in the Arctic, their innovations kept being developed at a breakneck pace. They had not only learned how to tame their harsh landscape, but had developed a dome to help handle the often frigid blizzard conditions, and make the Pole not only livable, but enjoyable. They had become partial to cold weather, and liked the snow, although they preferred it in less amounts and more gently falling. Once under the dome, they were able to keep the inside around the freezing mark, and opted not to make it too much warmer. Elves would become sluggish and less inclined to get things done when it was too warm.

Of course they also developed a more seasonal climate including spring, summer and fall. Like the rest of the globe, they enjoy beautiful days and can control the sunlight artificially. Especially since the sun does not appear for six months in winter. But even more important than the climate, in developing the dome which is many miles across, they had constructed a barrier that became impervious to both outsiders and natural disasters, up to and including meteorites.

During their development they had also discovered an interesting side affect to living at the North Pole. They began living much longer than their tallfolk counterparts. And not just by a few years, but decades, and later, centuries. Each new generation lived longer and longer. It was believed that because of the strong magnetic properties of the North Pole, it resulted in elves eventually living hundreds of years instead as a normal lifetime elsewhere.

Since they were now so long-lived, they became master craftsman in nearly any activity they pursued, often spending several decades working and perfecting their craft before being considered journeymen or women. They eventually abandoned the traditional way of being named outside of the North Pole. Many forsook their old last name and took on new ones, often adopting something pointing to the craft they were particularly good at.

Before long, only first names were given to newborn elves, and they were allowed to pick their own surname when they felt the time was right. Few ever changed it once chosen, but some waited nearly a century or more before making their decision.

Occasionally some elves would want to make a change for a time and move back south for a while. Some wished for their old geography, and were allowed to work on behalf of the North Pole in other areas. These elves could return whenever they wished. The only requirement was that they could not disclose the elves culture, or location, to the tallfolk. They were especially not allowed to bring any of the tallfok to the North Pole, and had to keep many of the advancements of the elves secret.

This continued for a great many years, and while elves kept abreast of what was happening in the other lands, they often just shook our heads and enjoyed their quiet peace in their secret habitat. Many of the elves that worked in other lands would load up a bag of toys after they visited and took them to the children of the area they returned to. Also, some elves would take a handful of toys and sweets to children of the tallfolk they traded with, and leave them quietly in various places where they would eventually be discovered.

As a matter of course, the elves would say nothing about the gifts and would just leave them secretly. Occasionally, a bag of toys would just appear in an area where children were known to gather and play.

Unknown to any of us at first, one particular tallfolk was doing the same thing. He had come from a lineage that began with a former bishop of early Christianity, originally from Turkey in Middle Asia. That bishop had been anointed to sainthood for his deeds and love of children. This good man, and then his ancestors, had already begun to have many tales told about them as they traveled throughout Asia and Europe.

The bishop of Turkey's sons spread into other European lands as did their influence. His ancestors had moved through Italy, France, Germany and the Netherlands. Each had begun many traditions in the lands they traveled, all culminating in events geared around the birth of the Christ child, just as their Bishop forefather had done. They had begun to be known by many names from each land they traveled like Papa Noel, Pere Noel, La Befana, Babbo Natalie, Sinterklaas and others.

Many of the toys the elves had left for children had been credited to this tallfolk. This never bothered them as it had taken the attention off the elves, and left them to distribute their gifts in peace. A couple times the elves were actually pointed to as the gift-givers. They just said nothing and walked away. The elves did not want the attention of the tallfolk for the gifts left behind.

Toward the close of the eighteenth century, one of the elves came up with the idea to approach the tallfolk gift giver and ask if he would help distribute the elves' toys to the children, as he seemed to be doing it anyway. Denny Sweetooth, one of the members of the Council of Elves, asked about enlisting the stranger for help. Immediately a great debate ensued over whether or not to break elven law and allow the stranger to visit the North Pole, and to witness the wonders of the elves and their land.

After all, he was a member of the tallfolk. Many argued that it was wrong to say that none of the tallfolk could ever be trusted. Others argued that dire consequences would take place if this was allowed to happen. In the end, and by a single vote, it was agreed that the elves would send a delegation to meet with the man. During this meeting, if the delegation agreed, they would invite him to the North Pole.

They had placed on this delegation some of their best and brightest including Carrow Chekitwice - who was known for his leadership and careful ingenuity; Denny Sweetooth – whose suggestion it was in the first place. Also, though Denny was a baker and chef by trade, he

was known for his big heart and wise council; Forrest
Hedemup – who was in charge of all the animals and
training in the North Pole and a lover of all creatures;
Whitey Slippenfall – who was not only one of the
principle elves that made the North Pole habitable, but
was in charge of the defenses of the Pole, including its
protective dome, and finally, Ella Communacado – who
was the chief information elf in charge of
communicating with the elves outside of the North
Pole.

Carrow was an ancient elf who had helped design and
build the village in the beginning. He was slightly taller
and thinner than many of the elves with a beard that
ran all the way down to his knees. His face carried a lot
of wrinkles and the elves weren't sure if it was due more
to his age, or his stern nature. Carrow always seemed to
be frowning and studying things, whether village plans
or simple toys, with the same unending scrutiny.

At the opposite end of Carrow, Denny Sweetooth was
always smiling and jovial. He was as round as he was
tall, and looked like a dwarf even to other elves. Denny's
passion was food. Cooking it or eating it didn't matter.
He just loved being in a kitchen or near it. He also was
known to have the biggest heart in the North Pole and
was always offering counsel and help to others with their
many concerns.

Forrest Hedemup was chosen for his stamina and
strength. While no bigger than an average elf, he looked
like a ranch hand and was stronger than nearly any elf.
He carried large bundles with no effort, and could
handle himself with tallfolk if the need arose. He was

chosen to help keep a protective eye on the delegation, and to assist with the animals they would need and their load. A good looking young man by elf standards, he was one of the few blond elves with deep blue eyes.

Whitey was aptly named, as he sported a full head of white hair that looked as white and big as a snow bank. He had piercing green eyes, and like Carrow, was taller than most of his village. Whitey was the protector of the North Pole. He handled the defenses and also the security within the Pole. Very rarely did anything untoward happen in the village, but if it did, Whitey was called to the scene. His keen senses were known throughout the village, and he had a great capacity for sensing what was right from wrong. It was for this reason, as much as any, that he was chosen for this important mission.

If Whitey was known for his intuition, Ella was known for being able to put thought into "sincere speech" as elves called complete truth. A pleasant looking woman with dark hair and dark mysterious hazel eyes to match, she was one of the more desirable ladies of the North Pole, and was often sought after by the single men of the village.

What made Ella important (and feared by less sincere men) was her ability to see through to the truth, or make sense of any garbled discussion, and put it into words that everyone could grasp. There are some that just have a difficult time talking with others. Ella could understand what they meant and spoke their thoughts in a concise manner. Just in case this tallfolk began saying things insincerely, or without clear meaning, Ella would be there to interpret.

When these intrepid five left the North Pole on their quest, it was an unusual time in history. As they headed for the Netherlands, Ella explained to the others that this was a time of turmoil in England. As they all knew, the English had colonies throughout the world, on every known continental land mass, but one of these colonies was rebelling against their home country and England was embroiled in a war with their own people.

Apparently 'Americans', as they were calling themselves, had decided they no longer wished to be ruled by England and wanted to be free and independent. The other elves felt an instant kinship to these people, as they had traveled to the North Pole for similar reasons, though elves would rather leave for places unknown than to create war on others for something as unimportant as land.

The troupe had spent most of the fall, and part of the winter, searching for their quarry through the Netherlands. He was known to be in Amsterdam for a time, but they were not sure he was still around. It seemed the man was anxious to avoid recognition and attention, just as the elves had done. Many times they were told that yes, someone had been by and left some food stuffs and toys, but he was gone before they could even thank him. They had been given a vague description of the man, but other then sporting a full white beard and mustache, and being of large and strong build, there was little else to distinguish him.

They finally caught up with the man they sought outside of Eindhoven in the south eastern part of the

Netherlands around mid-December. They found him on the road heading out of town. He looked like a peddler and was carrying a large pack on his back. He had a long beard, hair and mustache.

But what the elves also saw was that his eyes twinkled, and he had the reddest cheeks Ella had ever seen on a tallfolk. He called himself Kris Kringle, and he had a very pleasant demeanor about him. He was surprised when approached by the small band. While being of average height himself, he had not seen such a small group gathered together before. They said they would like to talk with him and invited him to dine with them at the local tavern.

Kris at first thanked the group, but told them he had to get his possessions to Tilburg, as he had children waiting for him. The elves pressed him further and said that what they had to say to him may help him reach a great many more children than just in Tilburg and Eindhoven. They also impressed upon that they had been seeking him for months and throughout the country. Kris finally agreed to have lunch with them and they all went to the tavern.

Once they sat down, it was an awkward beginning, as the elves didn't quite know where or how to start. They had spent so much time searching for the man, but never truly discussed how they would initiate the conversation once they found him. They were still apprehensive about sharing too much of their life in the North Pole, in case they decided against asking this stranger to join them, so they attempted to speak in generalities. Likewise, Kris wasn't sure what business they wanted with him, and while he was polite, he was a little impatient to continue on his way.

They found common ground when Ella asked Kris why he traveled around giving gifts to children and then watched as Kris' eyes lit up immediately. He explained that his ancestor had instructed as far back as 300 A.D., on how God so loved the world that he gave the greatest gift of all to the world. A child, a simple gift that would forever change much of the world and its beliefs. As Kris was the tenth descendant of the great St. Nicholas, he wanted children to know that they were still loved. So like his forefathers before him, he brought gifts to as many as he could, and especially during December to remind them of God's gift. He explained that between making, securing and delivering the gifts, his efforts filled the entire year. But it was around Christmas when he tried to have the biggest impact.

He said that many children lose their innocent nature too soon, and he wanted to help them keep a little joy even if just during his one visit each year. The elves and Kris got into a very animated and spirited discussion about children, and what made them the most special of all God's creatures. Forrest talked about how the best of any creature could be found in the eyes of a child. Denny regaled his stories about the joy of a child's expression in every sweet cake he gave them. Even Carrow who is normally of a stern nature, talked about the wonderment of a child as they handled one of the carefully constructed toys they were given.

The elves saw in Kris the virtues they had hoped; a strong and loving heart, a child's amazement of the earth and heavens, an innocence untarnished by the hardships of the world, and a vitality and enthusiasm that seemed boundless. With an indiscernible nod to each other, the elves began to talk in hushed tones about a wondrous land that was built almost entirely to serve children. They told Kris of their mission to find him and invite him to the North Pole.

Kris listened enraptured about the amazing things they were saying about their village and mission. Of course he had many misgivings about making such an argent journey to such a faraway place and during such an inhospitable time. Also, if he went he would need to bring his wife, and there were still the children in Tilburg that needed their toys, and what of Christmas coming? This time the elves were ready and met each of Kris' concerns with a solution.

It was finally agreed that first, they would assist Kris in delivering his toys to the children in Tilburg, then they would meet his wife and discuss the North Pole in more detail with both of them. Finally, if they both agreed, the elves would send another delegation to the Kringle's after Christmas, and they would all make the journey then. The elves promised that the journey wouldn't be as difficult as Kris envisioned, and they would bring very special clothing that would keep them both safe and warm during the trip.

After spending quite some time on the journey to Tilburg with Kris and then meeting Mrs. Kringle, the delegation was even more certain that they had made the right decision. Ann Marie Kringle was warm and enchanting with an easy smile and laugh, like her husband. They both seemed so very...jolly! They were comfortable to be around and they had an easy spirit wrapped in a blanket of endless faith. All had agreed to the plan as laid out by the elves, and set the date to begin right after the Epiphany, on January 7th of the New Year.

This accord would change history around the world for billions of children everywhere.

Read an excerpt from the 3rd Book

in The Santa Claus Trilogy

GLACIERS MELT
&
MOUNTAINS SMOKE

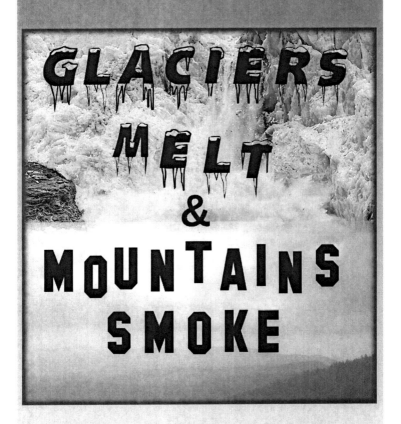

GLACIERS MELT & MOUNTAINS SMOKE

Joe Moore

PART ONE:

THE
DISCOVERY

Life is what happens to you

while you're busy

making other plans.

— **John Lennon**

Glaciers Melt & Mountains Smoke by Joe Moore

CHAPTER ONE
WATER, WATER EVERYWHERE

Jamie Hardrock stood looking at the wall before him. "It looks like it is alive," he commented as much to himself as the person next to him. "It seems to be moving back there. Perhaps you should stand back."

The younger man moved away without another word. He had brought this strange sight to his superior as he should, but he wasn't anxious to see what might lie beyond.

Jamie stood before the wall and picked up his heavy double pick. His muscular physique had wielded this tool millions of times over his 300 plus years. He took aim and firmly, but gently, struck the top of the wall

Immediately the ice at the top began to crack and rivulets of water flowed toward the floor. The crack began spreading in all directions and Jamie yelled, "Get everyone out – NOW!" As he got his own feet moving, he heard the rumbling and cracking behind him and felt sick to his stomach.

He and the other miner caught up to the others and Jamie just kept yelling, "Get out! Get out now!" They sprinted up the shaft toward the opening but were quite a ways from the opening when they heard a large boom and then the sound of a torrent of water coming rushing toward them. The water overtook them and soon the band of miners were swept away like logs in a flume. They were banging against the walls uncontrolled as they went rolled in the freezing water.

It spat them out of the mouth of the cave and the water flowed through the streets of the village. It began to taper off, but looked as if someone was draining a fire hydrant.

Jamie picked himself up, coughed out some water and shivered a bit, "Is everyone alright?"

"I think Whistler has a broken arm, and a few of us are pretty banged up, but other than that everyone seems okay," replied one of his crew bosses.

"Get him over to the infirmary. I need to report this at once," said Jamie, "This may have more serious implications than a flooded mine."

The younger miner that had been standing by him also coughed out water and replied, "You'd best get out of those wet clothes first before hypothermia sets in. Otherwise you'll be at the health center, too. That water is only 29° Fahrenheit."

Jamie nodded and walked off toward the Woodlands.

A half hour later he knocked on the door of the Kringle's home. The lovely Mrs. Kringle opened the door and said, "Hello Jamie, this is a surprise. Won't you come in?" Jamie's height was about two thirds of the lady before him and he tried to muster a smile.

"I'm afraid this is not a social call and I need to see both of you right away." Jamie said solemnly.

"I'll go get Nick. Why don't you wait in the study?" As Mary placed her hand on his back to lead him and she said, "Are you wet?"

He chuckled and said, "Only my hair and beard, I changed before coming. This is what we need to talk about."

"I'll get him and we'll be right in. Can I get you something warm to drink?" Mary now was concerned about both her guest and his news.

"Ah, no thanks, I had water before I came by. I'm fine right now." He moved to the room she indicated.

Mary walked to the workshop where her husband was working on a variety of projects and said to him, "Nick we have a visitor and it seems important. Could you please join us?"

As Nick rose he asked, "What's up?" He moved to Mary, and as was his custom, he gave her a little peck.

"Jamie is here and he's soaking wet, and I don't think it's from a shower," she said softly.

"Oh not again," Nick said in exasperation.

"I'm afraid so, but this is the first time it has involved the mines," she responded.

They both hurried to the study to hear Jamie's report.

Jamie stood when they walked in and Nick motioned him to sit down and be comfortable. As Nick looked him over he could see the beginnings of a couple bruises on Jamie's face and arms. And indeed he still looked water logged even in his dry clothes.

"Are you okay Jamie?" Nick asked concerned.

"I got a little banged up, and Whistler broke his arm, but we'll live," said Jamie.

"Okay, let's hear it," said Nick fearing the news but needing it nonetheless.

"We were working in the new shaft that is heading east. Jinxy came up to me and said he had come against a strange looking sight and was afraid to go any further

without my permission. When I came to the spot I could
see it moving behind the wall, so I gave it a little tap
toward the top to see how bad it might be, and the
whole thing gave way." Jamie shivered again as he
finished.

"Has it stopped?" asked Mary.

"I'm not sure," replied Jamie. "The water was flowing
when I left but not as fast or much. I'm afraid either
way, it is what we have feared. I believe the whole North
Pole is melting."

Nick raised his hands. "Now hang on a second, Jamie.
We don't know that for certain. Could it be that this was
an isolated pocket?"

"We've never come across one before." Jamie shook
his head. "And there is no reason to think this would
have been one, and in the middle of winter as well. That
water was below freezing and it should have been frozen,
but it was anything but. Plus if you add this to some of
the other goings on, it seems to point to the fact that
this whole area is becoming unstable."

Several buildings over the last year had begun to have
foundation issues, and a few had started to list a bit.
They knew that the North Pole was losing its ice shelf
at an alarming rate, but each winter the Pole had
refrozen and they hadn't developed a problem. Until
now. Many articles written from the States and Britain
had spread the word that the ice shelf was less than
50% of what it had been in the past, and they were
saying that the North Pole would be ice free within
another decade or so.

This was extremely bad news for the residents of the

North Pole, as there was nothing below the ice but ocean. Though the elves had brought tons of dirt, sand and other materials up in order to grow trees, plants and the like, it certainly wasn't enough to keep the village from being swallowed whole and disappearing forever beneath the surface.

The protective dome couldn't keep the ice from melting underneath their feet. Santa Claus had a big problem and the elf before him now proved how serious it was becoming.

He looked up at Mary. As the Chief Elf Organizer or CEO, it was her responsibility to keep the village and villagers safe. She looked at Nick and said, "We will have to reconvene the Council, right away."

Nick nodded his head and said, "We also need to bring in anyone who could advise us further." He suggested elves like Topo Geosphere, who was their primary geologist, and Whitey Slippenfall, who was in charge of the town structures and security be brought in. Whitey was already a member of the Council and would be there anyway.

Mary said, "I'll set up a meeting for the earliest possible time this week. Although I am not sure what can be done to hold back Mother Nature."

"I think the crux of the meeting will be more as to what alternatives we can come up with," said the current Santa Claus, "Aeon Millennium hinted that someday the North Pole, such as it is, might have to move."

"How and where would we move?" asked Jamie. "We have been here for hundreds of years, and our longevity is tied to the magnetism of the North Pole."

"These are questions and discussions for the Council," answered Nick. "And as always, with the combined intelligence of everyone we will figure out the answers."

Jamie correctly assumed that Nick did not wish to discuss the topic further right now, so he excused himself from the Kringles.

CHAPTER TWO
SHAKE, RATTLE AND FLOW

In another part of the North Pole Whitey Slippenfall was dealing with a different problem. "What happened in here?" he asked as he surveyed the damage in Egrid Shortpockets' Light Shoppe.

Egrid steadied himself against one wall and said in a shaken voice, "The whole building starting rocking back and forth like I was in some crazy fun-house! The lights fell everywhere and it sounded like firecrackers going off at my feet."

Egrid, afraid to move an inch because the house was so wobbly, clung to a shelf with one hand, his other plastered to the wall. "I think it happened to Priscilla's house, too," he nodded toward Priscilla Huffenpuff's Ornament Shop and home next to his. "She wasn't home when it happened, but I heard some loud crashes coming from there."

Whitey said "I think it is okay now. You can move out of your corner."

Egrid looked unsure and said, "What if it starts again?"

"I don't think that shelf is going to hold you if it does," answered Whitey. "Best you move outdoors for a little bit until I can check this out."

Whitey looked in and around the structure and was relieved to see it wasn't permanently damaged. He walked over to Priscilla's home and called her name. There was no answer so he walked through the shop door. Sure enough, shattered glass lay all over the floor and most of the normally full shelves looked empty.

Whitey moved through the building making sure Priscilla wasn't injured and laying somewhere in need of help. He found nothing but more broken ornaments and personal belongings strewn across the floor. He noticed a structure crack in the back of the house and didn't like the way it extended up the corner of the wall. *That's a load-bearing wall*, he thought to himself, *Not good, not good at all.*

Whitey was aptly named, as he sported a full head of white hair that looked as white and big as a snow bank. He had piercing green eyes, and was taller than most in his village. Whitey was the protector of the North Pole. He handled the defenses and also the security within the Pole. Very rarely did anything untoward happen in the village, but if it did, Whitey was called to the scene. His keen senses were known throughout the village, and he had a great capacity for sensing what was right from wrong.

He moved to the outside. He looked down to see another crack in the ice that ran through the back of the house and off toward the hills behind the house. When he returned to Egrid's, he found the same thing going in the opposite direction from the farthest corner of that home.

He had seen these cracks before in various places around the village. More often than not, they were associated with damage at or near any buildings close to them. This had happened too often in recent days. He had not witnessed the events, but the results were always the same. Damage, and lots of it. The worst so far had been at Britney Clearwaters' plant. Britney was in charge of the water flow through the North Pole. She and her staff controlled the amount of melt and the treatment of the water for purity, for the entire village.

A few weeks ago her plant experienced what was at first thought to be an earthquake. The pipes broke lose and water tanks ruptured. There remained a few places that were not getting any normal flow of water, still. And though no damage was done by the flooding, it was a major disruption that hadn't been fully repaired yet.

Whitey scratched his head and wondered why this was happening now. After centuries of peaceful existence in the farthest reaches of the world, away from tallfolk and their endless conflicts, now their peaceful village seemed to be cracking right under their feet. *And how can we stop it?* he asked himself.

If you would like to purchase the Trilogy books or any other books written by Joe Moore, you may buy his books at bookstores or Amazon.

You can also purchase autographed books through our website at

www.thenorthpolepress.com

or scan the QR code below

About The Author

Joe Moore has written millions of words over his lifetime. A graduate from California State University, Northridge, Joe is a former publisher, editor, advertising, marketing and sales executive. He worked on hundreds of campaigns and articles with thousands of proposals and stories for everything from fishing equipment to business magazines. This may help explain why he is able to write in so many genres.

Moore was a former feature writer for several Southern California periodicals. He has three books published in his Santa Claus Trilogy – *Believe Again, The North Pole Chronicles* and *Faith, Hope & Reindeer* and *Glaciers Melt & Mountains Smoke*. He is very excited to have his first three children's books also published. *Santa's World, Introducing Santa's Elf Series, Jamie Hardrock, Chief Mining Elf* and *Shelley Wrapitup, Master Design Elf* in the newly created Santa's Elf Series©. These books are produced for early readers, written in rhyme, and illustrated by Moore's wife, Mary. Moore has written a total of 25 children's stories for the Santa's Elf Series that will be published at the rate of two to four per year.

Moore is also venturing into new genre's of suspense/horror with *Return of the Birds* and is currently working on a ghost series.

Moore has been seen and interviewed on nearly every news program, such as Good Morning America, Fox News, ABC/NBC/CBS News and in numerous radio programs and newspapers. He also appeared on Disney Surfers, Nickelodeon, in numerous parades, on billboards and he and his wife were featured guests on

Wealth TV with the late Charlie Jones (NFL Media Hall of Fame announcer). As a professional Santa Claus, he currently is the premiere Santa Claus for Hello Santa digital Santa visits and works with daycare centers, visited dozens of homes and corporations, and spread his goodwill and joy with Mrs. Claus everywhere they travel.

Joe and Mary Moore, (as Santa and Mrs. Claus) also give of themselves, having contributed countless hours (and toys) to worthy charities including, the American Cancer Society, Children's Hospitals, Military families, Domestic abuse shelters, Community projects for schools, "Angel" programs, Hospice centers and more. Both Joe & Mary feel truly blessed by God to be able to bring such joy and happiness to others.

Moore's other passion is cooking! He enjoys creating spectacular meals for Mary and his friends. He also enjoys fishing, even though he admits his wife can always out fish him!

The Moores reside in the beautiful Smoky Mountains of East Tennessee.

CPSIA information can be obtained
at www.ICGtesting.com
Printed in the USA
LVOW10s1232101117
555753LV00001B/2/P

9 780978 712921